"What is the bedroom like?" she asked.

Wade pointed to the door at the end of the hall. "You tell me."

Roxy disappeared inside, and he followed. When she heard his footsteps on the hardwood floor, she glanced back at him. "This is a large room. I like that the windows are high, letting in light without letting anyone actually see into the room. Chefs keep strange hours, up before the roosters in the morning and back in bed while most people are just starting to party."

Wade's mind snagged on an image of her in bed, her hair tousled from sleep, a sheet sliding off her creamy shoulder; and his composure slipped. "The bathroom is over here."

"Again, it's large. This shower is to die for. Rain shower, dual heads. I could get used to that."

Great, now he was picturing her naked, in the shower with the water raining down on her, nipples beaded, rivulets of water slipping between her full breasts, over her flat tummy, between the crevices and folds at the juncture of those long, sweet legs. Damn, it had been eons since he'd been naked with a woman, and his body was rallying to change that even as he stood there trying to deny it to himself.

Acclaim for the Big Sky Pie Series

DELIGHTFUL

DELICIOUS

"Five Big Sky blueberry pies for this fabulous romantic page-turner...You'll want to savor each slice of this scrumptious series."
   —TheBestReviews.com

"Fast-paced and engaging...a wonderful addition to Lee's heartwarming series."
   —BookReviewsandMorebyKathy.com

DELECTABLE

"For a fun, light, and entertaining read about second chances, don't miss *Delectable*."
   —HarlequinJunkie.com

"I found *Delectable* so refreshing!...True love and homemade pies made this totally delectable!"
   —RandomBookMuses.com

"A nice second-chance love story with good main and secondary characters. I enjoyed the read and am looking forward to the second book in this series."
   —SexyBookTimes.com

"A positively charming romance that is incredibly heartwarming...a fast-paced and engaging novel that is sure to delight anyone who enjoys homespun love stories."
   —BookReviewsandMorebyKathy.com

Decadent

Also by Adrianne Lee

Delectable
Delicious
Delightful

Decadent

Adrianne Lee

FOREVER

NEW YORK   BOSTON

Copyright © 2014 by Adrianne Lee
Excerpt from *Delectable* copyright © 2013 by Adrianne Lee
Cover copyright © 2014 by Hachette Book Group

Forever
Hachette Book Group
1290 Avenue of the Americas
New York, NY 10104
www.HachetteBookGroup.com
www.twitter.com/foreverromance

Originally published as an ebook

First mass market edition: December 2014
10 9 8 7 6 5 4 3 2 1

OPM

Forever is an imprint of Grand Central Publishing.
The Forever name and logo are trademarks of Hachette Book Group, Inc.

The publisher is not responsible for websites (or their content) that are not owned by the publisher.

The Hachette Speakers Bureau provides a wide range of authors for speaking events. To find out more, go to www.hachettespeakersbureau.com or call (866) 376-6591.

For Maureen, your smile and laugh will live in our memories forever. You were always gracious, always fun, and always loved. We lost you too soon. We miss you every day.

Acknowledgments

Thank You:

Alex Logan—My amazing editor, who works so hard to help me make my books the best they can be and for easing my stress when life is determined to pile it on.

Karen Papandrew—For being free for a pizza lunch whenever I needed to take a break and for always believing I can do it, and for trying to help take the pressure off.

Gail Fortune—My fabulous agent. You know why.

To the Art Department at Forever—For giving the Big Sky Pie series those delectable, delicious, delightful, and decadent covers.

Decadent

Chapter One

~~~

Going home under these circumstances was like overindulging in decadent chocolate pie; the tummy ache outweighed the pleasure.

"There he is." Roxanne Nash directed the driver of the hired car to pull over in the parking garage. "I'll just be a minute."

"Make sure, lady, 'cause I don't want that cat decidin' my ride is a giant litter box."

"She won't." But would she? Roxy bit her lower lip and glanced toward the cat carrier at her feet. Tallulah, her adopted, purebred Ragdoll had a mind of her own. Another reason to quickly scratch this last item off her get-out-of-Seattle-forever list.

Chill air slipped through her thin jacket as she exited the dark sedan and glanced around. She half-expected some of the reporters who'd assailed her at the hotel a while ago to be lurking behind parked cars, seeking one

last sound bite in the final chapter of celebrity chef Roxanne Nash and Seahawks linebacker Ty Buckholtz. But
there was only herself, her driver, and the man in the
five-thousand-dollar suit.

She strode toward him, her high-heel boots clicking
on the concrete floor, echoing through the vast space
that was already filled to capacity with cars on this early
Friday morning. The man, her ex's attorney, was standing next to a brown Escalade with a grille the same
gleaming silver as her favorite sauté pan. She'd expected
to meet him in his office on the 29th floor and was
surprised that he'd suggested this instead. Although it
would expedite their transaction. And given Tallulah's
unpredictable nature, that was a good thing.

Roxy was here to pick up her half of the divorce
settlement. So why was the attorney holding a set of
keys and a file folder instead of a check-sized envelope?
More curious yet, the attorney's normally unflappable
manner showed signs of deteriorating. His tie was
askew, his pocket square rumpled, and despite the cold,
sweat beaded on his forehead. But most worrisome was
his expression. It belonged on a surgeon about to deliver
the news that his patient had died on the operating table.

A shiver that had nothing to do with the weather
snaked down her spine. Something was amiss. But
what? Myriad candidates leapt to mind, too many to pin-
point just one. *Stop it, Roxy. Whatever it is, it's not your
problem. Just like Ty is no longer your problem.*

Buoyed by that thought, she stopped before the attorney, a paunchy, middle-aged man several inches shorter

than her five-eleven. He'd applied his cologne with a heavy hand. The sharp odor mixed with the oily gasoline fumes and produced a nauseating stench. She stifled the urge to cover her nose as she ground to a halt. She didn't bother with niceties. Too much water had passed beneath the bridge between this lawyer and herself to pretend otherwise. Roxy held out her hand. "My check?"

The attorney shuffled from foot to foot, glanced away, then back at her like a shifty salesman about to offer her a bogus deal. Roxy wished her attorney were here, taking care of this, but that one-woman legal firm had decided to elope and take an extended honeymoon. *Probably on the money she'd earned representing me.*

The man cleared his throat. "Mr. Buckholtz has been trying to reach you since yesterday afternoon, Ms. Nash."

"Well, here's the thing about that," Roxy said, tilting her head to one side and smiling wide. "I no longer have to take his calls."

And she wouldn't. She'd blocked Ty's number on her cell phone.

"Or mine?"

Her silence seemed to grate on him.

"Well, Ms. Nash, if you'd answered our calls, it would have made this easier."

"Nothing could be easier than you giving me the money that I'm owed and me getting back in that car and catching the plane to Montana." She held her hand out again.

"I'm afraid I don't have the check."

He did not just say that. Exasperation twisted through her. "Why not?"

"There's been a... a complication."

She shivered, feeling the chill reach her bones. She should have opted for something warmer this morning, instead of choosing this lightweight jacket that matched her sage eyes and perfectly set off her layered mop of red hair, the style and shape likely slipping away in this damp air. But then, she hadn't planned on being outside this long. "What's the problem? Cut to the chase."

He pursed his lips, obviously more used to giving orders than taking them. "The sale of your house didn't close yesterday."

Of all the things she'd imagined being wrong, this had been low on the list. A knot began forming in her stomach. Ty had signed the closing papers yesterday morning. She'd signed an hour later, and the buyers were supposed to sign right after her. "What happened?"

"The buyers didn't show up at the title company."

"They backed out?" At the last freakin' minute? She tried calculating how much this would affect the plans she'd been making for her future in Kalispell, but she couldn't even assimilate the news.

"Well, no. They haven't exactly backed out. They just need an extension."

"On the closing?" They'd already been given two extensions.

"Yes." He looked as relieved as if he'd finally presented the problem in such simple terms a whole courtroom would understand, not realizing he'd omitted the important details. If he was a chef in her kitchen, she'd reprimand him for leaving out essential ingredients.

"The Dillons are already living in the house," she said, irritation clipping her words. Damn it. She'd trusted that couple enough to let them move into the house before the sale closed. Ty and her attorney had advised against this, but Roxy believed the Dillons sincerely meant to go through with the deal. *Obviously trusting the wrong people is a flaw I need to work on.* She didn't like being made a fool of. "They need to close as scheduled or get out so we can sell the house to someone else."

"Mrs. Dillon had a heart attack on the way to the title company's office."

Roxy froze, her ire squelched by contrition and concern. "Oh my God, d—did she die?"

"No, but apparently the situation was dire. Narrowed artery. Blood clot. She's having a stent inserted this morning, and she should be as good as new in a few days."

Relief flooded through Roxy. "Do you have the paperwork for the extension?" He gave it to her, and she signed it. Then she added, "You can FedEx me the check once the sale is finalized. And now, I'll take the check Ty is giving me for the bistro. I assume you have that."

The hired car's motor revved. Roxy glanced at the driver. He was scowling, pointing to his watch.

She nodded, then peered expectantly at the attorney. "As you can see, I need to get going."

The lawyer looked peaked, as if he might be ill.

"What?"

"Have you been hiding in a cave the past twenty-eight hours?"

What she'd been doing was none of his business. "I don't understand."

"Haven't you seen a news report or watched TV since yesterday?"

Her TV was on its way to Kalispell. And she had no interest in watching the news. It was bad enough dealing with the paparazzi outside the hotel this morning, shouting questions about Ty. Humming loudly inside her head, she'd simply tuned them out. "I've had all the media I can take for a while, thank you very much."

The driver of her hired car raced the engine, another prodding reminder that he wanted the cat out of the car and that the plane wasn't going to wait for her. She gave the driver an "I'm moving as fast as I can" glare, then told the attorney, "Look, I have to go right now. Please give me the bistro check."

"I can't."

"Why not?" What kind of trick was Ty pulling now?

"It's easier to just show you." The attorney produced an iPhone and pulled up an ESPN website. Finding what he wanted, he held the screen toward her.

Roxy protested, "I don't have time for this…"

Ty's name was a banner across the top of the national sports report. The sportscaster said, "Seattle Seahawk Ty Buckholtz is being benched for the next four games due to alleged substance abuse issues."

Roxy just shook her head.

"Don't worry, Ms. Nash. We're appealing."

"I'm not worried." Roxy blew out an angry breath. She wasn't surprised that someone with Ty's low moral compass might be doing drugs. But it had nothing to do with her. She said, "Not my problem."

"Well, it sort of is." The attorney gnashed his teeth. "You see, Mr. Buckholtz has no access to his financial accounts and can't come up with the hundred thousand in cash that he promised you for turning over the bistro to him. His salary is frozen, and will be until he's cleared to play again. But he isn't trying to get out of his obligation to you. He's giving you something of equal value for collateral."

Collateral? "I'm not a bank or a pawn shop. I don't want anything but that cash."

"I've already explained that cash is not an option at this time."

She frowned, her foot tapping like a butcher knife through a pile of onions.

The hired car's engine revved again. She waved at the driver, praying Tallulah was behaving and would continue to do so for a few more minutes. She glared at the lawyer. "What is Ty offering me?"

The attorney held up the set of keys and pointed to the SUV with the gleaming-grille. "This Escalade."

Her gaze went to the four-door, truck-bed Cadillac that shone like a gigantic chocolate diamond, the color more mocha than brown.

"It's a 2015 with every whistle and bell imaginable and more. It's worth as much as he owes you."

"Tell your client to send it back to the dealer and pay me the cash he owes me."

"He special ordered it. There's nothing wrong with it. He just can't return it. It's only until his salary is reinstated. Once that happens, Mr. Buckholtz will cut you a check and reclaim this vehicle. I have the legal documentation here. Already signed by my client."

"But I don't want it." She felt her plans slipping away like steam being sucked up a hood vent.

"I'm sorry, Ms. Nash." The lawyer shrugged. "It's this or nothing."

The dark sedan's engine revved once more. Roxy's nerves pinched. If she didn't leave this minute, the plane would be gone. She had to cut bait. Now. "How am I supposed to get the Cadillac to Montana?"

"I'll arrange to have it shipped." The attorney rattled off his intention of ordering a closed trailer to avoid road damage as he pocketed the keys.

Her mind was whirring faster than the blades of a blender. "I'd have to have the title in my name."

"That's already been done." He handed her the paperwork. She inspected the documentation, reading fast, glad to find there were no hidden clauses. She signed it.

"And you'll arrange shipping today?" she asked, returning his pen.

"As soon as I get to my office."

Could she take him at his word? Probably. He wouldn't stay in business long if he pulled something as unethical as not following through on a signed contract. But add Ty into the mix and all bets were off. What if she walked out of this garage with only the title and a signed agreement, and the vehicle somehow didn't get sent? What if she had to go back to court to get her hundred thousand dollars? She shuddered at how much that might end up costing. Her attorney would probably retire on it. She decided that—despite the eleven- to twelve-hour drive-time involved—the simplest solution was the best. "Or I could drive it to Montana."

The lawyer's brows lifted. "You could, but I must caution you to be extremely careful. The Escalade needs to come back to Mr. Buckholtz in exactly the same condition as it leaves here."

"Yeah, well, tell him to worry about himself. The Cadillac is under full warranty, and I'm holding the proof of insurance. So potential mishaps are covered." *Romance should come with collision and liability insurance,* Roxy thought. *That way when a woman collides with a potential love interest, she'll be covered when he becomes a liability.*

* * *

Wade Reynolds's Friday night was off to a bad start. He felt like he'd stepped on a bear trap, caught by inescapable jaws, the pain so fierce he couldn't release the screaming in his brain. He glanced at his twelve-year-old daughter for help, but the hopeful gleam in her eyes sent an arrow through his heart. *Et tu, Emily?* Damn. His beloved little girl was in on this, this...female setup. Why did everyone seem intent on hooking him up? Was he wearing a sign around his neck: Widower seeking mate? Hell no. Just the opposite. His wedding band should deter any such ill-advised action. So what if it had been four years since cancer took Sarah? He still didn't want anyone else. Not now. Not ever.

He stammered, "I, uh, I, uh, can't stay for dinner."

The sexily clad single mother of Emily's best friend dropped her smile like he would drop an overheated nail gun. "But the table's set and—"

"I have plans." It was the truth, but Wade felt his neck getting warm as he threaded the brim of his Stetson through nervous fingers, and he knew it looked like he was pulling excuses from his hat. He backed toward the door. "I'm sorry, but if I don't leave now, I'll be late."

The pretty blonde rushed toward him, her boobs bouncing in the V-neck of her sweater like bobbers on a lake, teasing that a strike was imminent. The thought sent a flash of fear through him. He said, "Emily, I'll pick you up tomorrow around noon."

"Awww, Dad." The look of disappointment in his daughter's eyes fueled his distress.

"I can bring her home," said the blonde—Tiffany or Taffy or Tippy—sashaying closer still, every switch of her hips suggestive, seductive.

Wade's blood began to heat, his body reacting to the stimuli. Hell, he was human. And hetero. And deprived. He saw a cold shower in his near future. "Sure. Okay. I'll call Emily tomorrow."

With that, Wade slipped on his hat and hastened out the door, making sure to shut it behind him. He stood on the porch, breathing hard, the cold air flushing relief through his overheated body. Biting wind swirled snow across the front walk and into his face. He'd only been inside ten minutes and already another three inches of the white stuff had piled onto the yard and street, big sloppy flakes, the kind that stick so fast they turn roads into ice rinks. He pulled up the collar of his sheepskin jacket and trudged to his pickup, arriving at the driver's side feeling like a snowman.

He kicked the compacted flakes from his boots, brushed off his hat and shoulders, the effort futile, the snow piling back on faster than he could smack it away. He climbed into the cab and got the engine running. The wipers *swicked* across the windshield, clearing a small quadrant of visibility. Still fuming mad, he clamped his hands on the steering wheel as he jammed his foot on the gas pedal. The pickup lurched, the tires skidding, the truck bed barely missing a mailbox. He eased off the gas, but anger continued to boil through him, anger at being set up, anger at himself for being unable to get past Sarah's death, to let go of the guilt. How could Emily have had any part in this? Yeah, she was a kid, but still...It seemed so disloyal to her mother.

This had Callee McCoy's handiwork written all over it. He thought back to earlier in the week. Callee, the wife of his best friend, was working as a design consultant on a remodel job he was doing. She'd come to his house to discuss a change to the kitchen they were overhauling. Emily had wandered in while he'd stepped out to take a phone call, and when he'd returned, the two females had their heads together, discussing something like crooks plotting a crime.

He hadn't known then that he'd been the intended victim.

He considered calling Quint, Callee's husband, and canceling his plans to meet them at the pie shop before heading over to Moose's Saloon for pizza and beer. But Quint would ask why, and Wade doubted he'd get any sympathy once he told him. Quint was president of the Get Wade Laid Club.

Wade tossed his hat onto the passenger seat. His friends meant well, but he wished they'd listen to him and just stop. Maybe he should skip the pizza and beer and grab a burger to eat at home. Alone. In that big empty house. Maybe a movie then. Alone. The thought made him queasy. Lately he'd been feeling it more and more, a deep loneliness settling over him that was thicker than the snow on his hood.

If he was honest with himself, he'd admit he missed having a woman in his life. Just saying it in his head seemed to unlock a floodgate and fill him with a yearning he'd denied for too long. Damn, how he missed female companionship, missed the interaction of conversation, missed the warmth a woman brought to a home. Missed the closeness. The sex. Especially the sex.

He twisted the gold band on his left ring finger. He'd tried dating a few weeks back, but had to end it when he realized he wasn't going to move the relationship beyond friendship. He didn't want a romance, didn't want to fall in love. Although he wouldn't mind someone to go to the movies with, and maybe a little more, occasionally—someone who didn't expect or want anything permanent from him. An image of the perfect candidate filled his mind: a tiny blonde, as demure and even-tempered as his Sarah had been.

* * *

Roxy squinted against the snow pinging like pellets against the windshield. The road was a solid sheet of white. Only the tracks made by other drivers assured her that she wasn't headed for a ditch, but the tread marks were quickly disappearing beneath a fresh layer of white. She yawned and rubbed at her weary eyes. Twelve hours on the road. If she'd known it would be snowing, she'd have stopped in Spokane and made the rest of the trip tomorrow, in daylight. One of the gadgets on the dashboard probably included a weather app, if she could figure out how to operate it, but there had been no time to study a manual. And besides, she'd been lulled into a false confidence by the ease of driving this luxurious, four-wheel-drive Escalade until it was too late to turn back.

She shifted in the seat, trying to relieve the numbness in her bottom and to get the blood moving in her legs. She longed for a place to get out and stretch, but then Tallulah would also want out, and just imagining the cat's reaction to all the white stuff made Roxy shudder.

No telling how the cat would react to snow. Fortunately, another mile should see them pulling up to her mother's house in Kalispell.

A sudden glare of light pierced her thoughts. Roxy jolted. Headlights roared toward the passenger side of the Escalade. Holy shit. A giant pickup truck was about to T-bone the Cadillac. She slammed the brakes. Her vehicle fishtailed, then started to pirouette like an ice skater. The scream she reserved for riding roller coasters filled the cab as she held the steering wheel in a death grip and slammed her eyes shut, bracing for the collision.

With every muscle clenched, she didn't realize for several seconds that the Escalade had stopped spinning. Or that she'd felt no impact. Nothing. Not a bump. Or a crunch. No air bags exploding. Just a sudden silence punctuated by the roar of her pulse. She opened her eyes. The Escalade was now pointed nose to nose with the pickup as if they were about to kiss. Her heart tried to escape through her throat. Her breath came in rapid punches.

Curse words spewed from her mouth as she stumbled out of her vehicle to confront the jerk driving the pickup, a mountainous man in a light-colored Stetson and sheepskin jacket. He emerged through the heavy snowfall like the Marlboro Man coming to rescue the damsel in distress. It had been a long, disappointing, frustrating day, and Roxy's temper was as shredded as a pile of cheddar. She didn't need rescuing. Especially not by some idiot who didn't know how to drive in snow.

"What the hell were you thinking, you jackass? Speeding in these conditions? Are you nuts?"

He stopped in his tracks, caught between the front fenders of the vehicles, the headlights exposing a handsome, amused face with a slow, sexy grin. "I'm sorry, ma'am. I just wanted to make sure you weren't harmed."

"Only by the grace of God," she huffed. The huge, fat flakes seemed to have muted the world around them, giving her the sense that they were alone in the wilderness rather than on a normally busy highway.

She reined in her temper with a struggle. She wasn't hurt. The Escalade wasn't damaged. She needed to calm down, but that was easier said than done given the adrenaline still rushing through her. "You're right. I'm okay. No harm, no foul."

"Exactly . . . and if you hadn't hit your brakes—"

"If I hadn't—?" A new flare of ire spiked through her. *Welcome home, Roxy, to good old redneck country— where macho reigns supreme.* "You're the one who came roaring out of the side road at breakneck speed, buddy. Not me."

"I wasn't speeding." He shook his head, eyed her license plate, and then offered up that slow, sexy grin again. "Driving in snow takes a certain skill that most Seattleites aren't familiar with."

She recalled the Escalade had the name of the auto dealership on the license plate frame. She narrowed her eyes wanting to call him on making assumptions, on jumping to conclusions, but then she'd done the same, assuming he couldn't drive in this weather. Instead, she opted to undermine his macho swagger. "I'll have you know that I cut my driving teeth just down the street from here, during an ice storm."

But he was no longer listening, or looking at her. His attention had snagged on the Escalade like a gourmand eyeing his favorite dish. He released a low whistle of appreciation. "It would've been a shame to damage this baby. It looks almost new."

"Almost?" Roxy choked on the word. *Try new, hot-off-the-showroom-floor-that-morning*. Ty hadn't even driven it yet—which offered the only trace of satisfaction she'd felt since discovering she wasn't going to get the money owed her today. "It was a consolation prize."

"Really." He sounded surprised. "If this is the consolation, what did the winner get?"

My life. "What she deserves."

That caught his full attention. He looked up, shoving his Stetson back enough to give her a glimpse of his eyes, some pale, warm color. Roxy squared her shoulders expecting him to ask her to explain the remark, but instead he yanked off the hat, plowed his fingers through hair the same mocha color as the Cadillac, and offered her a sympathetic, "I see."

He couldn't possibly "see" what she'd been through, but his kindness and unassuming manner pulled her off balance. He'd circled the Escalade and was trudging toward her from the rear. He said, "Since no damage has been done to either of our vehicles, we should probably get out of the middle of this road. All manner of fools venture out in this weather."

She stiffened. Was that another dig at her? Or was she just too tired and too sensitive? She swallowed a new knot of pique. Tallulah and she—"Oh my God, Tallulah!"

She lunged for the back door of the Escalade and yanked it open, almost slamming it into Marlboro Man's gut. A yowl escaped into the chilly night.

"Is your child hurt?" He hovered over her, alarm in his deep voice.

"Tallulah isn't a child. She's a Ragdoll." The interior light shone on the cat carrier. Its door was ajar. She reached inside. Empty. Alarm shot through Roxy. She tried backing up, but Marlboro Man stood too close, blocking her retreat.

"A what?" He leaned over her shoulder, peering into the Cadillac. "Is that some sort of gerbil?"

"Back up. Quick." Her heel sank into the toe of his boot. He jerked just as a ball of fur flew past the right side of Roxy's face. The tall cowboy gasped, then swore. Roxy spun around, frantic to grab the cat. Tallulah clung to the collar of the man's sheepskin jacket like a rabid raccoon, hissing, while Marlboro Man grappled to remove her. Roxy reached for the big feline, tripped on the toe of his boot, and fell hard against him, knocking him backward. He dropped to the road, his Stetson flying off, landing just beyond his head, brim side up.

Tallulah leaped for the hat as Roxy landed on top of the man. Air woofed from his lungs. And hers. She scrambled to lift herself from him, frantic to catch the cat before it escaped into the wild, but she slipped on the compacted snow and ice, landing on him a second time, her nose ending up buried against his neck. Oh Lord, he smelled like a fresh summer breeze with a hint of something spicy, and felt so male that her body clenched.

She pushed up on his chest, and his gaze locked on hers. She felt his arousal against her thigh and felt her face glowing with the heat of humiliation, her flesh alive with lust. A charged awareness passed between them, startling her. It seemed to startle him, too. He released a guttural moan, catching hold of her, rolling sideways, and then disentangling his long legs from hers. "Where's that critter?"

As he helped her to her feet, Roxy spotted Tallulah balancing on the brim of the Stetson, and she realized that, in the pale light, it resembled the rim of a commode. The cat didn't use a litter box. She was toilet-trained. "Oh, no, Tallulah, don't!"

But the cat wasn't paying any attention to Roxy. She assumed the position and relieved herself into the bowl of the hat.

"Oh God." Roxy grimaced.

"What the—?" Horror etched Marlboro Man's face, but he waited until the cat was finished, then snatched the hefty feline by the scruff and gently handed her to Roxy. "This is yours, I believe."

"Oh God, I'm so sorry," she said, silently admonishing Tallulah as she placed her back in the cat carrier and secured the latch. "I'll pay to have it cleaned."

He snorted. "Cleaning won't fix this."

"You're right, of course. If you'll give me your name and number, I'll buy you a new one. Exactly like this one."

He shrugged, shook the snow from his thick hair, and flashed that slow, sexy smile again. "Don't worry about it. Shit happens. The hat wasn't new, and besides, I have others."

"Are you sure?" This wasn't right. She had to make it up to him.

"Positive." He lifted the fouled hat by the brim, emptied it, carried it to his pickup, and tossed it into the bed. As he made his way to the cab of his truck, his cell phone rang. She heard him answer it. "Wade Reynolds speaking."

Roxy settled onto her driver's seat, catching one last glimpse of the sexy cowboy named Wade Reynolds as she backed away from his vehicle and pointed the Escalade for town. A moment later, his headlights filled her rearview mirror. Following. A sensuous quiver swept through her as she recalled her reaction to his inviting smell, and his reaction to her laying on top of him. She hadn't been with a man since figuring out she couldn't forgive and forget Ty's betrayals: she was beyond ready for a love affair or two or even three. And considering the sparks that had just flown between them, she was putting Wade Reynolds at the top of her "to-do" list.

Unless he was married, engaged, or involved. She'd be damned if she'd poach another woman's man.

"Wade Reynolds... hmm. Why does that name sound so familiar, Tallulah?"

The cat wasn't paying any attention. She'd gone back to sleep. The little monster had no conscience. As Roxy reached the outskirts of town, she remembered where she'd heard Marlboro Man's name. He was one of Callee and Quint McCoy's best friends. In fact, Wade and Callee were working on a home renovation together.

He wasn't married, engaged, or in a relationship. He was a widower, still grieving the loss of his wife, despite four years having passed since her death and despite his friends trying to get him to move on. Roxy began to smile. What could be better? He had to be as primed for some hot monkey sex as she was, and he wouldn't want any kind of clingy, messy relationship since he was still in love with his deceased wife. That suited Roxy to a T. She was never, ever falling in love again. Never getting married again.

But what else had Callee said about Wade? Oh yeah. "He's laced up tighter than the sneakers he wore winning the state basketball championship his senior year of high school."

Roxy smiled. "What do you think, Tallulah? Wouldn't it be fun to unlace the sexy Mr. Reynolds?"

Chapter Two

⁓

Big Sky Pie. Roxy stared at the shop that had once been the realty office of Quint McCoy, her best friend Callee's husband. What a transformation his mother had wrought. The plain storefront façade of the past had been updated to include bay windows and charming awnings. The no-nonsense gray siding was now a rich red with accent trim in beige and white, bringing to mind one of Molly McCoy's renowned cherry pies. It was even more inviting in person than in the photos Callee had shown her, especially on a snowy, winter afternoon.

Roxy parked across the street in the Kalispell Center Mall's lot, choosing a space near the road. She was meeting Callee and Quint at the pie shop. She should have her money from the sale of the house by next week, and she needed to get out of her mother's before she went cuckoo. Two days in and she was climbing the walls. She missed having her own kitchen more than anything. Missed the bistro kitchen. Missed the bistro and her staff. She'd hated abandoning them to Ty and his fiancée, but they had each understood her decision.

Still, what did her ex and Ms. Seahawks Cheerleader know about running an upscale restaurant? Worry swept her. How soon would all of those employees be seeking other employment? Resentment joined the worry, and she gave herself a mental slap. She couldn't go there. Couldn't let anything overshadow her new start.

New start. Yes. Concentrate on that. And the first step toward that start would take the talents of Quint McCoy, the king of location.

Roxy snapped on earmuffs and gloves, knowing her suede, four-inch boots were no match for the fat snowflakes that, again today, were piling up quicker than entrée orders in the bistro kitchen. *Welcome to winter in Montana.* People might complain about the rain in Seattle, but at least she hadn't needed thermal underwear there. She glanced back at the mall. Maybe she should duck inside and purchase something more adequate for this weather, like a heavy parka and waterproof boots, but she was already running late. Tomorrow, for sure.

As she exited the Cadillac, cold air gave her a bear hug, drawing shivers the length of her. Grumbling, Roxy trudged across the street. Her bad mood wasn't about the weather. Or about the life she'd left behind. It was her need to escape her mother's pitying glances and telling sighs, the unspoken message that this was her own doing, that she'd been too busy to hold onto her man. Like holding onto a man was the measure of a woman. *Why doesn't Mom get that I don't need a man? I don't want a man.*

Okay, that was a lie.

Keeping her marriage vows until the divorce was final had satisfied her sense of righteousness, yet done nothing to relieve or ease the ache between her legs. But she was single now. No ties or promises holding her back. How better to celebrate her freedom than with a fling or two? Wade Reynolds's image filled her mind, warming her middle. He was definitely *numero uno* on the list of candidates. Of course, after the Tallulah debacle, he'd probably run for the hills at the first sight of her.

A bell tinkled, heralding Roxy's entrance into the pie shop and drawing the glances of customers seated at tables scattered throughout the café area. Three private booths against an outside wall were also occupied. Everyone was indulging in yummy-looking desserts. Roxy closed the door behind her, but didn't move as her gaze swept through the room. She only half heard the soothing strums of a country guitar issuing from hidden speakers or the soft chatter of the café guests. The inviting décor, sweetened with warm tan, crisp white, and cherry red hues gave the shop a welcoming feel, but it was the sinfully decadent aromas that captivated her.

She'd loved walking into the waterfront bistro's kitchen, breathing in the heady tang of seafood fresh from Pike Place Market, of chopped garlic and organic vegetables. It was her oxygen. The juice that got her blood pumping. And she could tell by the clash of tasty fragrances rife in the air that this was also an establishment with a chef who loved creating dishes that tickled the taste buds.

Oh, my. What was she smelling? Her discerning palate detected chocolate and cream and mincemeat and pumpkin along with myriad spices and an overlay of espresso. A heavenly perfume. She sighed, pleasure sloughing through her as she crossed to the display case to view the tempting offerings—the high meringue on the chocolate cream pie, the delicate crust that looked as though it would melt against the tongue. Roxy's mouth watered.

Roxy decided to order a piece of that chocolate pie and caught the attention of a busy waitress, realizing belatedly that she knew this woman. She grinned in recognition. "Andrea Lovette."

The pretty blonde froze, studied her a moment, and then her warm, brown eyes widened and so did her smile. "Oh my God, Roxy. Callee said you were back. You look wonderful."

"Thank you. So do you. What's this I hear about you taking the plunge again?"

"It's true." Andrea held up her left hand, showing off an engagement ring that could serve as a solar panel. Roxy was acutely aware of the missing rings on her own finger. An unexpected pang squeezed her stomach. She and Andrea stood on opposite sides of the same garden gate, she realized, one entering and one walking away, one giddy with glee, one raw with regrets.

Roxy forced a pleasant expression. She wouldn't rain on Andrea's obvious happiness. The single mother of two already knew the probable pitfalls of wedded bliss. Roxy said, "I hear he's the son of a famous actress?"

"Yep." Andrea sighed. "And his dad is founder of iMagnus Studios."

"Have you met either of them?"

Andrea shook her head. "We're spending Christmas together, and frankly, I'm terrified. I mean, what do you call a movie star once she's your mother-in-law?"

"Mom?" Roxy suggested, then smirked, and Andrea burst out laughing, the frown line between her eyebrows smoothing out. "I'm sure your fiancé will have suggestions. Have you set a date?"

"Not yet. We're taking our time, getting to know each other better, making sure it's for keeps, giving the boys a chance to adjust to the idea." Andrea hooked her hair behind her ear, revealing a gold hoop earring. "But the boys adore Ian, and he feels the same about them. God, I love that man."

"I thought his name was Ice?"

"Oh, that's another story."

"I'll look forward to hearing it sometime." Roxy grinned, sucked in by Andrea's joy. She pulled off her earmuffs and gloves and shoved them into her pockets, then fluffed her wedge-cut hair with her fingers. "I'm supposed to be meeting Callee and Quint. Have you seen them?"

"End booth. Go sit. I'll bring you coffee. How do you take it?"

"Heavy on the espresso, please." Roxy headed for the high-backed booth, wearing a ready smile for her best friend, but it wavered as she spotted a lone man there, staring into a steaming mug of coffee. Before she could ask where Callee was, she spotted a black Stetson on the seat beside him and noticed his trim, mocha brown hair. A familiar sheepskin jacket stretched across shoulders as broad as Ty's and hung open to reveal a western shirt in a deep aqua. He lifted his gaze, his eyes two shades lighter than his shirt with green flecks at the centers. Her toes curled. Wade Reynolds.

He didn't seem to recognize her. She tilted her head and smirked. "I'm relieved to see it's true."

"Huh?" His brow furrowed. Not only did he not recognize her, he didn't know what she was talking about. Seriously? Had she made no impression on this man? At the thought, she winced. *You knocked him down, and your cat pissed in his hat. You made an impression, just not the kind you're thinking.*

Roxy pointed to the Stetson. "That you have more than one hat."

Recall dawned in his eyes like sunlight shining across a sea green pool, and her knees weakened. Damn, a woman could lose her mind in that gaze if she weren't careful, but then, did she care to be careful with this man? No. Not even.

Instead of his usual slow, sexy grin, the smile he gave her could freeze fire. "Oh yeah, the lady with the cat."

He spat the word "cat" like a curse, and Roxy nixed the subjects of Tallulah and cowboy hats. She wanted to charm this guy, not turn him off. But if he felt as much as a flicker of attraction or temptation toward her, he shut it down with the speed of flicking a light switch. One more guy, one more rejection. Her bruised ego winced. Had she totally lost it? Was she so absorbed in her career—as Ty claimed—that she'd developed a man-repellant vibe? She had laughed that off when Ty had said it, but now, with Wade acting like he wished she'd disappear, a needle of doubt pricked her self-confidence. It was like she had "touch me and your dick will freeze and fall off" etched on her forehead.

She swallowed over the lump in her throat and managed to say, "Er, I'm looking for Callee—"

"That's what I figured," Wade growled, his face darkening like a storm cloud. "Look, whatever she told you about me, it isn't true. I'm not interested in being set up."

Roxy's mouth dropped open. Had he forgotten his, er, *hard* reaction to her body stretched out on top of his during the cat debacle? Or that little sexual spark that had passed between them? She hadn't. And how dare he accuse Callee of setting them up? Her temper rallied to the rescue, flooding heat into her veins.

She leaned on the table until her nose was a whisper from his. The heady scents of rich coffee and pure male appeal knocked her a bit off balance, but she managed to meet his gaze with an equally fierce glare. He needed a dose of reality, a loosening up of that laced-too-tight nature of his. "As drop-dead gorgeous and flat-out charm-

ing as I'm sure you think women find you, cowboy, I'm
not interested either. I'm meeting my best friend and her
husband here. No setup. Or hookup."

"Oh. Oh, hell, I'm…I'm…" His Adam's apple
bobbed, and a red stain rose up his neck from the depths
of his collar as he lurched to his feet, awkward, quick,
banging his long legs into the table that pinned him at
mid-thigh. The cup wobbled, spilling a tiny bit of coffee over the sides. "Please excuse my manners. I had no
idea that…that you were Roxanne Nash."

"Roxy," she said, pulling back and standing straight
as she unzipped her jacket, giving him an eyeful of
curves that other men had drooled over, but that seemed
too much for him. Wade looked away while swallowing
as though choking on his libido. Good. Roxy loved
nothing better than a challenge, and her mind was already locking in coordinates—like meeting his defense
with one of her own.

"I'm sorry. I was so, er, such an, er—I'm Wade
Reynolds." He offered to shake.

Her hand moved to his as if it had a will of its own, as
if it couldn't wait to feel his big, warm, calloused fingers
engulfing it. It was only a quick how-do-you-do gesture,
over too soon. He released her and rubbed at the side of
his neck as if he could erase the telltale embarrassment
that still had it glowing a soft pink. He noticed the coffee spill then, daubed it with his napkin, and that's when
she noticed a flash of gold on his left ring finger.

She motioned him to sit back down, and as he sank
onto the bench cushion, she considered the conundrum

of why—four years after losing his wife—a man would still wear his wedding band. Love? A prick of pity slivered her heart. She'd lost a spouse, too, and as painful as the divorce had been, she couldn't imagine what losing your significant other to death must feel like, especially if you loved that person.

She did, however, know the loneliness of reaching across the bed and finding only cold, empty space instead of a warm body. Ty, however, was still alive. She could pick up a phone and scream in his ear if the mood arose. Wade's wife was beyond such reach. After four years, though, shouldn't he have accepted that she wasn't coming back? Shouldn't he be moving on?

Maybe unlacing this man wasn't going to be as easy as it seemed.

"I really am sorry," he said, contrition turning his eyes more blue than green. "I shouldn't jump to conclusions."

Hmm, maybe she shouldn't either. Maybe he only wore the ring to ward off blind-date setups. "It'll stay our little secret."

"Okay." Wade nodded, looking somewhat relieved, and a little shocked? His neck grew red again, and his gaze shifted away from her. Roxy shook her head. He wasn't just buttoned up; he was shy. No one had ever used shy or demure or laced-up to describe Roxy. In fact, she'd been derided for her too-loud laugh, her sky-high ambitions, and her red-hot temper. There wasn't much she could do about her laugh or her short fuse. To paraphrase Lady Gaga: she was born this way. And what was wrong with having a passion for cooking? Was it a crime to go after what she wanted, trusting when caution or consideration might be called for instead?

Maybe... considering where that had gotten her.

Andrea set her coffee on the table. "You going to sit down or what?"

"In a second. Thanks." Roxy glanced at Wade, who'd gone back to studying the brew in his cup. "Mind if I join you, cowboy?"

His head jerked up. "Yeah, sure." He started to stand again, and she motioned him to stay where he was, giving him her warmest smile.

What might happen if her maverick spirit unleashed itself on his reticent one? A sensuous scenario danced through her mind of the moon crashing into the sun, explosive, fiery. Whew. Had someone just jacked up the heat in this café? She peeled off her jacket and tossed it onto the empty side of the booth, but before she could sit, she heard Callee call from behind her. "Roxy."

Roxy spun around and was immediately wrapped in a hug with her much shorter, much-missed best friend. "Oh, I can't believe you're finally home. This is going to be the best Christmas ever."

Roxy found herself nodding in agreement, although she didn't feel like she was home. She'd lost the sense of that word, put it in storage with her furniture and other belongings. Maybe once she had her own place, she would get the feeling back. The sooner, the better. "I can't think of anyone I want to spend this holiday with more than you."

Callee squeezed her hand. "I'm going to be a few more minutes. Why don't you sit, drink your coffee, and I'll bring you some chocolate pie?"

"Dosed with Godiva cappuccino liqueur?"

"If I tell you the secret McCoy recipe, I'll have to kill you." Callee laughed, her bouncy chestnut hair shifting across her shoulders.

Roxy hugged her again. Chocolate had been Roxy's go-to comfort food since she was a gangly kid with Raggedy Ann hair and a spotty complexion. Ignored or bullied. She'd been subjected to both in equal measures until she grew six inches and developed breasts and her skin cleared up. Kalispell hadn't been the happiest place for her, but as a sweet, warm sensation filled her heart now, she realized she'd missed having her best friend so near. Happy tears blurred her vision. No matter what rocky patch a woman hit in life, the journey smoothed out with the help of her girlfriends and chocolate cream pie.

Callee pulled free and directed Roxy to sit. "Oh, hi, Wade. Ah, I see you've met Roxy. Good." She said to Roxy, "He's your man."

The statement had Roxy's gaze bumping Wade's. He looked startled and about to protest Callee's matchmaking tactics, but regardless of what Wade thought, Roxy knew her best friend wasn't in the habit of arranging blind setups. Yet, she had to admit, for a second there, she'd wondered. She said, "What do you mean...my man, Callee?"

Callee laughed. "He'll be perfect for your needs."

You can say that again. But given that she hadn't told Callee about her maybe-plans for Wade, this conversation wasn't about Roxy's love life. She shrugged, indicating that she still didn't understand.

"Contractor, remodeling."

"Oh, duh." Roxy grinned.

"Well, I wish you'd let me in on the joke." Wade's frown looked painful.

Callee punched his arm. "Geez, Wade, get over yourself. Roxy is planning to buy a house in town, and she'd like your professional advice. You know, for stuff like, is the structure sound, the plumbing good, the wiring about to short out and burn the place down? I suggested she talk to you about it."

"I'm only at the looking stage, but some expertise would be appreciated." Roxy gave him an encouraging, hopeful smile. "I expect to pay you for your time, of course."

"Of course." Wade rubbed the side of his face, and that's when Roxy noticed a long, thin red scratch from his temple to his very fine jaw. She'd know that claw mark anywhere. Tallulah. She wouldn't be surprised to see Wade hesitate, as if he'd rather drink vinegar than spend time with her, even if money was involved.

But since Callee trusted his honesty, Roxy didn't want to hire someone else. This had nothing to do with wanting to have hot monkey sex with him at some point. This was about her home. Her future business. "I am also going to be looking for a commercial space."

Callee grabbed a cup of coffee as Roxy scooted into the booth, her knees bumping Wade's, eliciting an apology from him.

Roxy didn't think she'd ever met a man as polite as Wade. She offered her own "I'm sorry," then said, "I'm not sure what I'll be doing yet, but something in the food industry."

"I can't wait. Kalispell won't know what hit them." Callee released a longing sigh. "I miss your Lobster Newburg."

Wade swallowed as if his mouth had watered at the thought, and his aqua eyes softened into a warm sea green, but he surprised her by not asking about her profession or what she'd require in a kitchen, or how soon he might get to taste her cooking. Instead his mind seemed to be on carpentry. Apparently, she'd finally brought up a subject he could discuss without fear of letting down his guard or dropping his manners.

He asked, "How many square feet are you going to need?"

"Not sure yet." Roxy told herself not to get excited about the friendly glint in his eyes; it had less to do with an interest in her than an interest in work. Offering him a job, or two, apparently was the way to his heart. Maybe sweetening the deal with food at some point would get him into her bed. She filed away the information and took a sip of her espresso before saying, "I need to see the properties Quint has lined up for me to view first. My decision on what type of business I'll open is going to come down to available space and location." And budget, of course. And the arrival of her money into her new Montana bank account.

"Did I hear someone mention location?" Quint McCoy sauntered up to their table, as in need of a haircut and shave as the last time she'd seen him. He preferred a skiff of whiskers on his strong jaw, and his blue-black hair perpetually kissed his collar. Today, he wore a chef's coat over faded jeans and Dan Post boots. He'd inherited electric-blue eyes from his mother, learned his salesman's mentality at his daddy's knee, and Callee loved him so much she'd even taken to fishing with him. *Fishing. Ewww*. A mini-shudder went through Roxy. She preferred to get her seafood at a marketplace, and God, she was going to miss Pike Place Market. It had every kind of fresh catch she could ever want.

She gave Quint a smile. "So the rumors are true. The king of real estate dabbles in flour dough as well as fishing."

He smirked, rubbing at his scruffy jaw. "Yeah, I'm a regular triple threat."

Roxy snorted. It was hard not to be sucked in by that McCoy charm, that twinkle in his eyes, that easygoing manner, but she hadn't quite forgiven Quint for the hell he'd put Callee through earlier this year. As far as she was concerned, he was on probation until he convinced her that he'd never hurt Callee again.

"It's a joy to watch him working side by side with his mama," Callee said, reaching up and wiping a touch of flour from her husband's cheek. He nuzzled her hand.

It wasn't until he'd almost lost his mother last spring that Callee had discovered her husband could bake a pie to rival Molly's. A secret that went back to junior high, thanks to some bullying kids and a teenage boy's fragile ego. He'd finally found his balls, though, 'fessed up, and claimed his talent. Roxy supposed he deserved props for that.

Callee said, "Hon, Roxy wants to hear about the properties you've lined up for her to look at."

Quint hugged Callee to his side. "I've got a couple of places that I think will meet your must-have list, but if not, your reaction to these properties will narrow down the hunt."

"Sounds great. Can we look at something now?" Roxy caught hold of her parka, anxious to move forward in this new beginning and to spend a little alone time with the tempting Mr. Reynolds.

"Uh, I can't leave for another hour or so, Roxy," Quint said. "Sorry. Jane went home early today, and Mama picked up a special order this afternoon for a last-minute social affair the mayor is throwing tonight. She and I are filling that order now."

"Anything I can do to help?" Roxy asked, more than eager to get back into a chef's kitchen than she realized. If she didn't know better, she'd swear olive oil pulsed in her veins.

"Nope," Quint said, "but thanks for the offer. We've got this one covered." Quint seemed to notice Wade for the first time, and he gave his friend a full-on, blinder of a grin. "Hey, buddy, how are you? Glad you could make it."

The men did a fist bump, then Quint added, "I was hoping you'd do me a huge favor and take Roxy over to look at Nick's loft."

A loft? Roxy hadn't even considered a loft—she'd been thinking small house or condo—but a loft sounded intriguing. The best part was Wade taking her to see it. The telltale rosiness crept up Wade's neck again. Despite his collar being unbuttoned, he looked as though it were choking him. Roxy expected an "I forgot I have an appointment that I'm late for" excuse to pop out of his scrumptious mouth any second, but either he was slow on his thinking feet or lacked a devious gene. He nodded like a dying man accepting his fate. "Yeah, sure."

"Great." Quint handed him a set of keys, then turned back to Roxy. "The loft is 1800 square feet. It has one large bedroom with a huge walk-in closet. The reason that I'd like our ace contractor to go with you to this viewing is that I know the kitchen isn't going to suit your needs, and the bathroom is probably too masculine. But in case you think the place has possibilities, then Wade can work up a ballpark figure of how much the potential renovations might cost."

Quint caught his wife around the waist. "By the time you two get back here, Callee and I will be free. Steaks are on me tonight."

"Damned straight they are," Wade told Quint, draining his coffee mug and scooting out of the booth just as Roxy did the same.

Quint caught Roxy's gaze. "Come say hi to Mama before you take off."

Callee squeezed his arm. "Let them go look at the loft first. Molly is up to her elbows in pies right now."

"Wife knows best," Quint said, his gaze full of love. To look at them now, Roxy might never know they'd almost divorced after the death of his father last year, but somehow they'd set aside their differences, got the pie shop up and running, and eventually found their way back to each other.

Maybe she was being too hard on Quint.

Wade waited for her at the door. They stepped outside into the cold afternoon. It had stopped snowing, and the beauty wrought by Mother Nature stole her breath. It was a real, live winter wonderland. Christmas shoppers poured into and out of the mall. Cars and trucks inched along Front Street, and the crisp air nipped at her ears and nose. She donned her fuzzy earmuffs and fur-lined gloves. "So, how far away is this loft?"

"Six blocks. You can follow me."

Wow, he really doesn't want to spend any time with me. She stopped and glared at him, the three-inch heels on her boots putting her eyes level with his. "I have an idea. Since we're both going to the same place and then returning here, why don't we do something really crazy, like take one vehicle?"

His Adam's apple bobbed as he adjusted his Stetson and pointed to the big white pickup that had scared her so badly the other night. It looked like it hadn't been washed since last summer. She pointed to the Escalade. "Let's take mine. You were itching to drive it the other night."

She held the Escalade keys toward him like a dangled carrot and saw his eyes light up, but then a shadow of distrust and hesitation dulled the gleam. What did he think she would do if he reached for the keys? Yank them away like Lucy in the Peanuts cartoon did to Charlie Brown's football?

"Is that cat still inside?" he asked.

Her eyes widened. Was he kidding? The temperature had dipped into the teens, and she'd been in the pie shop for a good half hour. Who left their pet out in weather like this? Not her. She didn't even try to keep the sarcasm from her voice. "Tallulah is nice and warm at my mother's house."

"Good."

"Good that she's safe and not freezing to death? Or good that you don't need to interact with her again?"

A "what do you think" smirk appeared as he fingered the claw mark on his face.

"Yeah," she said, reining in her temper, "that's what I thought."

He released the remote locks, approaching the Cadillac with the same reverence he'd shown the other night. It was the first time in her life she'd ever wished she was a vehicle, wished a man would look at her the way he was looking at this beautiful hunk of metal and chrome. What was it with guys and cars?

When he opened the passenger door for her, the retractable step emerged, an aid to climbing into the taller-than-usual vehicle, and he released a low whistle of amazement. "Now that's a nice feature."

"It is." Not that he needed it with his long legs. Neither did she. She slid inside and sank onto the buttery-soft seat, the scent of new leather rife in every inhaled breath. He swung up and into the driver's seat, settling behind the wheel as if the space had been built to accommodate his large frame. But he didn't put the key into the ignition. She said, "The gas pedal comes toward you, so that you can move the seat back to accommodate your legs."

"Sweet." His gaze shifted to the dashboard. "Looks more like the cockpit of an airplane than a car. What do all these gadgets do?"

"I haven't a clue. I didn't order this luxury ride. My ex-husband did."

He arched a brow at her. "And you took it away in the divorce? Is that what you meant by consolation prize?"

"Not exactly." She wasn't going to discuss her finances with him unless they pertained to his salary and her renovations. "Let's just say it's more of a loaner."

"Okay." For the first time since she'd met him, Wade Reynolds laughed out loud, and the sound went straight to her erogenous zones.

Chapter Three

❦

"That's the local gym," Wade said as he steered the amazing Cadillac through the snowy street toward the loft.

"For the record, I grew up in Kalispell." There was no reproach in her voice, but Wade felt heat climbing his neck. Either she was talking about his tour-guide conversation or the other night when he'd called her a *Seattle driver*, implying she couldn't drive in snowy conditions. *That's what you get for assuming, Reynolds.* He couldn't seem to say anything right to this woman. He wouldn't care, except she was Callee's best friend and his potential customer. He'd lost his shirt on the cherry ranch and could use as many jobs as he and his crew could handle. "Look, we got off on the wrong foot, but—"

She rushed to speak. "I'm sorry about Tallulah—"

"No. I told you, it's okay."

They fell silent again, and the oxygen in the Cadillac seemed to disappear. He could barely breathe, but he didn't know if it was the Escalade or the woman that had his nerves jacked. Maybe both. The buttery leather upholstery felt too alien, too new, despite it molding his ass like a well-worn saddle, and the gizmos on the dashboard would befuddle an electronic geek. He didn't like a truck to be smarter than him. Nick, however, would love this shit. Probably Quint, too. But Wade hadn't grown up playing Xbox or video games. When it wasn't basketball season, he went directly home after school and worked construction with his father and grandfather.

"Well, I'll be damned," she said, pulling him out of his thoughts. "The Broken Spur is alive and well."

"Yep." He glanced past her at the run-down saloon, easing his foot off the gas, slowing to a near crawl. "Still going strong."

"Strong?" She laughed, the sound as throaty and sensuous as that old Patsy Cline song his granddad used to play over and over. He swallowed, his mouth oddly dry, his palms damp. She said, "I don't recall that bar ever being anything more than a mediocre dive."

"Yeah, most of the patrons are the same regulars they were back in the day, but they're older and fewer every year." He nosed the Cadillac to the curb across from the bar, and her attention shifted to him, giving him the full force of those disturbingly beautiful, unnerving, sage green eyes. "Here we are."

Roxy peered out the windshield at the storefront door between two shops. Nick hadn't removed his logo yet—

Adz R Taz—and there was a sign giving the new location of his business. Wade climbed out of the Escalade and hurried around the front bumper to get her door, but she was already out and joining him on the sidewalk. Sarah had always waited.

He cleared his throat. "The only reason I mentioned the gym is that it hasn't been here more than six months. I wasn't sure if you'd seen it when you were last in town."

"I didn't. It's like two blocks that way, right?" She pointed toward Front Street, obviously familiar with this block.

He nodded. "Reasonable membership, too." God, what was wrong with him? Why was he bringing up the gym again? Prattling on like a teenager on a first date. Whoa. Where had that come from? This wasn't a date. He would never date someone like Roxy. She was, she was...not what he was looking for. From her wild red hair, to her blunt tongue, to her long legs that seemed to go on forever—she fell into the category of what his grandpa would've called the kind of woman you did things with that you wouldn't do with your wife.

Even as a teenage boy with zero sexual experience, he knew that meant any woman who got his dick standing at attention and his hormones racing by just looking at her. She definitely had that effect on him, and it was taking all his effort to resist her allure.

"It's an interesting location," Roxy said as he opened the door for her, catching a fruity scent wafting from her, the same fragrance he'd noticed the night she landed on top of him in the snow. She smelled like she'd been rolling in oranges. He hadn't known he liked oranges so much until he realized his blood was rushing south like a flock of geese for the winter.

Get a grip, Reynolds.

"Who is Nick, by the way?"

"Nick Taziano. He's done all the advertising for the pie shop, set up a website, and stuff. He did the same for me when I got back into building full time. He's great with logos and branding. Once you're ready to launch your new business, I'd recommend you talk to Nick."

"Thanks for the suggestion. I'll keep him in mind."

They stepped into the foyer, and Wade locked the door behind them and switched on lights, exposing a wide staircase straight ahead. Roxy's attention seemed to slide across the room and up to the second-floor landing, then back and into the spaces behind the stairwell. "I know this is Kalispell, where a lot of folks never lock their doors, but coming off five years in Seattle, I'm a bit skittish about all the nooks and crannies on this level."

"Nothing scary back there. Come on, I'll show you." He gestured for her to follow as he moved past the staircase and down a short hall. "This is an elevator, and that larger door directly across from it opens on the garage. As you can see, it's wide enough, high enough, and long enough to accommodate your 'loaner' rig."

She peered into the empty, finished space. "Nowhere for anyone or anything to hide."

Wade bumped his hat higher off his forehead, meeting her gaze as something she might need to know occurred to him. "There's no outdoor space for the cat, though."

Roxy nodded. "Tallulah isn't much for the outdoors. She was a city cat, starving when I found her pawing through the garbage behind my waterfront restaurant. I thought at first she was slumming, lured by the aroma of day-old seafood, but when no one claimed her, I took her home, and after that, she wouldn't go outside on her own. A vet told me she was a purebred, and that she'd been spayed at a young age, but no one answered my ads, and she didn't have any identifying chip. I don't know if someone abandoned her hoping she'd find a home or if she'd escaped and couldn't find her way back."

"Sounds like she was lucky she found you."

"And vice versa." Roxy's laughter echoed off the walls. That laugh again. Too loud, too throaty, too blood-stirring, sending his mind across the border of sanity and self-control and into the land of sexual imagery. Steam seemed to flush through his veins. Was probably coming out his ears. What the hell? If he didn't get control of himself, no telling what might happen.

He grappled for his composure, forcing his mind to the task at hand. He gestured toward the elevator. "Just step in and hit two for the second floor." He followed her into the small space, his gaze riveted on the swish of her curvy ass, his mind threatening to skid into the danger zone again.

"The elevator would be handy for moving in." She

turned toward him as she spoke and seemed disconcerted to find him standing so close. She tried stepping back, but there was nowhere to go. If they weren't both so tall, perhaps the space wouldn't seem so snug, or the air so full of her irresistible orange-y scent.

The short ride ended, and disappointment tumbled through Wade. The elevator door opened onto a wide landing. Roxy stepped out, then stopped, and he nearly rammed into her. She glanced over her shoulder and asked, "Nick Taziano...Isn't he married to Molly's pastry chef, Jane?"

"Yep." His gaze snagged on her hair, such a rich, bright red, like the juice of the cherries he used to grow. He fisted his hands at his sides to keep from touching it. "They're expecting a baby in a couple of months."

"Yes, now I remember. Callee did mention that." Roxy moved toward the door. "I suppose they needed more room with a baby on the way."

"Yep." Wade exited the elevator, joining Roxy beside the door. "The space they've moved into is another of the buildings that Molly owns. The first level has a large room like this for Nick's advertising business and a private area that will be perfect for the baby. Since he works out of his residence, Nick can pretty much set his own hours and take care of the baby while Jane is at work. He wants her to have the career she's always dreamed of."

Roxy's soft eyes widened in amazement, and a touch of regret revealed itself in their depths. "That's pretty great of him. Not all guys feel that way."

"Are you speaking from experience?" Wade knew he hadn't expected Sarah to work, but she'd wanted to own a cherry orchard.

"You mean my ex?" Roxy asked, giving a toss of her head, causing that fiery hair to shimmy. "He thought I put my career before him. It's the hazard of having a job you're passionate about, I guess. It's easy to get swept up in it and not even bother to check a clock. I missed a lot of appointments, dinner dates."

"And time is often shorter than we imagine it's going to be."

The words were like a guitar strum in the quiet—striking, attention-catching, melancholy. She touched his arm, nodding, understanding, a wealth of sympathy in the gentle pressure of her hand on his forearm, and it nearly undid him. He hadn't meant to let her into his personal sadness. He gave himself a mental shake, held up the key to the loft, and opened the door. A blast of hot air greeted them like a tropical breeze escaping.

Roxy said, "Whoa, someone isn't worried about their electric bill."

Wade caught the odor of fresh paint. "I'm guessing Quint or Nick was painting in here, and the heat is to help it dry faster."

"Well, I feel like I'm on a Florida beach in the height of summer." She pulled off her gloves and earmuffs, and then stripped off her jacket, draping it over a ladder in the middle of the room. Wade didn't mean to notice that her nipples stood erect beneath the tight sweater, seeming as if they might just poke through the fabric. His mouth watered, and his blood headed south. Roxy was right. It felt like the Gobi desert in here. He peeled off his sheepskin coat and placed it atop her parka.

But when he turned to look at her, he couldn't keep his eyes on her face; they kept wandering over her generous curves, rousing images of how she'd look naked, her skin a creamy pink with a scattering of freckles here and there. *God, man, get your mind out of your boxers.*

Think about something else. Anything. "I did the original remodel on this for Quint's dad before he passed away. So I can vouch for the electrical and plumbing. It's an open loft with a bedroom, bath, and kitchenette on one wall. But as you can see, it's big as a basketball court and the kitchenette could lend itself to a reconfiguration if the overall space suits your purposes."

He'd grown so used to coming here once or twice a week to share coffee and BS with Nick and Quint that the emptiness felt jarring. Time passing. Another reminder that nothing stayed the same, and if he didn't jump aboard life's ever-moving train, he'd never get back on track. Light poured in through factory-sized windows mounted in distressed brick walls. Roxy nodded, eyeing them with a look of pleasure on her face. "This is very unexpected. And I'm surprised how bright it is. I like that. And it is huge. It's not bad. Not bad at all." She strode from end to end as though pacing off footage, probably envisioning what she could do with the space to make it work.

"What kind of business are you going to open?"

"I'm not sure yet." She pushed a hand through her

layered hair, causing his pulse to skip. "I need to research what's working and what's not working in Flathead County. I don't want to make a hasty decision that I'll regret later on." A glint of remorse passed through her eyes that told him she'd done that before, leaped without looking and been slammed for it, but maybe not in business. Wade sensed it was a personal decision of some kind. Her marriage? Her divorce?

Although he wondered, he didn't ask, replying instead to her comment about scoping out the prospects before deciding on what business she wanted to open. "Nothing wrong with being cautious."

She sighed. "Yeah, restaurants are risky businesses, most failing before they can gain a footing."

"Yeah, a few restaurants have opened around the lake, but they don't seem to last long. This area booms in the summer, tourists everywhere, but the rest of the year you need to rely on locals to keep your business going. I know. I used to own a cherry business."

"I'm sorry. That must have been difficult."

"It was." The truth was, the cherry orchard had been Sarah's love, not his. She was the one with the green thumb. He couldn't grow weeds. "I wasn't raised on a farm. I had no feel for growing crops. I'm a third-generation builder. That's all I've really done since I was a kid, and it's just in my blood."

"I always knew I wanted to cook. I guess we're lucky that way. Knowing what we wanted young enough to pursue it. But now I'm up in the air. I wasn't prepared for the sudden shift in my life."

"Yeah, I know how that feels."

"Anyway, what you said about the restaurants is exactly what my research showed. Whatever I decide to do, I will need to cater it to the folks who live here year-round."

"Like a catering service?" He grinned at his own pun, but her eyes brightened.

"The funny thing is, that's what Callee and I talked about doing together when we were kids. But it turned out she doesn't have a passion for cooking."

"But she's a helluva designer."

"That she is." Roxy glanced at the kitchenette—appliances, cupboards, and sink all on one wall. "This would do for now, but not if I decide to make this my permanent residence. I'd need a huge island for one thing, a farmhouse sink, and at least a six- or eight-burner stove. A couple of wall ovens. And a gigantic double-wide fridge. Is there room for all that?"

He grinned, throwing out the widths and lengths from memory. She asked questions, smart about the process. Listening to her discuss potential changes that could be made in the loft reminded Wade of how he approached remodel projects. It wasn't so much that she knew what she wanted; it was that she could envision it. Perversely, he found that a turn-on.

"What is the bedroom like?" she asked.

He pointed to the door in the end wall. "You tell me."

She disappeared inside, and he followed. When she heard his footsteps on the hardwood flooring, she glanced around at him. "This is a large room. I like that the windows are high, letting in light without letting anyone actually see into the room. Chefs keep strange hours, up before the roosters in the morning and back in bed while most people are just starting to party."

Wade's mind snagged on an image of her in bed, her hair tousled from sleep, a sheet sliding off her creamy shoulder. The reaction of his body kept him from following her to the bathroom.

She let out a delighted sigh. "Ooh, this is so spacious, lots of countertop and storage and a giant shower with dual rain shower heads."

Great; now he was picturing her naked in the shower with the water raining down on her, nipples beaded, rivulets of water slipping between her full breasts, over her flat tummy, between the crevices and folds at the juncture of those long, sweet legs. Damn, it had been eons since he'd been naked with a woman, and his body was rallying to change that even as he stood there trying to deny it to himself.

"But a soaker tub, too?" Her face went all dreamy, and the muscles that allowed him to swallow froze. "I love bubble baths, candles glowing, a glass of wine. Pure heaven after a steaming hot day in the kitchen."

Wade felt steamy hot, in need of a long, cold shower. "Did you see the walk-in closet?"

"There's a walk-in closet? Sold."

She ducked inside, and Wade heard her squeal. He peeked in. She was hugging herself, and he wanted his arms around her. She spun toward him, smiling, catching the look in his eyes, and it seemed to immobilize them, as if time had suddenly stopped. She ran her tongue across her lips, and he couldn't look away from her mouth. She sucked in a breath, shook her head— once, twice—as though trying to break free of the spell that bound them.

She closed the gap between them, a smoldering light ablaze in her pale eyes. "You really are gorgeous, cowboy, and there's no denying that some kind of electric storm is raging between us. You feel it. I feel it, too. And there is nothing I'd like more than to encourage you to act on how we're both feeling." She'd backed him against the closet door frame. "Only you're not ready to let go of the past.

"But if you were, I'd stand really close to you like this, and shove my hands into your hair like this, and pull your head toward me, and kiss you like this." She kissed his mouth, hard, not sweet or gentle as he was used to being kissed, but with a pressure that ignited a fuse in him. Then her tongue was pushing inside his mouth, shocking him, the sensation at once foreign, yet damned pleasurable.

She pulled away, leaving him breathless, panting for more. She was also breathing fast. "If you were ready, I'd press against you like this, run my hands up your back like this, and I'd tell you that just touching you makes me weak in the knees and crazed with desire. And you'd push your hands under my sweater like this, up under my bra, to torture my tingling breasts." She shoved his hands beneath her sweater as she spoke, slowing, torturously bringing them to the rigid beads.

Her breasts were full in his palms, and an earthy groan slipped from between his lips. She threw her head back and moaned. "Oh, my..."

"And if you were ready, I'd unbutton your shirt and pull it loose from your jeans, then slip my fingers through your chest hair—God, I love a man with chest hair—and you'd put your hands on my bottom, like this." She placed his hands on her butt and pulled herself hard against his erection, their hips meeting, grinding, the need a pulsing, living entity.

She was kissing him again, working the buttons of his jeans. He'd lost his mind completely; all he wanted was to be inside this woman with her legs wrapped around him, as he drove deeper and deeper. But she was pushing back again. Pulling his hands from her, pushing away from him, trying to catch her breath. "It would be so nice, but you can see that it's impossible, right?"

"No." He grabbed her by the waist, urging her closer. "Why is it impossible?"

"On the surface, we'd be a perfect 'friends-with-benefits' couple, since I'm never falling in love again, never getting married again, and you're still in love with your wife. We're both looking for someone who will satisfy that itch five or six times a month without expecting anything more than a romp in the hay. I admit that it would be nice if that someone was a person I also had amazing chemistry with. The kind we're feeling right now. But you're not the kind of guy who has casual affairs. If you were, you'd have removed your wedding ring long ago."

His silence seemed to confirm it for her.

"Yeah, I thought so," she said, looking sorry to be right. "I hope your wife knew how lucky she was to have you."

Lucky? Wade almost laughed at the absurdity. The only thing keeping his ring on his finger was guilt, and giving in to his baser instincts with Roxy would only make the guilt worse. But at that moment, he wanted to grab her and kiss her so damned bad, it was killing him. Instead, he let her step back, watched her as she righted her bra and her sweater, her lips puffy and sexy as hell.

"I don't know about you, cowboy, but make-out sessions always give me one hell of an appetite," she said, a bit breathlessly. "Let's go get that steak Quint offered."

Wade watched her sashay to the ladder and don her outdoor gear. His considerable discomfort wasn't allowing him to move just yet. He had a hell of an appetite, all right. But not for steak.

Chapter Four

∽

Wade brought the hammer down so hard the nail head bent. Swearing under his breath, he wrenched it out with the prongs, then found another nail, and forced himself to show restraint. The idea wasn't to ruin the trim in Ian Erikksen's new kitchen, but to make the nail disappear into the dark strip of wood. Finishing touches. It was his favorite part of a project, when it all came together. Usually.

But everywhere he looked he was reminded of that crazy redhead. In the curve of the counter, he saw her curves, in the streaks of sage and rust-colored flecks woven throughout the granite, he saw her eyes, and to make it worse, there was a fruit bowl near the sink, sending off an orange fragrance every time he inhaled.

Footsteps on the new plank flooring brought Wade's gaze to a pair of stockinged feet that belonged to the owner of this kitchen. Ian Erikksen, aka Ice, hailed from

Malibu and had the dark tan and sun-streaked, cropped blond hair of a guy more comfortable on a surfboard than just about anywhere else. His parents were Hollywood big names, but from what he'd gotten to know of Ian, that was just a fact, not a definition of the man he was. Ian clapped his hands on the arms of his San Diego Chargers sweatshirt and swore. "It's so cold outside I think my balls left for Malibu."

"Well, let's put out an Amber alert, 'cause I'm sure this qualifies as missing little ones," Quint said, strolling in with a Big Sky Pie box.

Ian snorted and called Quint a name that made Quint laugh. Quint set the pie box on the dining room table that offered seating for six and was made from reclaimed barn wood. It stood next to a glacier rock fireplace with a heavy mantel and a gas insert.

"Maybe you should have opted for a wood-burning fireplace," Wade said.

"What he needs is a good pair of long johns until his body acclimates..." Nick Taziano stepped into the room, dragging a hand over his dark hair, his brown eyes crinkling at the corners, his deep dimples flashing. "Like in six years from now."

"Meantime, though I've never personally tried it," Wade said, getting to his feet and hooking his hammer onto his tool belt, "I hear a set of hand-warmers shoved into your underwear feels pretty good."

That elicited a few more rude remarks from each of the guys, and soon male guffaws were bouncing through the kitchen, Ian laughing hardest of all. But when the laughter quieted, Nick and Quint were checking out the kitchen.

Nick said, "This has really come together."

Ian beamed as if he'd done the actual work, then surprised Wade by saying, "The credit belongs to Reynolds. It's like he tapped into my vision of it."

"Callee did most of the tapping," Wade said, embarrassed by the praise, but also pleased that he'd satisfied such a fussy customer. He knew his work would be as good as any that Ian could find in California, but Ian hadn't known that; he'd taken Quint and Callee's word for it. It meant everything to Wade to validate his friends' belief in him. "I'm glad you like it, though I have to say, a six-burner Viking stove might be a bit of overkill for a woman who can barely boil water." Wade knew; he'd dated Andrea Lovette before she and Ian fell in love.

"I'm not marrying Andrea for her cooking." Ian grinned. "That stove is for me."

Wade scratched the side of his head. "My dick is longer than my cooking repertoire. I can bake a potato, fry eggs, and barbeque a mean steak."

"What more could a man want?" Nick said, eyeing the box on the table.

"Pie..." Quint said.

"You jokers want some coffee to go with that?"

The four pulled up to the table, and Quint extracted a pie with a golden crust and mile-high meringue.

"You guys know I'm not much on sweets, but I'm getting addicted to these weekly indulgences. What is that one?" Ian asked, gaze glued to the baked treasure that Quint was about to slice into.

"Chocolate cream," Quint said.

"Oh, hell, yeah," Nick said.

"Oh, man," Ian agreed, the look in his eyes contradicting his statement about sweets.

Wade's mouth watered as Quint extracted the first slice, exposing the rich, fudgy-brown center, and placed in onto a plate. It had to be the thickest chocolate cream pie he'd ever laid eyes on. He used to believe having dessert before noon was breaking some golden rule, but that notion crashed and burned the first time Quint brought one of Big Sky Pie's decadent treats to these guy get-togethers. Nothing better than one of Molly McCoy's specials of the month being consumed between chatter about fishing, cameras, surfing, and women. Throw in some coffee and a dollop of BS, and it was perfect.

Quint handed out the plates, giving Wade his pie last.

Nick lifted his fork, admiring the dessert with pride, obviously thinking his wife had made it. "Would you look at this crust?"

"Jane is an artist with pastry, Taz. She really is," Quint said, digging into his slice.

Nick nodded, grinning at the compliment, but sighing like a man even more pleased with what he was eating.

Ian made another joke about rude pig sounds, and a burst of gleeful male snorts and chuckles filled the room, but then silence reigned as everyone concentrated on eating. Nick spoke first, licking meringue from his upper lips. "Damn, I like chocolate cream pie, but this is the...fucking...best."

"Umm," Ian agreed.

Wade didn't think it got much better than this. Good buddies, great pie, and even better camaraderie, but the sweet treat wasn't sitting well on his stomach. Quint noticed him tracing lines through the chocolate. "What's up with you, Reynolds? Still a little green around the gills from the twenty-ounce steak you consumed the other night?"

Ian liked telling them about watching fat content and how healthy it was to eat more vegetables than beef. He eyed Wade as if he'd suddenly turned into Kermit the Frog. "You ate a steak that size by yourself? Whoa, do you know what that stuff can do to your arteries?"

To avoid a lecture on cholesterol, Wade said, "Quint was buying, and I wanted my money's worth."

Quint snorted. "Ha. He's still pissed at me for sending him to show Callee's best friend Nick and Jane's loft."

Wade glared at Quint. "You sent me with her in another 'get Wade laid' scheme, didn't you? Admit it."

Quint's amused expression rankled. "Hey, what's the matter? Roxy too much woman for your deprived libido?"

Nick tried to hide a grin, but his dimples gave it away.

"It's not funny, you pricks."

"Ah, man, you're the prickly one," Quint said. "Touchy as a porcupine these days. Nothing a generous woman couldn't cure."

Wade's neck burned as if he were standing in the sunlight instead of leaning on the table over a piece of half-eaten chocolate pie. Damn it to hell. They could read him like a blueprint. Maybe he should find someone to take the edge off, but he was too embarrassed to admit his lack of experience with women, to admit he'd never had sex with anyone but Sarah. If he told these yahoos that, they were likely to revoke his man-card. "She's not my type."

Why did that sound like a lie? Why couldn't he get her out of his mind? The memory of her kiss had him swallowing so hard that Quint noticed. "She's not my type," Wade repeated and knew instantly, by the light in Quint's eyes, that he had gone too far, protested too much.

"I don't know what you're so pissed off about, and it doesn't look like you're going to tell us. Are you?" Quint said, then seemed to get an idea. "God, don't tell me you're actually attracted to Roxy?"

"Judging by the color of his neck, I think you struck a nerve, McCoy," Ian said, smirking.

"No, he didn't," Wade protested. "Roxy is Callee's best friend, for one thing, and that would be weird."

"Why?" Nick asked. "Jane works for the McCoys and that's not weird."

"She's not my type. I-I-I like small, demure women. Roxy's loud, swears like a truck driver, and has a cat."

"A cat?" Ian's brows shot up. "What have you got against cats?"

"I'm a dog guy."

"You don't have a dog," Quint said, grinning, obviously enjoying Wade's discomfort.

"We had one at the cherry orchard."

"I thought he had to be put down." Nick took another piece of pie.

"He was old and in pain. It was the humane thing to do." But after losing Sarah, it had also been another painful death for Emily and him. He couldn't bear to think about replacing the dog, even though Emily had been asking for a puppy. "I've been thinking about getting another dog...for Emily...for Christmas. A Lab."

"I'm surprised Emily doesn't like cats," Nick said around a bit of pie. "Are either of you allergic?"

"No."

"Then what do you have against cats?" Ian asked again.

"Not against all cats. Against her cat. The damned thing pissed in my Stetson."

"What?" Nick Taziano burst out laughing, spewing pie across the table. "What the hell?"

Wade told them the story, and his best buddies collapsed in peals of laughter. Wade found himself grinning, too. It still irked him, but then it was also kind of funny. "Damnedest thing I ever saw. That cat perched on the brim, hunkered down, and let go."

"I could use that in a script." Ian got up and refilled his coffee. "It's funny."

"Bottom line, I have zero romantic interest in Roxy."

Quint didn't say anything, just stared at him, his eyes narrowed, obviously suspicious. "Callee said she noticed some sparks between you and Roxy the other night at dinner. I didn't think much of it when she told me, but—"

"No, no." Wade shook his head. "That was just my love for the steak you bought me."

"Yeah, if you say so."

"I guess, since you're all focused on my love life, you'll shut up when I tell you that I've decided to give dating a try again. But I'm not looking for romance, just companionship. Ideally I'd like someone a lot like Sarah. So if you can't resist fixing me up, please, keep that in mind."

"Like Sarah," Nick said, exchanging a secret look with Quint.

"Okay," Quint said. "Like Sarah."

Why, Wade wondered, did he have the feeling that his friends didn't think finding another Sarah was a good thing?

"Just as well," Quint added, "that you're not into Roxy. She's coming off a pretty nasty divorce. I don't think she's interested in getting involved with anyone yet. And to be honest, I don't think you're her type, either."

What did that mean? Why wasn't he Roxy's type? She'd seemed pretty into that kiss they shared. Pretty into their touching and . . . What the hell? He was hard just thinking about it. "What do you mean, she's not into me?"

Wade's best friends burst out laughing.

* * *

"What are you going to do?" Valentina Nash—all five feet, size two with mile-high, auburn hair—peered up at Roxy over the rim of her leopard-framed half-glasses. She had that look in her eyes, the look mothers give their daughters that doesn't require explanation. The daughter knows exactly to what her mother is referring. In this case, her mother was asking about Roxy's future, her very near future. She'd been home less than a week, but apparently, like last week's catch of the day, she'd already overstayed her welcome. It wasn't that the three-bedroom rambler couldn't accommodate the two of them. No, this had more to do with a certain twenty-pound cat, who used her guest toilet and shed white fur on her red sofa.

Valentina glared at Tallulah, confirming Roxy's suspicion, and said, "That beast belongs in a zoo. Some breed of wild cat, I tell you. She walked across the computer keyboard this morning and somehow deleted my 'Dear Valentina' column. My editor was already screaming for it, and now I need to rewrite the whole thing."

Tallulah meowed, jumped onto the red sofa, lifted her leg, and began licking herself. Mother made a disgusted face. "Seriously, Roxy. What are you going to do? I can't take much more of that…creature."

"I'm sorry, Mom. I'm trying to find a place."

"If you hadn't chased your husband away, you'd still have a place. And a restaurant."

And your column would be winging its way through cyberspace to your editor at the online news outlet even as we speak. The sister of the tummy ache Roxy had had the day she'd left Seattle showed up, making her want to scream in frustration. She forced herself to keep an even tone. "It's not my fault Ty cheated on me."

"Darling, it's always the woman's fault." Her mother lifted her chin, as if to say she'd managed to keep one husband clam-happy for thirty-five years without a hitch, not to mention being a paid professional at giving women advice on how to hang onto their men for almost as long. "You should have tried to patch it up."

A slow burn flared in Roxy's chest. She had tried. For two whole weeks. She'd gone back as her mother advised her to do. She accepted his promise to end it with the girlfriend, believed him when he swore he'd never cheat again, and even enjoyed a renewed honeymoon happiness—until the day she'd found the cheerleader's panties in their bed.

Roxy clamped her lips together. Mom didn't need all the sordid details, but the only way to convince her that a woman didn't need a man was to prove that she could take care of herself. But how did she do that without the cash to either purchase or rent a house or apartment?

She supposed she could ask Mom to loan her the money until hers came through, but it would probably only garner yet another lecture on why she needed a man. Besides, she couldn't decide if she wanted to rent or buy, if she wanted an apartment or a house or a condo. Or a loft. She groaned to herself as she carried her empty coffee cup to the kitchen and deposited it in the dishwasher, feeling a cloud of depression descending on her.

She needed to clear her head. She donned her new Uggs and parka, calling to her mother as she tied a scarf around her neck and grabbed her keys. "I'm going out for a while. Quint is showing me a couple of houses." *God help me for lying.* She had no idea where Quint was, or his friend Wade. "I'll be back in a few hours."

She stroked the top of the cat's head. "Behave yourself, Tallulah."

Tallulah purred innocently, but the cat had a mind of her own. No telling what mischief she might get up to.

Once Roxy was in the Escalade, she just started driving. The roads were slick, the sky gray and gloomy, not that different from a late December morning in Seattle. As she drove, questions plagued her. *What are you going to do? Where are you going to live? What kind of business do you want to open? What are you going to do about your feelings for Wade Reynolds?*

The last thought seemed to come out of nowhere. For two days now, she'd been avoiding the subject of Wade like she would a big, hairy spider. Images and sensations washed through her. Why had she behaved so wantonly with Wade? Now she couldn't stop thinking about him, wanting him. She must have been out of her mind the other night, all but seducing him. It was as if she'd been possessed. Okay, so he was undeniably delightful on the eyes, smelling as if his shirts were dried on a summer breeze, and that shy demeanor suggested a wild nature leashed so taut it might release a hurricane if she touched the right button. And God, she'd wanted to find that button.

Her mouth watered, and her pulse ticked a beat faster. The craziest part was that they had some kind of chemistry that seemed to hum on the air, unheard by the naked ear, a kind of carnal radio frequency. A siren's lure. But he wasn't ready. He wasn't a one-night stand or a fling kind of guy. She'd made him realize that. Right?

"What are you going to do?" Recalling her mother's words sent the sexy longings fleeing.

Decisions, decisions, decisions. When she'd left Seattle, she'd planned to hit Kalispell running, get a home, settle on a business, restart her life. But without her money, that plan had gone up in smoke before she'd even left Seattle. The weird thing was, though, once she was here, something changed. Like a switch being flipped. Roxy couldn't believe how indecisive she was, how insecure she felt about the choices she needed to make regarding her future. Usually she was so sure of what she wanted and didn't want. But it was as if she'd had the rug yanked out from beneath her Crocs, robbing her of her self-assurance, self-confidence, and independent nature.

She seemed almost afraid to make a choice for fear it would set her back another five or six years. She'd been on the verge of getting the career recognition she'd worked for since her teens, and then the whole thing blew up in her face like a pressure cooker. She'd tried balancing love and career, but cooking always won out. And now it was all she had. But did she want to cook just anywhere? She didn't know. She really didn't know.

Her palms felt damp inside her gloves. What if she

screwed up again? What if she bought a home in Kalispell and then regretted it? What if she started a business and lost everything this time? What if she couldn't kill the attraction to Wade?

She thought she might upchuck her breakfast. She couldn't go on like this, worried every minute that she'd make another serious mistake. She'd end up with an ulcer. There had to be somewhere she could turn to for advice, other than to her mother. She glanced up and realized she'd driven to the pie shop.

Hmm. Maybe her subconscious was smarter than she was.

She entered the kitchen of Big Sky Pie through the back door. She'd expected to come across the whole staff this time of the morning, but only a woman with spiked red hair stood at a professional-grade, stainless steel stove, stirring ingredients into a large saucepan. She wore a chef's coat and was humming along with a soft Latino ballad playing on the radio.

"The aroma in here should be illegal," Roxy declared, drawing in a deep breath, while admiring the cream-colored cabinets and the huge marble island, feeling as though she'd walked into a villa in the south of France. Her own kitchen had resembled a coroner's morgue with its many stainless steel surfaces.

Molly McCoy, the pie shop's energetic proprietor, spun around as though to see who'd come barging into her work space unannounced, and the heaviness in Roxy's heart lifted instantly at the delighted expression that spread across Molly's face.

"Roxy, now aren't you a sight for sore eyes. I was hoping you'd stop by and see me. I've been dying to catch up with you, but I couldn't stick around the other night. I had to deliver the pies to the mayor's party, and then I went home to bed. I'm not allowed to overdo these days. Oh, I'm so glad you decided to move back home. We've all missed you, especially Callee."

"I've missed you all, too," Roxy said, though she wished she could find the joy in this homecoming that others wanted for her. Maybe if she didn't feel like a rudderless ship, spinning round and round on waves of indecision.

"Why don't you help yourself to some coffee, then come visit with me."

Roxy thought if she had any more caffeine today, she'd hyperventilate. "No thanks. You wouldn't have some bottled water, would you?"

"In the fridge," Molly said over her shoulder. She was slowly pouring milk into the saucepan.

"Is this the recipe you shared with me a few years ago?" Roxy found a bottle of water and stood to one edge of the stove, watching Molly work.

"The very same."

Roxy nodded, knowing the saucepan contained sugar, cocoa, cornstarch, and salt. She could make this recipe by heart. She watched Molly stirring the mixture on a medium-high temperature until the sauce was thick and bubbly, then reduce the heat, and stir another two minutes. Molly removed the pan from the burner, scooped a cup of the hot filling into some pre-prepared egg yolks and stirred. She returned that to the saucepan and brought the pie filling to a gentle boil, cooking for two minutes more. She removed the pan from the heat and mixed in vanilla. "I never get tired of this pie."

"I know what you mean. I think I'm getting high on chocolate fumes," Roxy said, drawing a laugh from Molly. Quint's mother had had a triple bypass last spring, but now she looked so healthy, and was thinner than Roxy remembered. A lot thinner. "How can you work here every day and not gain five pounds a week?"

"It's that darned cardiologist. Controls my diet like a dictator," Molly humphed, pulling unbaked pie shells from the refrigerator and placing them on the island. "Taken all the fun out of eating."

"All things in moderation, huh?" Roxy asked, commiserating.

"Well, it's not as much all things as some things." Molly had a disarming twinkle in her bright blue eyes that could lighten the cloudiest day.

"If it's any consolation, the results are incredible. You look amazing."

"Thank you, dear." Molly's smile said the compliment was appreciated.

Roxy's gaze drifted around the room again. "This is such an inviting work space. It must be a joy to come to work every day."

"Miss your bistro kitchen, do you, dear?"

"I do." Roxy sighed. More than she'd thought she would, and she'd thought she would really, really miss it. "It probably sounds strange, but it was my touch-stone, and now I'm feeling off balance, as if the ground keeps shifting beneath my feet."

"I felt something similar when my Jimmy died, like there wasn't a solid piece of flooring or ground any-where. You just need some time to figure it out, dear."

Exactly. Roxy took a deep breath, moving out of the way as Molly began to pour filling into the pie shells. Molly said, "Tell me, how did it go the other night with Wade Reynolds?"

In mid-swallow, Roxy nearly choked, the question taking her by surprise. Heat climbed into her face, giv-ing away any shot she might have had at acting cool. "What do mean?"

"The loft? What did you think?"

You mean that place where I almost seduced Wade? The memory rushed her, almost robbing her breath. "It's interesting. It might even suit me, if I could figure out what I wanted to do business-wise."

"You'll figure it out when the timing is right."

"I suppose."

"What about Wade? How did you get along? Isn't he a darling man? And he's so lonely." Molly kept her gaze on her task, not on Roxy. "But I suspect it's too soon for you to be considering dating yet, right?"

Wrong. She didn't want to say that, however—not to Molly anyway. Damn, how she wished she could abandon her concerns about having a fling with one of Quint's best buddies, but she couldn't. She didn't need her life to be more complicated than it already was, no matter how divine making love to Wade might be. She was glad she'd called a halt to it. Glad, but not glad. Double damn.

The back door bumped open, and Roxy swung around to see a very pregnant strawberry blonde with the sweetest face entering. She was frowning as if she carried a heavy burden, although the tiny purse she was white-knuckling couldn't weigh much. She spied Roxy and stopped cold, her cheeks glowing hot pink.

"Oh, I'm sorry, I didn't mean to interrupt," she began, looking apologetic for barging in, though clearly this was Jane Wilson-Taziano, Big Sky Pie's other pastry chef, and she belonged here, not Roxy.

"It's fine, Jane dear." Molly made the introductions and said, "Roxy was just stopping by to say hello."

"So nice to meet you. Callee's spoken of you often." Jane continued to look flustered, wringing her hands. "Molly, I need to speak to you. Maybe in your office. If it's okay?"

"Are you all right, Jane?" Molly set the saucepan aside, forgetting about the pies, her gaze fully locked on the young mother-to-be. "You look a little peaked."

"I'm so sorry, Molly." Tears began to roll down Jane's cheeks. "The doctor says I must. I tried to explain to him that this is our busiest time of year, and that, that I can't leave you without a pastry chef, but he insisted and I . . . I don't know what to do. I'm sorry."

Molly wiped her hands on a dish towel, then hurried to Jane, guiding her onto one of the stools around the work island. Roxy found some tissue and brought the box. Molly dried Jane's tears. "There now, dear. It's going to be okay. The baby is all right, isn't it?"

Jane nodded, blowing into a tissue.

"Then that's all that matters," Molly's voice was heavy with relief. "Now, tell me what it is the doctor said. Nice and slow this time."

Jane sniffled, and her face crumpled again. "He says I might not carry the baby to full term if I don't go straight home, get into bed, and stay there until she, or he, comes."

"But you and the baby are okay?" Molly obviously wanted more confirmation. Family first. Always. It was why she was so beloved.

Jane nodded, sniffling. "So far."

The news could have been worse, Roxy thought, so much worse.

Molly hugged Jane's shoulders. "Have you told Nick yet?"

"No," the word trembled out of Jane. "I didn't want to scare him."

"Would you like me to call him?" Molly asked.

Jane nodded, but her eyes were filling with fresh tears. "But what are you going to do without me here?"

"I'm sure Quint and Rafe can fill in until we find someone else through the holidays."

"But..."

"No, my dear, you are not to worry about it another moment. Your health and the baby's take precedence."

Roxy had faced similar kitchen staff problems at the bistro, and they invariably came at the most inopportune

times, right before a huge special event or the holidays
when skilled staff was a must. Finding that staff at a
moment's notice, however, wasn't always easy. And that
had been in Seattle. How likely was it that Molly could
find the help she needed in Kalispell? She recalled
Callee telling her how difficult it had been finding a
good pastry chef until Jane showed up. What was Molly
going to do?

That question again. *What are you going to do?* Roxy
hadn't had a chance to discuss her dilemma with Molly
yet, to seek her wise counsel, but maybe there was no
longer a need to do that. Maybe the universe had sent
her to see Molly today, at just this time. She mulled the
idea that was forming and found she actually liked it. It
would keep her busy, giving her some distance from the
divorce and time to figure out the answers she couldn't
yet find.

While Molly saw Jane out to her car and then went
into her office to phone Jane's husband with a heads-up,
Roxy washed her hands, found an apron, and made the
meringue for the pies Molly had not finished, then she
put them into the pre-heated ovens.

"Oh, no, my pies," Molly cried as she exited her office at a run. She stopped short when she spied Roxy
and realized what she'd done. The stress line between
her brows disappeared, and a big smile crossed her
face. "How would you like a job as a temporary pastry chef over the holidays, Roxy? I can't pay you what
you were making in Seattle, but it's all the free pie you
can eat."

"If you hadn't asked me, I was going to ask you," Roxy admitted.

"Welcome aboard." Molly opened her arms for a hug, and Roxy bent over to participate. Then Molly stepped back and twinkled up at her. "And my doctor thanks you, too. He doesn't like me worrying about the pie shop."

"Don't worry, be happy," Roxy sang, feeling as though she'd finally leaped off the gyrating steps at the Carnival Fun House and landed on solid ground. One problem solved. She wasn't sure how she was going to solve the biggest problem. Her unwanted attraction to Wade Reynolds.

Chapter Five

For the first time since she'd returned to Kalispell, Roxy woke with purpose and a budding hope in her heart. She twisted her wild hair into a knot at the back of her head, dug out her favorite Crocs and chef outfit, and found herself humming as she fed Tallulah and headed out to the Escalade. On a cold, snowy day like this, she was grateful for the warmers in the leather seats.

As she drove through the dark streets at four a.m., excitement started to pump through her veins, a feeling she hadn't felt in ages. Confidence? Yeah, that. She parked in back and saw lights already on inside, surprised that Molly had beat her in. *Probably anxious to show me the ropes*, Roxy thought, realizing also that she needed to ask for a key.

She knocked on the door and it opened, but instead of Molly McCoy, a tall, broad-shouldered Latino man with dreamy dark eyes and longish ebony hair was framed in the doorway. Her celibate self took note and jotted him down on the "to-do" list, but if this was Rafe, and it likely was, he was off-limits. She didn't date coworkers. No one needed that drama in the kitchen.

The guy was still staring at her in confusion, spouting Spanish, none of which she was catching given how fast the words were zipping from his sexy mouth. Several of Roxy's cooks at the bistro had spoken Spanish, and she'd quickly picked up a few phrases. But this was a dialect she didn't know.

"Hi. I'm Roxanne Nash." She stuck her hand out to shake, causing him to stop midsentence. "You must be Rafe."

"*Sí.*" He seemed leery that she knew his name and on the verge of slamming the door in her face.

"I'm going to be filling in for Jane," Roxy explained, trying to duck past him, but he took on the dimensions of a solid wall.

"Ah, *Señora* Jane, *sí*," he nodded, finally catching on.

"Yes, yes." Roxy nodded too. "*Sí.*"

Rafe shook his head. "She no here."

"I know that. I'm here to take her place."

"*Señora* Jane no here."

Roxy swallowed a knot of frustration, the chill dawn air seeping into her thin pants. She had to get through to him. She decided to try another tack. She made a half-circle from beneath her breasts to her lower abdomen pantomiming a pregnant woman. "*Señora* Jane is having a bambino."

Rafe frowned. "A *bebé*?"

"Yes—er *sí*—a baby. I," she pointed at herself, "am taking her place until she has the babe."

"You have also *el bebé*?"

"No. Jane is—" Roxy broke off, shivering in her jacket. It was no use. He didn't understand her. She thought of something else, hoping he'd at least get the gist of her question if he didn't understand it completely. "When does Molly usually get here?"

"Ah, *Señora* Molly." He began nodding again.

"*Sí, Señora* Molly." She pointed to her wristwatch.

Rafe frowned. "She no here."

"I figured that out all by myself, pal." The spark of confidence Roxy had felt on the drive over here was deflating. Rather than stand there freezing, she considered retreating to the Escalade and phoning Molly, or Quint. Surely one of them could get through to this man. Right? But it was so early. Maybe Molly routinely came in much later since having the bypass. She should have thought to ask. As she turned to go down the stairs, however, headlights spilled across the Cadillac and a Subaru pulled in beside it. Molly. A sigh of relief swept through Roxy.

"Oh, good, I see you and Rafe have already met." Molly moved toward her with purpose, looking surprisingly refreshed at this early hour. She gave Roxy a quick hug.

"Uh, not really. I'm afraid he doesn't understand what I'm trying to tell him."

"Don't worry. He speaks the most important language. Pie." She hurried up and into the pie shop, greeting Rafe with a cheery "*hola*" as he stepped aside to make way for the shop's owner. Roxy hurried in on Molly's wake.

Roxy was immediately struck again by the sweet aroma that lingered in the air like a subtle perfume, a mix of spices and chocolate with a pinch of espresso. The passion she felt for cooking swelled through her like a wave, breaking apart a wedge of ice that had been forming on her heart, lifting a bit of the grief that had followed her from Seattle. It wasn't her bistro kitchen, but at least she was cooking again. To her, there could be no more rewarding, fulfilling job than being a chef. It was who she was.

She listened to Molly trying to explain the situation to Rafe, realizing that he didn't seem to get her explanation any more than he'd gotten Roxy's. All he seemed to understand was that Roxy would be working now and Jane would not, which was close enough as far as Roxy was concerned.

"*Señora* Roxy, *sí*," he said. "*Señora* Jane, no more."

Roxy exchanged an amused glance with Molly and smiled at Rafe. That worked. He could think whatever he wanted as long as there was harmony in the workplace, and he didn't lock her out again.

"*Senorita* Roxy," Molly corrected, letting him know that Roxy was not a married woman.

Rafe's dark brown eyes swept to Roxy, over Roxy, assessing her as a hetero male assesses a woman, as he had not done before. A devilish smile transformed his face into an even more handsome one, and the room seemed to grow a little warmer, but then, that might just be the heat of the furnace kicking in. Rafe nodded. "*Sí, sí.*"

Molly directed Rafe's attention away from Roxy, and he set about cleaning the marble island top, then putting out the rolling pins, parchment paper, and flour. As he did that, Molly said to Roxy, "Come on. You can hang your coat and purse in here."

She led the way to a long hallway lined with cupboards and doors. Inside the coat closet were also a couple of shelves with chef coats in clear plastic wrap, in a variety of sizes, and three or four aprons. Next was a bathroom for the employees. It was small, but spotlessly clean. Then a couple of pantries with flour and sugar and salt. And a broom closet with mop, bucket, brooms, and cleaning supplies.

Molly kept moving toward the end of the hall. "This is our cold room where we keep the fresh fruits and berries when they're in season. This second SubZero is for cream and butter and pies that need to be kept refrigerated, and the freezer is full of frozen cherries and other fast frozen sweet fruits and berries.

"There are extra pie plates and tart pans on those shelves. If you can't find something, don't hesitate to ask, or just snoop through drawers and cabinets until you discover where I've put it."

"It's similar enough to my kitchen in the bistro that I shouldn't have any problems picking up the routine quickly."

"Rafe starts the coffee first thing most days, and Andrea makes espresso, if you'd rather have that, but she won't be here for a few hours yet. She oversees the café, does the billing and accounts receivable, and she orders any supplies we need. So if you notice we're running low on something, make sure to tell her. This is my office, but mostly Andrea works in here."

Roxy had had a decent office in the bistro with a small window that overlooked Puget Sound. She could watch the ferries coming and going, if she didn't have a lot of paperwork to do. This space barely qualified as a tiny walk-in closet, but she had to admire the attempt to maximize every inch of it. Shelves reached to the ceiling and were laden with recipe books, and a tidy, compact desk held a laptop computer and an all-in-one printer/fax/copier and a pencil holder that looked to have been made by a child.

"Well, that's it," Molly said. "Time to get to work."

Roxy felt the first twinge of anxiety, but it didn't stick around. Her pastry training kicked in within the first twenty minutes, and that spark of confidence caught hold and began to flame brighter. For one thing, the pie recipes required much fewer ingredients than the things she prepared at the bistro, and Molly wasn't doing dozens of different dishes each day, just a few of the same recipes over and over.

Roxy worked, rolling out the dough to the beat of the soft Latin music, Rafe catching her eye on occasion, flirting with her, but instead of his dark brown eyes, his handsome face, she saw Wade's aqua-green eyes and his sexy mouth, which brought back the memory of his kiss.

Molly said, "I like to use the smaller pieces of left-over dough to make pielets and tarts. I'm hoping to introduce a line of diabetes-friendly, sugar-free pies soon, but I haven't hit on a recipe yet that meets my taste standards."

"Maybe we can work on that together." Roxy was loving the feel of the flour on her fingertips as she fit dough into a pie tin and crimped the edges, the scent homey and rich. This work was returning the sense of being centered that she'd lost along with her husband.

"We've been doing a pie of the month special every month since we opened. As you've probably guessed, this month is the chocolate cream meringue, but it gets a bit boring, and I'd like to spice it up a bit, add a twist of some kind. You know?"

Roxy thought a moment, and then said, "What if we added a shot of crème de menthe? Chocolate mint pie?"

"Ohhh, that does sound yummy, and folks in this town do like their pie with a shot of liqueur."

"Then we could do any number of variations on our theme. There are some great coffee and chocolate liqueurs that range from orange flavored to the darkest black chocolate."

"Would you mind running by the store on your way home today to see what liqueurs this town offers for a couple of decadent-minded pastry chefs?"

Roxy readily agreed, but she could have told Molly her decadent mind wasn't on liqueur, but on a shy, sexy cowboy, and no matter how hard she tried, she couldn't shake him loose.

* * *

Wade could still hear the guys laughing at him over Roxy. It annoyed the hell out of him. He was in the loft, doing a couple of repairs Nick had told Quint about. A sticky cupboard door, for one, and a drawer in the bathroom that was losing its front facing. It was all he could do to step into this loft without thoughts of Roxy coming at him the way she'd done, hell bent on setting him straight about why they should ignore the attraction they were both feeling. Telling him they should stay away from each other. She was right. He wasn't ready for a relationship or an affair . . . or was he?

No. He wasn't. He was as sure of that as his own name. At least he'd thought he was until her lush lips brushed his and made him want to taste every part of her, to do things he didn't even know how to do to her. God, he was hard again just thinking about it. He had to get her off his mind. But that seemed the most impossible thing of all. She kept haunting his thought every few seconds, like she was on some digital auto feed that he couldn't shut off.

He was horny. That's what it was. He really needed to get laid. He had to find someone willing to put him out of his misery and make him stop thinking about a woman he didn't want to want. But how did a guy find such a woman? He thought about TV shows, movies he'd seen. Where did guys find loose women? In bars. Sure. He could go to a bar, someplace no one knew him . . . like The Broken Spur right across the street. Sit at the bar, order a beer, and wait for a woman to approach him. There was bound to be that type of woman in that dive. Probably.

If that didn't work out, he could...um...work out... at the gym. He had a membership there, even though he seldom went. He usually got enough exercise every day on the job. But he recalled there being a few pretty hot females at any given time. The image of Emily's friend's mother, the little blonde with the revealing sweater, crossed his mind. For some reason, despite his body having had a favorable reaction to her that night, the thought of her now didn't do anything for him. He'd rather have Roxy.

He yanked on the bathroom drawer too hard and pulled the whole thing apart. Shit. Now he needed to rebuild the dumb thing. Maybe he should go get that beer now. But first, he had to pick up the pieces of the broken drawer. He didn't hear anyone come into the loft until it was too late. He jerked around and got halfway to his feet when something flashed past and leaped up to his chest, digging in sharp claws. He let out a loud groan.

"Tallulah!" Roxy cried. "Where are you?" She appeared in the bathroom doorway and froze. "Oh, crap. Tallulah..."

"Your cat," Wade said, peeling the big furball from his chest. He felt a trickle of something wet on his cheek. He touched it, looked at it. Blood. "This feline needs to be jailed. She's lethal."

"Quint said no one was here."

Quint must be having himself a real laugh about now,

Wade thought, plotting mayhem on his best friend. "He probably forgot I was going to fix a couple of things for Nick this afternoon."

"I guess." She seemed to have some suspicions of her own where Quint was concerned. "I'm still considering taking the loft, but first I wanted to see how Tallulah reacted to it."

"I'd say she qualifies as an attack cat."

"I'm really sorry. She usually just hides when strangers are around."

"Is that so?"

"You're bleeding. Oh, no. Let me see. I've got something in my purse." She disappeared and was back a couple of seconds later with a bandage, a tissue, and a little tube of antibiotic cream.

"Do you always carry a mini-first aid kit with you?"

"I do. You never know. Like a boy scout, I believe in being prepared." She led him into the bathroom, sat him down on the toilet lid, dampened the tissue, and cleaned the spot on his temple. She straddled his legs, tilted his chin toward the light, and leaned in to examine the damage. The aroma of ripe oranges filled his nose, making his head feel light. He tried to think of something vile to ward off the urge to kiss her. But the only vile thing to come to mind was her cat. And somehow, even that reminded him of how much he wanted Roxy. She arched back slightly, smiling at him with those enchanting sage green eyes, all warm and inviting, scrambling his brain. She said, "It's not much of a scratch, more like a jab mark, but I bet it stings like crazy, huh?"

He wasn't going to admit to that and sound like a wuss. He put on his tough face, the one he gave ornery building inspectors. "Naw."

She squeezed a little of the antibiotic cream on the wound, then with the tip of her finger, gently rubbed it in, her touch sending a charge straight from his big head to his little one.

God help him, if her cat didn't kill him, Roxy would.

Her gaze met his, held a beat too long, told him she still felt the pull between them, too. She seemed to shake herself, stepping back too quickly and bumping against the shower. She glanced at his pants, took in his uncomfortable condition, and closed her eyes, as if she wanted to erase the image of what her nearness had caused. His neck seemed on fire.

She opened her eyes and kept them on his face. She stammered, "I, ah, what is it that you're fixing?"

"Nothing major. A drawer." He pointed to the pile of wood that had been the drawer before he lost his cool.

She frowned. "Gee, what happened to it? Nick lose his temper one night and use it for a punching bag?"

"I dropped it. It hit the tile and broke apart. I need to take it home and fix it." He stood up, but now the bathroom seemed to close in on them, making everything so much more intimate. Keeping them both locked in place. He couldn't help himself. He came at her like she'd done to him the other night. "I need to know something."

He didn't ask, or wait, he just leaned in and kissed her. She didn't move, didn't make any attempt to touch

him, or fight him, or participate. She just allowed it, let
him shove his tongue into her mouth, let him deepen the
kiss until need raged through him.

He pulled back, breathless, angry, frustrated, confused. All at the same time. "That's what I thought," he
said, and stormed out.

* * *

Roxy stood outside his door, double checking the address that Callee had given her. This was embarrassing
enough without getting the wrong house. Wade's home
was an old craftsman style with a large front porch and
a swing. She imagined how wonderful it would be to
own a house like this, to sit on that swing on a warm
evening with someone you loved, cuddling, talking, listening to the night sounds of crickets. Her childhood had
been spent in a house like this, with a swing like that.

Nostalgia is for fools, she told herself. *You can't go
back. Nothing is ever the same*.

She forced herself to see the house without the rose-
colored glasses. It had seen better days, but for someone
with Wade's skills she was sure it would, at some point
in time, be brought back to something of its original
beauty. As she understood it, he'd only moved back to
town last summer. And since then, he'd been busy doing other people's remodel jobs, with probably not that
much time for his own.

She knocked on the door and stepped back to wait,
or maybe to escape if her nerve betrayed her. Two days

had passed since Wade had kissed her in the loft. Two days and she had thought of little else but that mind-blowing kiss and his parting words. What had he needed to know? Why had he turned her body to liquid fire and just walked out?

She shouldn't ask, wouldn't ask, no matter how much she ached to do just that. It would only complicate matters between them. And as it turned out, she needed his help, if she could convince him to risk spending a little more time with her. She had to keep their interactions professional, ignoring that tug of attraction that kept seducing her better judgment and ending up with her lips ravishing his. So why had she come here when she could have called him? What was the point?

The point was in the box she'd brought. She rapped harder on the door. She heard someone approaching, giggles sounding from within, and a second later, the door popped open. Two preteen girls stopped laughing at the sight of her.

"Who are you?" They asked in unison and burst out laughing again.

Roxy smiled, remembering when she and Callee were this age, looking much like these two—Callee the pretty one, Roxy the lanky, ugly duckling, giggling over some private joke. "I'm Roxanne Nash. I'm a friend of Callee McCoy's. I'm looking for your dad," she said, her gaze shifting between the two girls, unsure which was Wade's daughter since neither looked much like him.

"Dad, someone's here to see you!" the awkward girl shouted. *Wade's daughter.* The thought sent a strange tingle through her. It was one thing to know he had a child, another to stand here facing that child, not some vague image in her head, but a real live person whose world started and ended with her only parent. Roxy's heart wrenched for Emily. She was on the brink of the toughest time in any girl's life, a time when a girl most needed—and mostly hated needing—her mother. There was no substitute for a great dad, but when it came to teaching a teenager about hair and clothes, about handling the heart-bumps of boys and friendships, mom was the go-to parent.

At least her mom had been.

And despite being hot as hell and ripe for plucking, Wade still wore his wedding ring. He wasn't looking for a stepmom for his daughter, or a wife to replace Sarah. He was stuck in the past, and as long as he was, so was his daughter. A twinge she couldn't name pinched the edges of Roxy's heart, made her want to grab and hug this girl, made her want to shake Wade until he saw what his refusal to move on was doing to his child.

She stuffed those feelings, squared her shoulders, fidgeted with the box. Wade Reynolds was not her problem. His daughter was not her problem. She forced a smile. "You must be Emily."

The girl nodded, looking at Roxy with the wide-eyed gape of a fan meeting their favorite rock star. "I wish I had hair like yours."

"Ah, thank you." Roxy tried not to grimace. Her hair had always been the one thing she hated about herself. She'd learned to tame it, if not love it.

"It's sick," Emily said on a sigh that sounded like envy.

Chapter Six

❧

Dork." Emily's girlfriend elbowed her in the ribs, and both girls blushed, then started giggling and ran away from the door. Emily called over her shoulder, "Come on in. I think Dad's still in his room. I'll go get him."

As Roxy stepped into the foyer, the girls disappeared up a staircase to the left, Emily calling, "Dad! Someone's here to see you!"

Roxy noticed a rug with boots set neatly side by side. She removed hers, and padded across wood floors that looked old, maybe original, that had been restored to a high sheen. A dust-bunny family huddled beneath an antique coat rack set against the banister. The less than pristine housekeeping brought a smile as she removed her parka and moved into the living room. A river rock fireplace with a wide mantle held a group of framed photos. She crossed the room to examine them.

The first was of a much younger Wade in a tuxedo,

looking as if someone held a shotgun to his head, or like he might lose his cookies. A pretty, petite blond, whose head reached the middle of his chest, stood beside him in a wedding gown. This had to be Sarah. That twinge around Roxy's heart returned, only this time a flutter of sorrow accompanied it. The next photo was of Sarah, very pregnant with Emily. Then Wade holding baby Emily, an unlit cigar in his mouth and a smile in his eyes. The rest were more family photos, but nothing newer of Emily since she must have been around eight.

Tears filled her eyes. It was as if, with Sarah's death, this family had ceased to exist. But it hadn't, and it wasn't fair to Emily to not have these years in between documented and displayed with as much love as her younger photos. Roxy shook herself. This was none of her business. She stepped away from the photos that were making her sad, taking in the living room décor.

The furniture, floral and feminine, didn't seem to suit Wade. Probably selected by his late wife without any thought to the comfort of the man of the house. She pictured Wade in big leather sofas, in a rich brown or burgundy or saddle colors. In the dining room, she had the same impression. The vast space held an undersized table and delicate chairs.

Music and voices were coming from behind a door just beyond the dining room. It might have been more polite to stay at the door and wait for Wade, but the more she saw of his house, the less she felt she should be there. Besides, it was dinner time. She didn't want to disrupt his cooking. Although it smelled as if he were already burning whatever he had been attempting to fry.

She pushed the kitchen door inward and froze. Wade stood near a gas range, waving a spoon over a casserole dish that had smoke rising from its center. He looked as if he'd just stepped from a shower and tossed on a t-shirt, worn blue jeans, and some white socks. Her heart did a barrel roll inside her chest. The music was so loud that he couldn't have heard her enter or heard Emily calling for him. But he startled as if suddenly sensing her presence. He turned, a frown pulling his brows together. His hair was slicked back; a drop of shaving cream clung to one sideburn, and those aqua eyes seemed to blaze when he saw her. Like fire on water. Her whole body went wet with desire.

He cranked down the blaring iPod.

"Hi," Roxy said, her voice resonating with a telltale huskiness. She struggled to find her poise, to stop thinking about kissing him, to defuse the three-alarm fire racing through her body. She tore her gaze from his, noting absently that the bright yellow walls recalled a field of sunflowers. It was an old-fashioned farmhouse kitchen, with large windows over the sink and a round table in the center of the room. "Smells like you could use some help with that meal."

"Oh, he has plenty of help already," a female voice said as a blonde popped into view from behind the door. She was medium height, held a beer in one hand, and had balloon-sized boobs threatening to bounce right out of her low-cut sweater as she gyrated to the rock beat still humming through the room. Roxy felt like a nun in her loose-fitting, turtlenecked cable knit.

Wade's expression took on the signs of an approaching storm. *Warning. Severe weather on the horizon. Run for cover now.* He pulled the casserole off the flames, stomped to the shelf with the iPod, and lowered the volume to a whisper. He was still holding the spoon, his gaze back on Roxy like he couldn't figure out what she was doing in his house. In his kitchen.

The box she carried suddenly seemed to weigh twenty pounds, the string biting into her fingers. She wished she'd brought Tallulah instead of what was in the box. Her cat would defend her honor. Or maybe just bite her for being a fool about this guy.

The blonde sidled up to Wade and patted his butt. Wade jumped, red flashing on the tips of his ears. Roxy didn't know if he was embarrassed or upset at the blonde making it clear that he was *her* man. *Hands off, you red-headed intruder.*

The blonde took the spoon from him and hovered over the casserole, saying, "Aren't you going to introduce us, babe?"

Wade's neck had joined his ears and turned a bright, cranberry juice red. He stammered, "Roxy, this is Taffy..."

"Tabby," the blonde corrected tersely, her frosted-pink lips pouting.

"Yeah, Tabby. She brought dinner for Emily and her daughter, Missy."

"Misty," the blond said.

"Yeah, Emily's friend."

"I met them," Roxy said lamely, trying to figure out some way of just leaving without extending this awkward moment. But her mind was blank. All it wanted to do was notice the details in this room—like how much it could use some updating. The cabinets were straight out of the eighties, the black appliances might be circa 1990, and the checkerboard flooring was linoleum. What charm it could have if it was renovated with modern appliances, but cabinets and flooring that reflected the original era. It could also use a good scrubbing, for her tastes, but something had to give when you were Mommy and Daddy to a preteen, taking care of the house, the cooking, the laundry, and working more than eight hours most days. And juggling women.

Oh, hell, that wasn't fair. He was single. She didn't even want a relationship with him. Just a fling, remember? What he did in his spare time, and whom he did it with, was not her concern. No matter what Tammy or Tippy or whoever she was thought.

"What are you doing here?" Wade asked.

The blonde was staring at her, hand on her hip, obviously wanting to ask the same question.

Roxy said, "I, er, I needed a favor."

His eyebrows shot up. "Oh yeah?"

"Ah, Quint, er, you know what? Never mind. Quint can help me with it—" she broke off, glancing at the blonde, whose eyes were shooting daggers at her. "Sorry to have interrupted. Nice to meet you, Taffy."

"Tansy," Wade corrected.

"Tabby," the blonde huffed.

"Look, you're about to eat dinner. I should have phoned."

"Yes, you should—" the blond started to say, only to be cut off by Wade.

"We've got plenty. Tabby, please put another plate on the table."

If Roxy was any judge, Tabby would rather dump the casserole on her than set her a place at the table that already was set for four.

"Have a beer." Wade reached into the fridge for one.

"No thanks." Roxy hurried out of the kitchen as he turned his back to dig into the refrigerator. The music grew loud again as Roxy arrived in the foyer. She set the box down, pulled on her parka and boots, and dashed out into the night. Her face burned with humiliation. How could she have been so stupid to not even consider that he might be dating someone?

Maybe that was what he'd meant the other night when he'd said he needed to know something just before kissing her. Maybe he'd wanted to compare kissing her to kissing Tiffany, or whatever the hell his girlfriend's name was. And Tilly, Tally—whoever— had obviously won out. Just like the cheerleader had won her husband Ty.

Roxy burst into tears, for no damned reason that she could discern, and wept as she drove, crying as if a floodgate had opened. She pulled to the side of the road until the tears subsided. She'd thought she was done crying about the divorce months ago. Then why the waterworks now? Was she feeling sorry for herself? Why? Because some shy, tall drink of water with sexy-ass eyes and mind-numbing kisses wanted someone else? No. That couldn't be. She didn't want anything but a fling with Wade. A fling didn't involve the heart. It was a romp. Fun and games. No one getting hurt.

She was pulling into her mother's driveway when it hit her that she'd left behind the box.

* * *

What a fiasco. Wade could not get the look of dismay and embarrassment on Roxy's face out of his mind. She had nothing on him. Tabby had shown up uninvited, dressed for sin, bearing food and beer. If she'd come alone, without her daughter, he would have turned her away at the door, but she was already in his kitchen when he came down from his shower.

And she'd already set the table for four. What was he supposed to do? Toss her out on her ear? Sarah would have been horrified if he were less than hospitable, and Em would be mortified. He'd accepted a beer, then tried hurrying dinner along, but only managed to burn the bottom of the damned casserole.

Then next thing he knew, Roxy was standing there, and Tabby was acting like she and he . . . *Shit*. A slow burn raced over him as he recalled the pat on his ass. After that, his manners took a hike. He didn't care what Tabby thought. All through dinner, he gave her questions one word answers, but even then she didn't know when to stop trying. Insisting on helping with washing the dishes, rubbing up against him every chance she got.

As she was leaving, she pulled him into a kiss on the porch—where anyone in the neighborhood or driving past might have seen—again rubbing herself seductively against him, his hungry libido rallying to the possibility, until she reached for his fly, with the girls just upstairs and still awake. That had sobered big and little heads at the same instance.

The weird thing was that her kiss hadn't elicited the same response that Roxy's kisses did. He hadn't wanted to drag Tabby upstairs into his bed. Damn. He thought what he was feeling for Roxy was horny, that any woman could cure what ailed him, but maybe that was wrong.

He didn't even wait for Tabby to drive away. He darted back inside, shutting and locking the door, turning out the porch light, *hiding the welcome mat,* just in case the nymphomaniac returned. He'd had all the uninvited, unexpected company a man could deal with for one night. What kind of name was Tabby anyway? Like a cat, like Roxy's hellcat. He touched the scratch on his cheek. He had no doubt that blond female had claws just as sharp, if provoked. He gulped, feeling the need for another shower.

The only shower he'd needed after kissing Roxy had been icy cold.

Roxy. Just the thought of her stirred desire. What had she been doing here? After the other night, he figured they weren't likely to encounter one another for a long time, but there she'd been, knocking his socks off, her flame red hair looking windswept, messy in a perfect kind of halo. Halo, hah. Deceptive. She was no angel, and she brought out the devil in him.

Taffy, or Tacky or whatever, displayed her sex like a neon sign, everything flashing in your face, the too-low sweater, the too-tight jeans, but Roxy didn't need skin-hugging garments to showcase her curves or to turn a man's head. She had an earthy sexiness like a subtle vibration in the air. He didn't want to want her, but God help him he did. He couldn't lie. She had him reeling, confused, and constantly aroused.

He stumbled back into the foyer and almost tripped on a big box on the floor beside the coat rack. Where had this come from? Was it Misty's? He carried it into the light, spotting a familiar logo. Not Emily's friend's. He tugged the string aside, lifted the lid, and pulled out a bunch of tissue paper. Nestled in its depths was a brand-new, camel-colored, cattleman-style cowboy hat. His size. Just like the hat the devil-cat had destroyed. A note tucked inside the band read, "From Tallulah with apologies."

He burst out laughing. He plunked the hat onto his head and went into the downstairs half-bath to check it out in the mirror. He tweaked the brim this way and that and did another assessment, deciding that it looked a smidge better than the original, but as he continued to stare in the mirror, his own image faded. The glass seemed to be a movie screen picturing a steaming-hot redhead with an ornery cat and kisses that boiled a man's blood.

He went to bed with a smile and a hard-on that no amount of cold shower had squelched, but at least he no longer smelled Tabby's perfume on him.

Wade scrambled out of bed the next morning, groggy from dreaming of chasing after Roxy and running away from a quick, blonde Tabby cat. His daily morning routine started with making sure Emily ate breakfast and got to school on time before he headed to his job sites to check on his crew. Today he had two preteens to get moving. Hard enough with only one.

As he drove them to school, he overheard Emily and Misty discussing their teacher, Ms. Vedelman. Emily said, "I hope she moves back to Idaho."

"I wish. But she's not going to." Misty pulled a comb through her yellow hair. "My mom heard her tell someone at the grocery store that she's buying a house in Kalispell."

"Oh, no," Emily groaned.

"Em, your mom wouldn't approve of you gossiping about your teacher," Wade said, feeling like a hypocrite. He'd met Ms. Vedelman and pretty much shared his daughter's assessment of the old crone.

"Ah, Dad." Emily's cheeks reddened, and Wade realized he'd pulled a super no-no, berating his daughter in front of her friend. Lord, why didn't teenagers come with rule books? Maybe he should check the library for a "Teenage Daughters for Dummy Dads." He always seemed to step on his tongue trying to figure out what was okay to say or do and what landed you on the Worst Parents list.

"Who was that lady with the red hair?" Emily asked, sounding as innocent as a rattler that hadn't shaken its tail. He met her gaze in the rearview mirror and knew instantly that she wasn't just switching subjects; she was getting retribution, putting him on the hot seat.

"Yeah, who was she?" Misty sounded eerily like her mother. Had Tabby texted her kid, telling her to wheedle information from him about Roxy? He wouldn't put it past her.

"She's a friend of Quint and Callee's. Callee's best friend, actually. She grew up in Kalispell, but has been living in Seattle. She just moved back to town."

"I heart her hair," Emily said, clasping her hands over her heart. Both girls burst into giggles.

Then Misty said, "Is she your girlfriend, Mr. Reynolds?"

"No." Wade blanched. "I just met her."

"Then what was she doing at your house last night?" There was an accusatory edge to Misty's voice that had his hackles rising, but before he could respond, the little blonde added, "Is that new hat you're wearing what was in the box she brought last night?"

Wow. Even Emily hadn't picked up on that. Misty was definitely a chip off her mama's block. Thank God, they'd arrived at the school. He pulled to the curb. "Ah, here we are, girls."

They scrambled out and joined a bunch of kids near the front door, Emily hanging back from the group as if leery of them. He sat there for a long minute, loving on his daughter. She'd grown so tall, like a colt, all long, lanky limbs, that awkward stage where nature begins to shift gears and hormones start stirring. He dreaded the changes ahead as much as he welcomed them.

Emily hugged her books to her chest and tangled a lock of hair around her finger, the confident girl she'd been minutes before slipping away like a ghost into the shadows. He caught one of the girls in the group raking a gaze over Emily, then nudging the girl next to her and pointing. They began to chuckle. What the hell? They were laughing at his daughter. The urge to do something about it had him reaching for the door handle, but he froze, sensing this would be one of those times that a parent butting in would only make the situation worse. The rose-colored glasses slipped from his eyes. His daughter didn't fit in. But why?

His gaze shifted between Emily and the other girls. Her height? No. It wasn't that, at least not that alone. Compared to her friends, even Misty, Emily's hair and clothes, he realized, hadn't changed since grade school. Jeans and t-shirts. The other girls wore tights and long sweaters or skirts. Their hair had style, while Emily did little more than brush hers into the same ponytail she'd worn the past three years. Kids didn't like drawing attention to themselves, especially at this age, but he realized now that she stood out like a six-inch nail in a box of tacks. Pain skated across his heart, the helpless ache of knowing a problem existed, but having no clue how to fix it.

Obviously, Emily didn't know either, since the clothes were what she'd chosen on their school shopping trip last August. A woman would know. Callee? Emily's words came back to him, *"I heart her hair."* Roxy. Could he ask her advice? He touched the brim of his hat. He did owe her a thank you, and hadn't she said she'd come to his house to ask a favor? Maybe they could exchange favors. Maybe he'd visit the pie shop on his ten a.m. coffee break.

* * *

When it comes to love, I'd rather fall in chocolate, Roxy thought, not sure where she'd heard that phrase originally, but deciding to adopt it as her mantra after inhaling the sweet cocoa fumes in the Big Sky Pie café. The only smell she liked better was...The answer that popped into her head threw her. She wanted to name a dozen other fragrances—her special marinara sauce, shrimp scampi, Gouda cheese, lilacs on a summer breeze, a freshly uncorked Cabernet, pie dough—but no, the one scent she wanted to imbibe was his. Wade's. That woodsy, soapy aroma, a mix of fresh sawdust and fresher breezes, like standing in a forest clearing.

"You're wearing the look of a woman with a man on her mind," Callee said, pulling her back from the edge of insane yearnings. "Aren't you going to tell me who he is?"

Roxy squirmed on the bench seat, glad the high sides

of this end booth afforded some privacy. Andrea was waiting tables and handling takeout customers that were eager to snatch up the first of the day's pies. "My love life continues to be a dry wasteland."

"It's too bad you and Wade didn't hit it off, but then, I can't imagine he'd be much fun. He seems as stuck as gum in cat fur, as my grandmother used to say."

"Oh my god, I'd forgotten that one." Roxy laughed. Callee's grandmother hadn't had a funny bone in her body, but she'd used plenty of bizarre similes. Recalling the photos on Wade's mantel, Roxy considered it an apt comparison. "What I know of him, I'd say that is Wade to a T. It's not as much that he's still in love with his deceased wife, as that he acts like he died with her."

"Yes. Like since she died, he's not supposed to laugh, or have fun, or keep on living."

"I feel sorry for his daughter," Roxy said, not sure why she'd been so touched by his child.

"Ah, poor Emily. She really could use a woman's guidance, but I don't like to butt in. Wade can get his back up when it comes to his little girl."

"That's a shame. I only met her for a few seconds, but she is at such a vulnerable age. Aren't there any female family members around who might come to her rescue?"

"Sarah's mother, but hers isn't the council that little girl needs to thrive. Sarah's father is a minister, and her mother is pretty involved in the church. They babysit from time to time, but for my money, Greta Jacobs is rather pious and dresses like a nun, the sort who never liked sex or anything else that Mother Nature has cursed the female gender with."

"That's a shame. Was Sarah much like her mother?"

"Yeah, sadly."

No wonder Wade is laced up too tightly.

"Well, unless he asks for your advice, I don't see what you can do." Roxy had to stop fretting about this. Emily wasn't her problem. She wasn't getting involved with Wade or his daughter. She yawned, stretched, achy muscles easing. After starting at four a.m., this long day of making pies was getting to her. She needed this break. She took a deep drink of coffee, savoring the dark flavor, feeling the caffeine begin to recharge her energy. "It's so great to be able to see you during the workday. I'm really glad you came in."

"Well, it wasn't just for a chat. Quint asked me to give you this key. He said you and Wade can take your time, look over that house you wanted to see, and let him know what you think."

She didn't tell Callee that she hadn't asked Wade to check out the house with her. How could she ask him after last night? It was too awkward. Thinking he was maybe interested in her and then finding out he was actually seeing someone, a possessive someone, felt too much like poaching another woman's game. Like what had happened to her. She wouldn't do that. Not ever. "I was kind of hoping you'd come with me to see the house. If I like it, then we could discuss whatever changes I might want and you could work up some sketches for me."

Callee smiled, her chestnut curls bouncing across her shoulders, and a gleam that befitted girls-night-out fun danced in her green eyes. "Oh, darn. I would like that, but I am booked solid all week, and I know you're anxious to make a decision."

"Yeah, especially since Tallulah decided to sharpen her claws on Mom's red sofa this morning."

"Uh-oh."

"The trouble is, the thought of making any kind of long-term commitment has me wanting to curl into a ball and suck my thumb. I'm not sure how I'll feel in three months or six months. I don't want to lock myself in on a lease or mortgage and then discover it's another bad choice."

The light dropped from Callee's eyes to be replaced with sympathy. "I'm sorry, sweetie. Obviously, you still need more time to regroup. Maybe you should consider renting something instead of buying? Something short-term? Maybe in the spring you'll feel renewed again and ready for that fresh start."

Roxy mulled this over, finding the idea much to her liking. Given her reservations and hesitations, it might be the best choice for now—like taking this temporary job—it gave her breathing room. She could move out of her mother's house, get her own space, and take a long look around Kalispell for the right home and the right business. And maybe by spring, like Callee suggested, she'd be ready to take a stand. Relief spread through her, releasing the tight knot in her stomach and the pinch in her neck. She nodded, giving her friend a huge smile.

"Would you ask Quint to text me some short-term rental listings to consider? Meanwhile, I'll look at this house since you brought the key. It'll give me a different perspective to consider for later on."

"That sounds great," Callee said, as a shadow fell across the booth.

Roxy and Callee glanced toward the man standing there, and Roxy's pulse began to thrum. In the new Stetson, Wade looked as delectably delicious, as delightfully decadent, as the dark chocolate pies she'd created today, and the desire coursing through her veins told her that he would taste every bit as sweet. God help her. The only thing she was sure about lately was how much she wanted this man.

Chapter Seven

Callee said, "Well, speak of the devil. Good morning, Wade."

"Callee," he said, giving a nod of his head, then reaching up to remove his hat with a blush as if the manners police were lurking nearby, ticket books at the ready. That shy, sometimes awkward trait held way too much appeal for Roxy's comfort. She couldn't believe how good the new hat looked on him, the perfect shade to set off those aqua-green eyes that were searching her face as if he'd forgotten what she looked like since last night.

Callee seemed to pick up on the unspoken energy or weird vibe that passed between them. She cast Roxy a curious, we'll-talk-later-girlfriend glance, gathered her purse, and started saying good-byes, acting like they hadn't just discussed Wade being stuck in time and his emotional unavailability. So why did her best friend think there would be anything to discuss later? Nope. Nothing to share about this sexy cowboy that Callee didn't already know.

Roxy stood and gave Callee a hug, and whispered, "Nothing is going on between Wade and me."

"Yeah, sure," Callee said, a knowing glint in her eyes.

Roxy sighed and glanced at Wade. "I should get back to work."

"Could you...would you sit with me a minute?" He reached to grasp her arm, then withdrew the attempt just as quickly.

Oh, God, this wouldn't be about that Tabby person, would it? Maybe it was. Maybe she'd laid down the law about him accepting gifts from women. On second thought, that couldn't be it. Otherwise he wouldn't be wearing the new hat.

"Please," he said.

She glanced toward the kitchen, hoping to see Molly or Rafe standing there waving her back into the trenches, but they weren't. Why would they? The last of the day's pies were baking. Nothing left to do but clean up the work space and make the dough for tomorrow. The refrigerated display case would need to be restocked at some point, but a variety of desserts awaited this purpose in the kitchen.

Resigned, Roxy sat down. Andrea zipped over, greeting Wade with a warm welcome and asking if he wanted anything. "Coffee, regular, and a slice of pie."

"What kind?" Andrea asked.

He glanced at Roxy. "What do you recommend to-day?"

She blinked, her nerves twitching. Why had he deferred to her, and why couldn't she remember one of the pies she'd baked earlier with those sea green orbs zeroed in on her?

"The chocolate mint meringue is amazing," Andrea suggested.

"Sure." Wade nodded, smiling. He sat, placing the hat on the seat Callee had just vacated. He stirred a couple of spoons of sugar into his coffee, keeping his eyes on the steaming liquid a long moment, as if considering how to word whatever it was he wanted to say.

Roxy waited, more uneasy as the seconds passed. Her coffee was getting cold, her patience thinning.

He looked up, started to speak, and Andrea interrupted, sliding his dessert onto the table in front of him. She added a napkin, then hurried away. He ignored the pie, his gaze on Roxy. "I, er, ah—thank you for the hat."

This was why he'd wanted her to sit with him? He could have thanked her while she was still standing. "The hat is not from me. It's from Tallulah."

He shook his head, the corners of his sexy mouth lifting slightly. "That cat..."

"Owes you more than a new hat." Her gaze slipped to the scratch on his cheek.

"Let's call it even." He glanced at his coffee again, but didn't touch it.

"I, uh, I really should get back to work."

His hand fell on top of hers—large, warm, rough, and

yet, surprisingly gentle. His gaze said *Don't go. Not yet.*

"What?" she choked, nerves twitchy. *What do you want from me? What do I want from you?* She ran her tongue over her dry lips, recalling his moist, sweet kisses, and a fiery need filled her. *Forget about him. He's taken.*

As though he were sensing the direction of her thoughts, he cleared his throat, lifted his hand. "Last night, when you came to my house, you, er, you said you wanted to ask me a favor, but you left without telling me what it was."

The tension in her neck eased slightly. She exhaled, giving a dismissive wave and adopting a flippant tone. "Oh, that—"

"Don't say it was nothing," he interrupted. "You wouldn't have come to my house if it were."

She laughed that off. "I only darkened your doorstep to deliver the hat."

"Bull."

The blunt response called her a liar and brooked no argument. Since she couldn't deny it, she bit her lower lip, meeting his bold stare with one of her own. "Okay, I admit it. I wasn't sure you were still speaking to me after—well, you know, after the way things went down at the loft."

He glanced at his cup, his natural shyness lassoing her heart like a roped calf, surely and firmly caught by this handsome cowboy with the sure, quick hands. Why did she feel like her whole body was tingling? As if in anticipation. He tilted his head sideways and looked at her. "I'm sorry about what happened at the loft. I didn't mean to...take advantage."

Sorry? Disappointment spread through her. But of course he regretted the kiss. He had a girlfriend. She nodded. "Yeah, okay."

He stared at her mouth, sending mixed signals. Was he sorry, or not? He asked, "So, what is the favor you want?" His gaze said that she could ask him anything and he'd give it to her.

A thrill shot straight to the hot spot between Roxy's thighs, and she couldn't find enough liquid in her mouth to swallow. Was she breathing faster? Oh Lord, she was. She tried to find her composure, but it seemed to have left with Callee. *What favor can you do for me? Kiss me senseless. Strip off my clothes. Run those big rough hands over every inch of my man-deprived body. Fill me, make me feel alive again, love me hard and fast until I cry out your name.*

She squirmed on the booth cushion, wrangling with thoughts gone wild. He was still waiting for an answer. She gulped her cold coffee, the liquid releasing her tongue from the roof of her mouth. "There's a house I want to look at across town today. Quint is booked all day, but he gave me the key, and I was hoping you might..."

"Go with you."

She nodded, shrugged. "But I'll understand if you're too busy."

He sighed, stirred his coffee again, and finally took a sip.

"If it helps, Tallulah isn't coming with me," she said.

A charming, crooked smile appeared. "Well, in that case ... okay."

Really? He was going to do this? A warm, fuzzy feeling slipped through her. But she reminded herself not to take it to heart. He was a contractor helping her out. Nothing more. He had a possessive girlfriend who would probably scratch the eyes out of any female stupid enough to make a play for her man. She wondered if Tabby realized that Wade was emotionally unavailable, wondered if the woman even cared.

Wondered why *she* cared, considering all she'd originally wanted was to have hot monkey sex with him. His being emotionally unavailable would have made her cheer then; there was no risk that he would develop any unwanted attachments to her. Instead, now that she'd gotten to know him a little, she felt a mix of pity and sadness for him, a desire to help him overcome the roadblock he'd built in his life. But she wasn't going to act on that urge. Or any other urges that she had for Wade Reynolds.

"What time do you get off work?" He scooped his fork full of chocolate and meringue. The moment it was in his mouth, he sighed, a look of pure pleasure spreading across his handsome face. "God, this is really fantastic."

"I'm glad you like it. Molly and I are trying some slight variations on the special of the month."

He gave a nod of approval. "Sometimes a little is a lot."

Their gazes collided, and her insides turned as squishy as the dessert he was downing. Sweet and hot and decadent. "I get off at one p.m."

"You want me to pick you up?"

"How about if you meet me there?" She didn't want anyone to see them riding off together, and by anyone, she meant Tabby. No telling what that blonde might do if she added one and one and got three. Although several scenarios popped into her mind, Roxy brushed them aside. She gave Wade the address, then said she had to get back into the kitchen. She felt he wanted to say something more, but Andrea was hovering, or at least it seemed like she was.

* * *

Wade kicked himself for losing the nerve to ask Roxy for help with Emily. He just couldn't figure out how to bring up the subject. He didn't even know if Roxy liked kids, teenage kids, but she had style, style that Emily obviously thought was cool. Or sick. Or stoopid. Whatever the kids called "great" these days. Yeah, it might have been better to ask Callee, but damn, he'd kind of shot himself in the foot with her when it came to his daughter. She'd offered advice when he hadn't wanted to hear it, and now that he realized he probably should have listened, he didn't know quite how to admit he was wrong without coming off like a class A jackass.

He headed into the kitchen, needing to spill his guts now before he chickened out again. But as he cracked the door open, he spotted Roxy standing very near Rafe, Molly's new assistant. The guy was classically tall, dark, and handsome, looks that could land him on the cover of *GQ* if he were a model, and he was staring at Roxy like she was one of the pie shop's special desserts. He couldn't blame the guy. Although she wasn't his type, he couldn't deny that Roxy did get a man's juices flowing, his fantasies pumping. She wasn't obviously sexy like Andrea, or too obvious like Tabby, but in his book, that had always been more alluring. She left a lot to the imagination, and his imagination was enjoying the hell out of that. After all, it wasn't everyone who could manage to look sexy in a chef's coat. But she did.

Watching Rafe watching Roxy, Wade battled the urge to punch the assistant chef in his perfectly straight nose. The violent feeling gave him pause. He wasn't a violent man, but he realized he'd been bruising to punch something since he'd seen the way the other kids were treating his daughter this morning. His bad mood had nothing to do with whatever was going on between Roxy and Rafe. Just his own frustration over not knowing how to help Emily. He backed away and bumped into someone standing right behind him.

"Whatcha looking at?" Andrea asked.

"Nothing."

"Oh yeah?" Andrea cracked the door, peeking into the kitchen. Wade rolled his eyes as she spun back to him like a curious cat. "Roxy?"

He frowned, shaking his head. "No way."

"Yes, way." She wore a knowing grin. He had dated Andrea around Thanksgiving time. Although they'd soon realized it wasn't going to be a romance, they'd become pretty good friends. And apparently, she could read him like a menu.

But he denied it anyway. "I don't have any interest in dating Roxy."

"Too bad," Andrea said, tucking her blond hair behind an ear. "She'd be terrific for you."

Wade made a face as though disgusted by the suggestion. "She's not my type."

Andrea sighed and placed her hand right over his heart. "You really ought to consider rejoining the world, my friend. It has a lot of new and wonderful things to offer—if you're willing to open your eyes and your heart to them."

Once, not that long ago, he would have recoiled at this suggestion, but now, he only shrugged. "Hah. Just because you found love you want everyone else to do the same."

"Not true. Not everyone. Only those who really deserve it." She left him to mull this over, hurrying to greet some newly arrived café customers.

Andrea had no idea that her words roused the monster-guilt that lived deep in his soul. She didn't know his secret, couldn't know he didn't deserve the kind of joy that she'd found with Ian. His friends only knew the version of his life with Sarah that he presented. It hadn't been paradise. He'd paid for a mistake by doing the honorable thing, and his reward had been misery and grief. He feared happiness and love like others feared poisonous spiders and snakes.

The only female who would ever own his heart was Emily.

As if to slap him for the lie, an image of Roxy—her lush lips swollen from his kisses, her blouse open, lacy red bra askew—filled his mind, and the next thing he knew he was hard and aching for her again. Damn it. He was not falling for her. She wasn't his type. He just needed her help with Emily. That was it. Nothing else.

Then why couldn't he stop thinking about kissing her again as he finished his morning work routine, and all through lunch? Why then did he stop at home to shower and change into a fresh denim shirt and jeans before driving over to meet her? Was he that horny? That desperate to get laid? He groaned. God, maybe he was.

But he didn't want a relationship with anyone, and Roxy was coming off a divorce. She was too vulnerable, even if she didn't realize it. But even knowing that didn't diminish the longing he kept feeling to drag her into his bed and screw her senseless. Damn, what was the matter with him? He couldn't even think straight anymore.

He pulled up to the address Roxy had given him. She wasn't here yet. The house was on a quiet street, a cul-de-sac, and sat on a narrow lot. It appeared to have been empty for a while. His first impression was that the place was decent enough: a split-entry built in early 2002, he guessed, with a small front stoop, two-car garage, and fenced yard front and back. Good for a cat. It had curb appeal, but that didn't mean it was without issues. He knew this builder, a guy who cut corners whenever he could get away with it.

He stepped out of the truck, deciding to take a look at the foundation. Montana winters could be harsh. But he'd just opened the gate when the Escalade came into view. He stood where he was, watching Roxy drive onto the garage apron. Looking at his rundown pickup next to her Cadillac, he felt as if he were being shown the most important reason why he shouldn't even get involved with this woman. She was out of his league. In the next universe. He had no business even toying with the thought of toying with her.

"Am I late?" she asked, stepping down. She'd changed clothes too, he saw. Knee-high boots with fitted pants that made her legs look even longer than they were. His pulse skipped. His mind might know he shouldn't be interested in Roxy. His body didn't care. Her unique scent reached him, mixing with the cold snowy air, and smelling sort of like frosted oranges. He closed his eyes, drew in the fragrance, then said, "No. You're not late. I just got here."

"It's freezing out here," she said, slipping past him and across the walk to the porch.

It might be freezing, but lady, you look hot enough to melt the icicles hanging from the eaves.

As she slid the key into the lock, she said, "Apparently, it's a three-bedroom, two-and-a-half-bath that was updated last year. It's a bank-owned, short-sale property. So the price is right."

"Yeah, but you realize that actually buying it could

take anywhere from two to six months or more with these kinds of properties?"

"No. I didn't know that." She made a face. "I need to get out of my mother's ASAP. She's as fond of Tallulah as you are."

"Hey, I'm not saying anything bad about your cat. She has great taste in Stetsons." He tipped his hat.

Roxy laughed. She pushed the door inward. It opened directly onto a landing with staircases going up and down. They headed up. Laminate flooring stretched throughout the living and dining room areas. "I'm not a fan of this floor."

"It's pet friendly."

"I don't need pet friendly with Tallulah. She doesn't scratch the flooring like a dog might."

"I'd have the fireplace flue checked before you purchase."

"I should make a list." She pulled her phone from her pocket, opened an app and spoke into it, then said, "Let's look at the kitchen."

"Recently redone. But they went cheap. Laminate counter tops and low-end appliances, though they are new."

"I could change that, but I can't change that it's a narrow galley style."

"And unless the backyard is large enough to extend the back of the house, there's no real room for expansion. That wall there is a load-bearing wall, so you can't even open it up to the living area."

She sighed and puckered her lips in an expression

that should have conveyed disappointment, but that only managed to draw his interest to her mouth. He fought to control the baser urges scrambling his brain. She caught his hand. "Come on. We might as well check out the bedrooms and bathrooms so that I can tell Quint I gave it a chance. He is trying to find me something."

Wade followed Roxy down the narrow hallway, his gaze clued to the natural sway of her hips, as mesmerizing as a metronome. He couldn't look away. Couldn't haul his mind back to the reason they were here, didn't care if this house was well built, didn't care what could be done to make it something that would work for her. All he wanted to do was hold her, kiss her, and bury his aching cock deep inside her.

She entered the bathroom and released that loud, from-the-heart laugh that had unnerved him a couple of weeks ago, but that he now understood belonged to a person who didn't hold back, who lived in the moment. In all her moments. He'd never done that. He'd never just let go, not since . . . that one fateful hayride, a month before high school graduation.

Would she teach him how to let go if he asked?

He entered the bathroom on her heels, and when she suddenly turned around she bumped into him. Her orange scent seemed to explode, overriding the musty bathroom odor. Her eyes met his, and he saw a glimmer of desire, felt an echoing shimmer deep within himself. She licked her lips, and he lost his control. "Roxy, oh, oh, Roxy, I, I . . ."

"Shut up and kiss me, cowboy."

And he did. As he deepened the kiss, pulling her against him, Roxy moaned sensuously. She murmured his name against his mouth, and the cold house heated as though they stood beneath the sun. Wade peeled off his jacket, unzipped her parka, and took her lovely face in both hands, his fingers reaching into her glorious red hair, her skin like silk against his fingertips. She pulled back and began undoing the snaps on his shirt front, her mouth trailing down his jaw, to his neck, nipping little bites that sent impulses straight to his nerve endings. Jesus, what was she doing? *Oh, lord, don't let her stop.*

His breath came quick and then quicker, everywhere her hot tongue moved drove him more and more insane. The roaring in his ears was like the tide of the ocean, matching the pumping of his blood. She lifted her head; her eyes were glazed with need, and his heart pounded harder. She unbuttoned her blouse, one button at a time, and his gaze locked on the gift she was unwrapping. Mounds of pearly flesh rose against the scrap of black lace holding her breasts. She lifted his hands from behind her, bringing them to her breasts, and as his fingers touched her budded nipples, desire washed through him.

His jeans grew smaller, tighter by the second, his erection begging to be freed.

Roxy flicked the front of the black bra, and it fell away, revealing nipples ripe for him, eager for his touch, his taste. As he bent to the feast, she shoved his shirt from his shoulders. Her back was to the open bathroom door, and as Wade moved toward her, he spotted someone standing behind Roxy.

It took him a second to realize he wasn't having a vision. Heat barreled up his neck, setting his ears on fire. Holy shit. Someone, two someones, were gaping at him. At them. And one of them was Emily's teacher, Ms. Vedelman.

Chapter Eight

$\backsim$

Wade straightened, yanking Roxy against him, hiding her nakedness from the intruders, ignoring Roxy's surprised gasp and his body's reaction to her pert nipples against his naked chest.

"God in Heaven, what are you two doing?" a shocked, intolerant voice squawked.

Roxy stiffened against him as she realized they were not alone. Her hands moved him back enough so she could grasp the edges of her blouse and hold them together.

"Mr. Reynolds, is that you?" Ms. Vedelman asked, sounding impossibly more shocked than a moment before.

"Ms. Vedelman," a man said, reaching for the teacher's arm to pull her away from the bathroom. "Let's take another look at the living room."

Wade cringed, embarrassment scorching through

him. He knew that voice. It was Quint's buddy, Dave the Realtor. Oh dear God. Wade's eyes rolled back in his head as myriad consequences raced through his brain, as if Emily's teacher would vanish while his eyes were shut. But when he looked at the doorway again, she still stood there, her mouth as twisted as the braid dangling near her nape. She wielded indignation like a shield, refusing Roxy and him the courtesy of a couple of minutes' privacy to compose themselves. Her hand was on her mouth, but her gaze suggested someone waiting for the payoff in a peep show.

She grunted, then said, "What kind of a father are you, anyway? This explains a lot about your daughter. I'm going to see that Child Services checks into your home life."

What the hell did she mean, it explained a lot about his daughter? He wasn't quick to lose his temper, but that remark had it boiling over. Roxy placed her hand on his chest, holding him back.

Dave seemed to find his balls. He grabbed the teacher's wrist and pulled her from the doorway. "Get your hands off me, David!" *Slap!* Then Ms. Vedelman's clumping footfalls echoed through the hallway, down the stairs, and finally the front door slammed. They heard Dave shout, "Wait up! I need to lock the house."

Roxy was shaking. Wade thought she might be crying, and he started to apologize for putting her in this situation, but he realized she was laughing. Laughing? Didn't she realize what a problem this was? He stepped back, snapping the closures on his shirt, unable to contain the dismay he was feeling. "It's not funny."

"It kind of is," she said, hooking her bra, then starting on the buttons of her blouse.

"No. It's not." Wade shoved his shirttails into the waistband of his jeans. "That bitter old biddy is going to sic Child Services on me."

Roxy reached up to stroke his face, her eyes soft with kindness. "They won't find anything wrong at your house, Wade. From what I observed, you're a great dad. Your friends and family will confirm that. Besides, you're a grown man and have a right to engage in consensual foreplay, anywhere, as long as you're not doing it in front of your daughter."

He wasn't convinced that Child Services would see it that way. "Did you see who was with her?"

"I didn't see anything but your impressive chest." She dipped a finger into his shirt collar, and his heart gave a glad leap.

But Wade wasn't going to give in to temptation this time. Not here. No telling who might walk in next. "The realtor is a pal of Quint's. He'll tell Quint."

That seemed to stop her laughing, and even to sober her. "Why do you care if he tells Quint?"

He shook his head, reddening, ignoring her question. "I thought we locked that front door."

"We did, but it has a realtor key box on it..." she said, looking chagrined. Finally. "But I didn't know anyone else was looking at the house. Quint didn't say. Maybe he didn't know."

"God, everyone in town is going to hear about this."

Roxy bit her bottom lip, looking suddenly distressed. "Even Tabby."

"Tabby?" Why would he care if Tabby heard about this? Actually, he'd be glad. Maybe then she'd leave him the hell alone. "It's Emily that I'm worried about. I don't want her hearing that her dad was caught half-naked making out in a house his teacher was thinking about buying."

He groaned, imagining the conversation he was going to have to have with his almost-thirteen-year-old. Not the usual birds and bees chat. Lord. He shook his head, not believing that he'd gotten swept up in his desire for Roxy. That had never happened to him with any other woman. He was a logical, unemotional kind of guy. He didn't wear his heart on his sleeve. But he'd felt himself spinning out of control, driven beyond sanity by her every kiss, her every touch, and damn, he'd found it more exciting than anything he'd ever done.

What did that say about him?

Roxy started to laugh again, her eyes flashing, the rusty specks in their sage depths glittery. She touched his jaw, stared at his mouth, and smiled. "I'm sorry, but the look on your face is priceless. And precious. Sometime soon, cowboy, we need to finish what we started."

* * *

Big Sky Pie maintained its warm ambiance after closing, giving Roxy the sense that even in the shit storm of controversy and gossip, this was a safe haven where the worst could be weathered, calm waters reached. It didn't hurt that every breath held a scent of sweet spices and chocolate. Hearing the back kitchen door open, she sat straighter in the booth, anticipating the arrival of reinforcements, welcome allies.

"I brought my favorite wine," Callee said, popping into view and holding up a big bottle of Merlot. She set the bottle on the table and tugged off her coat. "And I hope it's okay, but I didn't come alone."

Roxy tensed, fearing she'd see Quint coming through the door.

"I also brought wine," Andrea said, holding up a big bottle of white. "Riesling."

"And I brought dark Cabernet." Molly trailed behind Andrea, holding up a small wine box.

Roxy breathed a sigh of relief, grinning. This wouldn't have happened in Seattle. She didn't have close female friends there to rally around when she needed them. A strange warmth flowed through her chest, the kind of wonderful sensation that enjoying a favorite dish gave her, only this felt even better, something tangible that wouldn't end when she finished eating. *I could get used to this.* As coats were shed and purses set aside, Roxy grabbed four mugs from the coffee counter and set them on the table. "Will these do, ladies?"

"We used to drink wine from canning jars when I was in my teens," Molly said, a faraway look in her eyes.

"We used jelly jars when Donnie and I were living on

the rodeo circuit." Andrea shook her head, her memory obviously not as sweet as Molly's.

"Let's not forget this." Callee produced a corkscrew from behind the cash register counter.

Roxy eyed her with a grin. "Looks like just about anything goes on in this pie shop."

"I'll never tell," Callee said, with a shy grin and pink cheeks.

They started with the Cabernet, Molly letting them know she was only allowed one glass of vino a night.

Roxy slid into the booth opposite Callee, and Molly scooted in next to her. Andrea sat next to Callee. Andrea filled their cups, then Roxy lifted hers and made a toast, "To the power of girlfriends."

They clinked cups, nodding and murmuring, "Here, here, and amen."

Roxy pushed the key to the split entry house across the table to Callee. "Tell Quint it's not for me. It would require a complete remodel, and I'm not sure I want to buy anything just yet. I'm thinking I should rent something until after I get my business started. Whatever the hell that might be."

"Have you considered a catering business?" Callee asked. "We used to talk about doing that."

Roxy sighed. "I have. Not sure yet about the long-term viability of a catering service in Kalispell."

"Another restaurant?" Andrea asked.

"No. That's too risky."

"You know, dear," Molly said, a drop of Cabernet on her upper lip. "I've been thinking about expanding

Big Sky Pie...just a little. Sort of a variation on a theme."

Roxy shifted toward her boss.

Molly licked at the drip of wine. "The building on the other side of this wall would be perfect for what I have in mind, you see. Of course it would need to be brought up to code and have a kitchen installed, something similar to the kitchen here, but slightly smaller."

"Why is this the first I'm hearing about this?" Andrea managed the accounts at Big Sky Pie, and from the look in her brown eyes, she could see profits flying out the window and wasn't about to let Molly get carried away without a say in whatever this expansion idea was.

Molly patted her hand. "Why dear, you're hearing about it now. I've just been mulling it around in my head until a few minutes ago, but I think the idea has merit. I've got some samples that Rafe made today." She got up and went into the kitchen. She was gone a couple of minutes and returned with a tray that held something that looked like tartlets, but that smelled like beef pot pies. "Rafe and I made these this afternoon. Our version of beef pasties."

Everyone reached for one. Roxy liked the texture, and the taste was delicious, but as she savored the blend of meat, veggies, and spices, she considered what she'd add or deduct to enhance the flavor. "These are very good."

"My guys would love these," Andrea said.

"Most guys would. Meat lovers' pies," Callee said.

Molly agreed, pointing out how much better they

were than store-bought beef pies since the dough was
Big Sky Pie's special flakey crust.

Callee said, "Plus these take-out sizes are convenient."

"Why not just add these to the menu instead of opening a separate shop?" Andrea daubed her mouth with a
napkin. "It would be cheaper."

Roxy said, "For one thing, it would change the
smell in this shop, and that isn't something you want
to lose."

Molly nodded and sipped her wine. "Not only do
I not want to change this shop at the moment, I also
don't want to risk cross-contamination of foodstuff in
the kitchen. Meat and fruit don't mix. I'm thinking the
new shop wouldn't do just beef pasties, though, but say,
fish turnovers, chicken pot pies, buffalo tarts, and every
other kind we can think up."

"You're out to lock up the pie market in Flathead
County." Callee laughed.

"It has great potential," Roxy said, liking the idea
more as she considered the possibilities. "It's different
and might not work in a lot of areas, but here, in a town
with so many men who love meat, I think it would be a
winner."

"Of course, I'd need someone to run it." Molly's not-
so-subtle point was not lost on anyone. "Rafe is a great
assistant, but he can't run the place."

Roxy took a gulp of wine, feeling as if she'd just
planted a foot squarely and firmly on Kalispell soil for
the first time since returning. She might be making a

commitment. Or seriously considering it. "You want me to run it?"

"Exactly. With your skills, Big Sky Pie Too can't miss. I was thinking we might be partners, and if at some point you wanted to buy me out, that would be okay, too."

Molly was staring eagerly at Roxy, as were Callee and Andrea. Roxy was trying to take in this unexpected gift that had been dropped in her lap. She had to admit the idea was tempting. The location couldn't be beat. The proximity to Molly and access to her help, should it be needed, was ideal. Partnering, instead of owning alone, was much less scary. But hesitation gripped her. "I'll need to see the building, what the renovation will require, and—"

"You don't need to give me your answer tonight or even this week," Molly interrupted. "Just think about it."

"Thank you, Molly. It's a generous offer and an intriguing one." Roxy felt like a light had switched on inside the dark attic she'd been residing in since the divorce, and even though its brilliance had her blinking, she finally saw something to focus on, to grab hold of, to pull herself toward. But still she hesitated. "My first priority is getting my own place to live."

Callee lifted her glass for more wine. "I'll have Quint see what's available in the rental market."

"Something cat friendly," Roxy reminded her.

"Of course." Callee smiled and gave her hand a loving squeeze. Andrea opened the Riesling and filled the three younger women's wine mugs.

Molly, still nursing her allotted portion of the dark red, set her mug down with a little thump. "So, are we going to talk about the elephant in the room or keep dancing around it?"

The younger women gaped at her. Molly shrugged and said, "Life is short, have dessert first."

"What?" Roxy said, confused.

Molly huffed. "Wade Reynolds qualifies as dessert in my book, and apparently in yours too."

Roxy cringed at the "I told you so" grin Quint's mother wore. *Hell, I can't deny it. I was caught in the act, and now half the town knows about Wade and me. Even her own mother, who had had a few choice words on the subject of getting naked with men in public places.* Roxy sighed. "I can't believe Dave spread the word."

"Far as I know, the only one he told was Quint."

"And his mother," Molly said. "She told me."

Roxy rolled her eyes. And Quint told Callee and Andrea, and here they all were, hoping to get the dope. Well, she was tired of bitching to Tallulah about her love life, and at least with friends, she'd get some feedback that she might even be able to use. Or at least some sympathy. "I guess I should back this conversation up to the beginning."

She told them that she'd sworn off sex after discovering her husband had cheated on her, that she'd remained celibate until the papers were final, and that she had every intention of ending the drought with some yummy cowboys once she was settled in Kalispell. "Yeah, the best laid plans…" Roxy took a deep breath, a swallow of wine, then went on, "That first night, as I was driving into town during the big snowstorm, I ran into Wade on the highway. We almost crashed, actually." She explained what had happened. The part about Tallulah peeing in Wade's Stetson had them all howling.

Andrea dried her eyes as her giggles subsided. "There is no denying that Wade is total man candy."

Roxy laughed. "Rest assured, my friends, I put Wade right at the top of my to-do list. Fling number one."

"Good choice," Callee said. "You're both in need of a good…fling."

"Wade is also adorable," Molly said, not to be left out of the conversation.

"He's one of the good guys," Andrea said. "He doesn't need his heart stomped on."

"No, but he could use some loosening up," Molly said, draining her cup.

"I didn't have any luck in that department," Andrea admitted. "But then, I wasn't really trying, and there just wasn't any, you know, chemistry between us."

"Well, apparently that's not the case with our resident redhead." Callee stared at Roxy, eyebrows lifted, silently encouraging her to get back to the story. It was obvious they were all eager for some juicy details by the looks on their faces.

Roxy grimaced, though in fact she knew she'd feel the same if this was one of them sharing. She pouted. "Well, then I discover Wade was one of Quint's and Callee's best friends, and that put the kibosh on any fling. It would just be too easy for a few sessions of mattress bebop to end up complicated. I don't want complicated. Or a relationship. Not again."

"Ah." Andrea chewed another of the beef pasties. "That's what I thought, too, but then I met Ian."

"Yes, dear," Molly said, "but you were single for enough years to put that first marriage behind you. It's still too fresh for Roxy."

"Yep." *But no amount of time will change my mind*, Roxy thought. "When Wade came with me the first time to view the loft, when we were alone, well, there were some seriously smoldering glances exchanged. I won't lie: we do have this strange, provocative chemistry that is as tempting as a vat of chocolate, but as I'm getting to know him, I realize Wade isn't a guy you have a fling with. If and when he gets involved, it will be with all of his heart, and I would only break that heart. I told him that night that there would be nothing going on between us. Unfortunately, I made the mistake of kissing him, of letting him kiss me."

The memory had Roxy shutting her eyes and smiling.

"Ooh," Callee squealed. "That looks like trouble."

"With a capital T," Roxy admitted. "But he's not really available, even if I wanted him to be. Do you guys realize that all of the photos of Emily on his mantel were taken before Sarah died? There are none of Emily since then. It's like his life stopped with Sarah's. He must have loved that woman...still loves that woman..."

"I'm not sure about that," Andrea said, putting her elbow on the table and crooking her thick blond hair behind one ear. "While he and I were dating, from the way he spoke about Sarah, I got the impression that she was passive aggressive. Sweet as sugar on the outside, ramrod steel on the inside. Wade doesn't like to rock the boat, or break rules, or let himself go. He was married right out of high school, and I don't think he'd dated much before then. It's like he never sewed any oats, and now that he can, he doesn't know how to let loose."

"Maybe he just needs someone to give him a kick start, like a rusty old motor," Molly suggested, gazing pointedly at Roxy.

Roxy gave a nervous laugh. "I had no intention of seeing him again."

"But," Andrea said, obviously sensing there was a but.

Roxy shook her head, bit her lower lip, then said, "I was giving the loft a second look, taking Tallulah there to see how she reacted to the place. Unknown to me, Wade was already there, doing a couple of repairs. He didn't know I'd be there, especially not with the cat, or I'm sure he'd have been gone before I arrived."

Callee arched an eyebrow. "But my husband knew you'd both be there at the same time, right?"

"Probably."

Callee just shook her head. "That man..."

"What happened?" Andrea was leaning across the table, eyes wide and eager.

"Tallulah startled and attacked him, clawing his face."

"Oh, no," everyone said in unison.

"Oh, yes." Roxy shoved her hair back. She'd swear her mouth was still swollen from this afternoon's kiss-a-thon. "I cleaned the wound and put a bandage on it, and he grabbed me and kissed me—a deep, mind-boggling kiss—then turned on his heel and walked out."

"Whew. I didn't know he had it in him. Go, Wade." Andrea sat back against the booth.

"I'm not sure what that kiss was all about except I knew he was pissed off and not just at the cat. I think he resented my telling him that we were not going to get together, and he was trying to prove to me that I wanted to get together no matter what I said."

"Knowing you, you didn't leave it at that." Callee was reaching for the corkscrew, and Roxy realized the Riesling bottle was empty. No wonder she felt so mellow.

Roxy held her mug out for some Merlot. "I bought him a new Stetson to replace the one Tallulah destroyed." She told them about going to his house, encountering Tabby there fixing dinner, and leaving without speaking to him. "I'd gone to apologize and ask if he'd come look at that house with me today, but figured I'd have to find another builder."

"Who is this Tabby?" Andrea inquired, frowning. "I've never heard of her."

"She's the mother of one of Emily's friends. Anyway, Wade showed up here this morning to thank me for the new hat and insisted he would view the house with me after I got off work. I met him there. It was going good until we got into the small bathroom—then, well, we just…"

Callee's eyes were wide, her imagination running wild. "Dave was right? You made love?"

"No." Roxy choked on her wine. "I don't know what Dave thinks he saw, but we were still dressed. Partially. Let's just say we were on our way to something along those lines when Dave and Emily's teacher showed up and caught us, and now Wade is afraid the whole town will soon know about this."

Andrea had her hand on her mouth, trying not to laugh. Callee seemed more mortified, but was also smirking. Roxy found herself agreeing with them. It was still funny. "That's exactly how I reacted. Wade didn't appreciate it. He's afraid Quint and the guys will never let him hear the end of it. But mostly he's worried about Emily."

"Well, sure." Andrea nodded. "He's probably going to have to tell her. God, I'd love to be a fly on the wall for that conversation."

Callee said, "I'd rather be one hearing the conversation Quint is having with Wade right now."

* * *

"Seriously, you of all people were caught with your pants around your ankles?" Quint cast a shit-eating grin at Wade. Wade wanted to rearrange his face.

"I'm gonna kill Dave. No one had their pants down. My pants weren't even unzipped." Considering how hard he'd been, he doubted he could have gotten the zipper to work.

"Well, if you're gonna lose your reclaimed virginity, you could do a hell of a lot worse than Roxy," Quint kept on. "She's sexy as hell."

"Don't talk about her like that," Wade said, surprising Quint—and himself.

"Okay. Okay." Quint raised his hands in surrender. "I understand, but you realize you're going to get a lot of wayward glances from the fine citizens of our fair city when news gets out that you're something of a Romeo?"

"Not funny."

"If you say so." Quint chuckled, swigged some beer.

Wade swallowed from his bottle, thinking whiskey might have been a better choice given his mood. "What am I going to tell Emily? I can't let her hear about this from her classmates, or that old biddy."

"Shit, I don't know. Tell her that she might hear some things about you that aren't as bad as they sound. And if she has questions about the gossip, that she can come and talk to you and you'll tell her the truth."

"I didn't ever want to be a dad that she had reason to doubt or couldn't be proud of. I feel like I've let her down."

Quint shook his head. "Man, cut yourself some slack. It's sex. Adults are allowed to have sex. It's natural and healthy, and you've been abstaining for so long, you're a little crazed is all."

Wade lifted his gaze, frowning, hearing his friend's advice, knowing logically that Quint was right, but emotionally…damn, he was all over the place. He wanted to take Roxy up on her offer, wanted to make love to her so bad it was killing him. Make love to her? Not just jump her bones? He groaned at the realization. "If it were only sex, I might not be so tangled up about it."

"You have feelings for Roxy."

"I don't know. Shit, maybe. Yes. But she doesn't want, isn't ready for, won't..."

"Man, you're overthinking this. It's just sex. Enjoy it."

Wade sat down with his head in his hands. "You don't understand. Sarah is the only woman I ever... you know, and she, well, wasn't that fond of sex. Once a week, same time, same place, no frills, no preamble. Just do the deed and done."

Quint's face was a mixture of stunned disbelief and pity.

Wade felt worse for the revelation, not better. "I wouldn't have told you, but you're my best friend, and damn it, McCoy, I need some advice. Sarah was so, so conservative, and Roxy is so...not, that I'm out of my league. I mean, she makes me feel things that I don't even recognize. I want to do things to her, with her, and I'm not even sure what those things are. She makes me feel like there's this wild beast inside me, and once I let it free, I might not be able to look myself in the mirror after."

Quint rubbed the scruff on his jaw, staring at his Dan Post boots, then finally back at Wade. "That's a hell of a problem to have, my friend, but I'm betting you'll like the man in the mirror more than you do now."

Wade wasn't sure how giving in to one's baser nature would have that result, but Quint seemed as serious as a judge passing down a life sentence.

There was a knock on the door. Both men glanced at it. Quint said, "It's probably the moral police come to arrest you."

Wade swore at him as he padded over in his stocking feet and yanked open the door. Tabby stood on the porch, buttoned up against the night weather. The porch light shone on her blond hair. Her cheeks were bright pink, either from the cold or too much rouge. She was holding a Crock-Pot. She beamed up at him. "I made you a pot of vegetable soup."

There was no lid on the Crock-Pot, and the steaming liquid smelled delicious, but he wasn't up to dealing with Tabby tonight. Forgetting his manners, he didn't invite her inside, but stepped out onto the porch, shutting the door behind him. "Tabby, I—"

"Oh my God, it's true, isn't it? What people are saying about you and that, that redheaded skank. Is she in there now? Is that why you don't want me in your house? Of course she is. Wade Reynolds, you are not the man I thought you were." With that, she yanked the Crock-Pot back and then swung it forward, hurling the hot soup at him. She swore, let loose a cackling laugh, and stormed off, leaving him standing there with carrots, potatoes, and green beans dripping off him onto his welcome mat.

"What the hell?" Quint had cracked open the door. His eyes were huge, and a grin was spreading across his face. "Man, still waters do run deep. What'd you do to that woman?"

"Nothing. That is one crazy bitch." Wade pushed past

him, peeling off his wet flannel shirt and wetter jeans as he stomped into the foyer. Down to his boxers, he balled up his clothes, including his socks. "I'm lucky I don't have second-degree burns."

Quint was still laughing. "I've been feeling sorry for you not getting any, Reynolds, but I guess I underestimated what a true ladies' man you really are."

Chapter Nine

Decked out with twinkling lights and sprigs of pine wrapped in ribbons, Big Sky Pie resembled a gaily wrapped Christmas box planted in the snow, Roxy thought. She crossed the mall parking lot, her gaze drifting to the vacant storefront next door to the pie shop. *Small, but full of possibility?* The more she considered Molly's proposition, the more she liked the idea. But could she commit to a partnership? That kept being the hang-up. She hadn't even found an apartment to rent. Although Quint had shown her a few great possibilities, she'd found flaws with all of them. Why? It wasn't like any of the leases bound her up for more than a couple of months. Quint had even offered her the loft on a short-term lease. But she hadn't jumped at it.

She entered the pie shop, finding it just as festive inside as out. A miniature tree, decorated with ruby garland and gold ornaments, stood on the display case, and there was another on the shelf above the cash register counter, while bright red and green candles decorated the café tables. Classic country tunes honored the holiday, and weary shoppers, fresh from the trenches of hard-core gift hunting, filled the tables for a reward of sweet offerings. She smiled and greeted those she knew, refusing to be daunted by the slowly dying gossip about Wade and her. She filled a mug with coffee and went into the kitchen to find Quint and Molly finishing up the last of the pies and chores. Andrea was seated at the work counter, poring over paperwork.

"Life is good," Molly said when she spied Roxy.

"Oh?" Roxy replied, smiling at her boss. Molly looked as tired as she felt after their early morning start to this long day. For most people it was afternoon. For bakers who started at four a.m., it was evening.

But Molly wasn't acting tired. She seemed as giddy as a kid going to a carnival. "The orders are pouring in, gang."

Andrea seemed less positive that this was such a good thing. "What if we get more demand than we can supply?"

"What?" Molly burst out laughing. "I never thought I'd hear you worrying about too much business."

Roxy smiled at the irony. Andrea's bean-counter brain was always worrying about the pie shop's bottom line, always coming up with ideas on how to improve it. She should be happier than anyone about this windfall.

"I know." Andrea shrugged, smiling and frowning at

the same time as she held up a fistful of papers. "But all these orders came in today. At some point we need to have a 'no more large orders' cutoff date."

Quint looked up from the dough mounds he was preparing for the next day's pies. "Lovette's got a point, Mama. With Jane out and only Rafe to assist, we're limited on what we can deliver before the big holiday celebrations. Christmas is ten days away."

Molly apparently didn't want to hear that. She glanced at Roxy, deferring to her because of her restaurant experience. Roxy set her mug on the work counter. "Holidays are always busy times in the food industry. I resigned myself to having my holidays a day or two after everyone else in order to keep the restaurant open on, say, a Thanksgiving or Christmas or Valentine's Day or Mother's Day. A lot of people like to take their families out and not have the hassle or mess of a home-cooked meal. I suspect it's the same with dessert. Our pies offer them a decadent treat while giving them one less task to handle during an already busy celebration."

"Yeah, I suspect business will slow down again in the new year." Andrea looked a bit crestfallen at the idea.

Roxy said, "The lucrative times will pull the business through the leaner months. It evens out in the long run. It's just the extra work that can be stressful and unnerving when things are this crazy."

Roxy was just glad the mini-scandal she and Wade had kicked up hadn't kept anyone away from Big Sky Pie. If anything, it had increased business right afterward. But she hadn't seen or heard from Wade since.

Four days and counting. It was like he was avoiding her, even though she'd pretty much invited him to have some hot monkey sex. Maybe he was avoiding her for Emily's sake.

"So are they right or wrong about the orders?" Molly asked.

Roxy smiled. "They're right. It's great that everyone seems to have discovered Big Sky Pie suddenly, but with call-in orders, texted orders, and e-mail orders coming in from the website, we'd have to be a huge factory to deliver it all. And the thing that folks love about your pies is that they're not manufactured in an assembly line."

Although saying that seemed odd, given that it had felt exactly like a mini-assembly line the past few days.

"Callee told me when we were launching the pie shop that it's all about the quality, not the quantity," Quint said, pulling a strip of plastic wrap from the roll. "And it is. But that's a good thing, Mama. The less we offer in order to be true to our brand, the more in demand our product will be. We just need that 'gotta-have-it' attitude to spill over into the after-holiday months."

Molly checked the timer on one of the ovens. "Okay then. Andrea and I will go over the orders, figure out what we can and cannot fill, and let people know."

Andrea's frown disappeared, and she scooted off the stool, heading into the office. "I'll have Nick post to the website that we are not taking any more holiday orders."

Quint gave his mother a bear hug from behind, careful not to get his hands on her, and kissed her cheek.

"Did I ever tell you what a wise woman you are, Mama?"

Molly was clearly pleased by her son's show of affection, but she shirked him off, telling him, "Foolish man. You're cross-contaminating everything."

"Slave driver." Quint chuckled as he went back to wrapping the last mounds, and Molly carried a pie out to the café to place in the display case.

Roxy sank onto one of the stools at the work island, letting the ease of being off her feet shift through her weary body. A warm bath awaited her later today, if she could manage it. She sipped coffee, her mind wandering, until she felt Quint's bright blue gaze drilling into her.

He said, "Have you seen Wade lately?"

She jolted as if he'd tapped her with a rolling pin, but she didn't look at him. "Not since last week."

He cleared his throat. "You mean at the viewing of the split-entry?"

She lifted her gaze, but there was nothing teasing, nothing judgmental in his expression. Just friendship and a serious curiosity. What was he asking? What her intentions were concerning his pal? The very idea brought out the smartass in her. "He doesn't write, he doesn't call, I'm not his cuppa…"

Quint went serious. "I wouldn't bet on that last."

Her stomach squeezed. It was what she wanted to hear, what she didn't want to hear. Quint stared pointedly, as if trying to read her response, but she'd be damned if she was going to discuss her love life, or lack thereof, with her best friend's husband. "Whatever. I'm not losing any sleep over him."

Liar. She'd lost more than she'd admit to, and when she did sleep, she dreamed of Wade—that damn man with his mind-shredding kisses and branding-iron touches.

"None of my business."

Then why had he brought it up? She wanted to kick him. Men. All of them were as annoying as swamp mosquitoes. Her glare was wasted on Quint, however, as he stowed the dough mounds inside the Sub-Zero. Molly came in and went to the sink to wash her hands. Quint strolled over to his mother, offering her a towel. "Mama, I'm taking you home now. No. No protests."

Roxy watched as Molly dried her hands and then shoved her arms into the coat her son held up for her. Maybe it was the season or the fact that she was bone tired, but the compassion and love Quint showed his mother sent an unexpected yearning through Roxy. She missed having a strong man in her life, one who took charge, one who took care of her. Oh, she didn't want that all the time, but on a day like this, when her muscles ached and her feet screamed, and she had to go home to a disloyal cat—who seemed to be switching loyalties to her mother—that was when the longing rose up inside her like an ache.

Wade was cut from the same cloth as Quint. He would be a take-charge, take-care kind of guy, too. Images of Wade teased her—that smile that could break a heart, the shy endearing blush when he was embarrassed, the fierce gleam in his eyes when he spoke of his daughter, the pride and ages-old knowledge when he spoke about the craft that he'd learned at his grandfather's knee.

She didn't like to admit it, but she was growing more attracted to him than was good for her. She should never have told him she'd be available to finish what they'd started at the split entry. Not that he'd made any attempt to take her up on the offer. Of course, given his shy nature, he might not know the fine art of romantic pursuit. *God, can you hear yourself? You're making excuses for him, sounding like you want more than a roll in the sack with him. Do you?*

Look at his response to what had happened between them. Complete retreat. What would he do if they actually made love? Move to Wyoming?

Quint and Molly left, and Rafe set straight to cubing the butter they needed for the next day, but now that they were alone, he kept tossing her overheated glances, obviously still crushing on her. Of course, she was flattered by the attention, especially from a gorgeous man who radiated testosterone and confidence. Why wouldn't she be after the ego battering she'd taken by her betraying ex? But she didn't do romantic entanglements with coworkers. She was going to have to make him understand that his affections were wasted on her.

Andrea had come in without Roxy hearing and stood by her shoulder. "You know, it looks like a liquor store in here with all these bottles on the counter."

Roxy glanced up at her. "A liqueur store, you mean. Have you tasted any of the new pies?"

"Not yet. What do you recommend?"

"Well, let's see, we've put a little rum in our pumpkin raisin rum pie, a little brandy in the mincemeat pies, a little crème de menthe in the chocolate fudge meringue, and a little coconut liqueur in the banana cream pie. So I guess it's up to which sounds best to you."

"A person could get drunk on a few of these tasty concoctions. I think I'll take one of these home to Ian tonight. Speaking of homes, did you find a place yet?"

"Not yet." Roxy sighed, giving the first excuse that popped into her head. "I don't have time to move right now. My mom is okay with it. She understands that work comes first. My fickle cat has been cozying up to her, probably because Mom is feeding her some kind of seafood treats, and that changed the immediate need to find my own place."

"A cat. I always liked cats, but the boys all want a dog. Ian and I are thinking about getting Lucas and Logan a puppy for Christmas."

"So, you and Ian, that's really working out, huh?"

"It is. I didn't believe there was a Mr. Right for me. You know, the perfect guy who rings my chimes, loves me outside the bedroom, and adores my sons as if they were his own. A man my sons would trust and look up to and aspire to be like. A pretty tall order. And you'd never have guessed by looking at him that Ice Erikksen would fit that criteria, but wow, he was full of surprises. Great surprises." Andrea sighed, tears glistening in her eyes, a secret smile tugging her lips up at the corners. "And this morning, Lucas called him 'daddy' for the first time. That's why I want to treat him to a little celebration tonight with one of these pies."

Roxy was happy for her friend. Maybe one day she'd be happy again. As she stepped away, she said, "Well, I don't have a man in my life or a new place to live, or a vet for my cat yet, or even a beauty salon for a good hair dresser."

"I'm not the one to ask about a cat doctor, but I highly recommend Trula's Trendy Tresses." She gave Roxy the address. "They do walk-ins, too, which is great this time of year."

"Thanks."

"As to a man in your life...what about Wade?"

* * *

Trula's Trendy Tresses sat in a strip mall near the Wal-Mart, two doors down from The Flower Garden, Betty and Dean Gardener's floral shop. Callee had told Roxy the story of the senior couple who had been lovers in their teens, but their parents had objected and separated them. Most of their lives were spent apart, but recently they'd found each other again, discovered they had never stopped being in love, finally married, and held a big reception last month, serving pie instead of cake at the celebration.

Roxy had no such delusion that she and Ty would find each other again in their senior years and remarry. They shouldn't have married in the first place, she realized more every day. Love, phooey. It was for everyone but her. The thought gave her pause. Was she getting grumpier by the day? She swore she was. In fact, her mind spent more time thinking about sex lately than anything else, but not sex with anyone. Sex with one tall, shy, maddening cowboy contractor.

Maybe getting her hair cut would lift her spirits. But as she gazed at the shop, a wayward sorrow swept through her for her Seattle hairdresser, Jean-Louis. His downtown salon made you feel like you were stepping into a Parisian spa on the Left Bank: very high-end, very expensive, but he was a perfectionist. Well worth what he charged to keep her unruly mop manageable.

But you're not in Emerald City anymore, Dorothy. Establishing a core of service people in the town where she lived was essential to her survival here. She had to do this. It ought to be simple enough to follow the lines of Jean-Louis's haircut. And yet, trepidation filled her stomach as she caught a glimpse of the interior paint that looked even darker than the purple slopped on the outside façade. She couldn't be sure, though, given the windows were plastered with flyers about local causes or events, some of them a year old.

She meant to take a step forward, but actually backed up a step. Maybe two. Maybe this wasn't such a good idea. She took another couple of backward steps and slammed into something solid that hadn't been there before. A man. A very tall man. He caught her arms, steadying her on the slippery pavement.

"This could be a replay of the night we met."

Wade. His breath fanned her ear, and her heart almost exploded in her chest. She couldn't move. Didn't want him to move. Even though they were standing in a parking lot just off a very public highway, even though this could start a whole new round of gossip.

Chapter Ten

Roxy couldn't breathe with Wade this near. "I, I was…"

"Going to get your hair done up?" he said, his voice a whisper.

Done up? She smiled and almost leaned back against his chest, the instinct so natural she didn't know where it came from. This man was definitely a throwback to another era in some ways—his old school manners, his uptight morals, his shy sexuality—and that combination seemed to be working a number on her. The dipping temperature kissed her cheeks with icy lips, but she barely noticed with the heat generated by Wade being so close.

Her gaze fell to the storefront, to what she could see inside Trula's Trendy Tresses. What was Wade doing here? Not for a haircut. Although a lot of Seattle men patronized a salon like Jean-Louis's. In Kalispell, a man's man used a barbershop or he ran the risk of being cattle-prodded out of town by his buddies. Except Quint, of course. Callee trimmed his hair, and he liked it over the collar.

Roxy found some solid footing and turned to face Wade, her lady parts dancing at the sight and smell of him. She ignored the party her body wanted to have with Wade, kept her expression as bland as she could manage, and answered his question about having her hair *done up*. "I was thinking about it."

"Looked to me like you were retreating."

"What brings you here?" She eyed his hair. Short and neat. No trim required. Could she hope he was headed to the florist for an "I'm sorry I haven't been in touch since almost making love to you last week" bouquet?

He cleared his throat and glanced at his boots, tugging on the brim of the Stetson. When he lifted his face to hers, he looked perplexed and unsure, like a man stepping through a field of mines, not knowing when or if he would land on a live one. Of all the scenarios that might explain his dilemma—all relating to her, of course—she didn't expect the one that came out of his mouth. "Emily's over there, in my truck. She's turning thirteen on New Year's Eve, and she wants to get her hair done up in a new style. Andrea recommended I bring her here, but now she's chickening out. Making up silly excuses not to go in. I think she's afraid they might laugh at her."

Roxy felt a sudden deep kinship with Emily. Hairdressers had no idea how intimidating they could be.

Despite their expertise, their vision of a woman's hair might not match the one inside the client's head. The end result could be an epic victory or a major fail—that the customer would have to live with for weeks. She shuddered. "I totally understand."

Wade glanced toward the shop, his mouth scrunched in indecision. "I thought I'd go in and see if they have a brochure or something that Emily could take home to look over."

Roxy smiled at the possibility that he might also end up with a handful of the flyers that were in the window. She had a better suggestion. "I think Emily needs to come in and see for herself that it's not as terrifying as she imagines."

Roxy wasn't sure if Emily needed the reassurance or if she did. Hell, they both did. An idea struck her. She touched Wade's arm. "Maybe she'd come in with me, and we could do this together."

Wade's eyes warmed to the shade of a tropical lagoon, filling with gratitude, the edges of his sexy mouth twitching in a half-smile. "Are you serious?"

"You were right when you thought I was retreating. It might sound silly, but trying out a new hairstylist scares me as much as it does Emily. Maybe I won't be so scared if we do it together."

Another guy might have told her that she was being a fool, but Wade grinned, seeming to like that she'd shown him a vulnerable side. "Let's go ask her."

Emily was slouched in the passenger seat, her arms crossed in the proverbial hostile teenager pose, her hair swept into a severe ponytail that did nothing to flatter her high forehead or the shape of her face. She eyed Roxy with suspicion. "Did my dad tell you to meet us here?"

Roxy wasn't sure where that had come from, but either Emily was upset with her over the gossip she had likely had to endure or she thought her dad and Roxy were conspiring against her. "No, he didn't. I just happened to be here for the same reason as you."

"Did you have yours done already?" Emily's narrowed gaze shifted to Roxy's head.

"Not yet. I got to the door and chickened out."

Disbelief ruled Emily's scowl. "Your hair doesn't look like it needs to be styled."

"Nope. Just trimmed. But my beautician is in Seattle, and since I can't drive there whenever I need a little clip and reshaping, I have to find someone here to do it. Andrea says this place is the best. But I'm used to my old hairdresser, and frankly, I'm afraid someone new might not get the cut right." Even if all they had to do was follow the current shape. "You see, if it's not cut properly, it looks like an unruly red mop."

She felt Wade's gaze on her hair, probably trying to picture that. She glanced over at him, nodding. "It's true."

"It doesn't look wild at all," Emily scoffed.

"Ah, that's the trick, you see. Great product and a great cut."

Emily considered that, the crossed arms going slack. "What kind of product? Can they do something with my hair?"

"There are products for all sorts of hair textures."

"There are?" A teeny glimmer of hope began to nip at the doubtful expression, then quickly died. "How much does it cost?"

"We won't know that until the hairdresser tells you which will work best for your hair. And that will depend on what you tell her you want your new style to be."

"I don't know what I want." The frown between her brows had smoothed into a thoughtful line, and an "I'm considering it" light shone in her eyes.

Roxy held out her hand, and Emily stared at it. "If you won't go with me, I won't go in either. I'm too scared to do this alone."

Emily looked taken aback. She had just been given the responsibility of the decision. And it seemed to cause a shift in her. She straightened her shoulders, uncrossed her legs, and took Roxy's hand tentatively, then more firmly. "We could make it a girls' day out kind of thing."

"I'd like that." Roxy nodded, grinning. "You'll go with me then?"

"Dad, can I have enough money for product, too?"

Wade didn't hesitate. He withdrew his wallet and offered her his credit card. "Whatever it takes to make you happy, baby."

"Dad, I'm not a baby..." Emily rolled her eyes.

"Sorry," Wade said, giving Roxy a grateful look that could have melted the ice from the top of Tall Mountain and had the same reaction on her, turning her blood to lava. She and Emily set out for the salon. She called to

Wade over her shoulder, "I'll bring Emily home afterward."

Roxy had a comrade in arms, but she was still scared about the experience ahead and would bet Emily's palms were as damp inside her gloves as hers were. Inside the lively, purple den with mirrors at every station, the butterflies in her stomach took flight, crashing into one another. They were greeted by a young woman with rainbow hair, makeup to match, and clothes extremely mismatched. And yet the look worked. She introduced herself as Trula's daughter Zoe, and looked around nineteen. Roxy felt Emily's tension lift like a magic curtain. But the girl was eyeing Zoe's hair as if she might be considering doing something similar to her own.

Roxy figured Emily's views on life and style were influenced by the same things that had influenced hers at this age: actresses and the popular singers of the day. Zoe resembled the girl-singer of a hard rock band Roxy had once adored.

Roxy could only imagine how Wade would react if she brought his little girl home with rainbow hair. She stifled a wicked grin. The point was to enhance Emily's hairstyle, not make her unrecognizable. She leaned over to Emily and whispered, "Are you sure you want to do something that extreme first time out?"

Emily thought about it, then shook her head. "I don't want to be so different that everyone points and stares."

"Me either," Roxy said, but there were a couple of customers casting sidelong glances at her as though they'd heard all about Wade and their split-level nudity, and now, here she was with Wade's little girl. *God knows what the grapevine will be saying about me to-morrow. Who cares?* But suddenly, she did care. For Emily's sake. She didn't want to hurt this girl in any way.

Roxy lowered her voice and asked Zoe, "Who do you recommend for a trim? Who gives the best haircuts?"

But before Zoe could speak, a woman who looked like an older version of her, sans the rainbow hair, spoke up. "I'm Trula, owner of Trendy Tresses."

"I'm Roxanne Nash and this is Emily," Roxy told Trula. "I work at Big Sky Pie."

"Oh, Roxy, Molly speaks very highly of you. Glad to finally meet you." She eyed Roxy's hair. "Need a trim, huh? I know she looks young, but my Zoe's been cuttin' hair since she was ten. I wouldn't let her do it in the shop until she got her license, but she's legal now, and although I don't tell her, she's the best in the salon. After me, of course."

"Really, Ma?" Zoe looked like a balloon that might float away with her chest puffed with pride, her cheeks rounded with a big grin.

Don't judge a book by its cover. Roxy asked, "Is Zoe free for a new style for Emily and a trim for me?"

"I'll do your trim," Trula said. "Zoe can do your daughter."

"She's not my mom," Emily blurted out. "She's my dad's friend."

"Oh yeah?" Trula nodded, her friendly gaze suddenly curious. "How does the young lady want her hair cut?"

"Let's let her and Zoe figure that out," Roxy said, squeezing Emily's shoulder.

Emily's chin came up, and she seemed less intimidated about the procedure. She asked Zoe, "Will you be using some product?"

As Roxy settled into Trula's station chair, she had the strangest feeling that she was about to get the third degree about Wade from a master gossip-extractor.

* * *

"So, let me get this straight," Quint said, pressing into the high back of the end booth at Big Sky Pie and giving Wade the evil eye. "You haven't even spoken to her since the split-level thing, but you've foisted your kid on her instead of handling Emily's problem on your own. Is that it?"

"It's a beauty shop, man." Wade had expected some sympathy, even a little understanding from his best bud, not a lecture. He cut into one of the meat tarts—they were taste-testing for Rafe—and mentally retraced the accidental run-in with Roxy at Trula's, remembering how it went down, remembering the zing that went through him as their bodies collided, remembering how her orange-y scent charged into him, heating his blood, firing his desire, recalling how sweet she'd been to his child. All of it wound together into a big mess of want and need and affection. "You're making it sound bad. It wasn't."

Wade bit into the flakey crust, the flavor somehow

richer or spicier with the beef center, the texture savory, his taste buds falling in love. "Damn, these are good."

"I know." Quint chewed, then said, "Did you say anything to her about how you're feeling?"

"I'm thinking I might want to marry Rafe."

Quint laughed, but he'd raised an eyebrow, still waiting for an answer.

Wade took another bite, mulling over the question. "I don't know how I'm feeling about Roxy."

"The hell you don't," Quint said, wiping his mouth with a napkin. "You get a boner every time that sexy lady walks into the room."

"Hey. Don't talk like that about her."

"Yep, you got it bad, my friend." Ian clapped Wade on the shoulder as he arrived at the booth. The shoulder bump, though light, felt charged with meaning. Ian shucked off his jacket and squeezed in next to Quint. He spotted the sample tray and reached for a beef tart. "I recognize the signs."

Ian and Quint high-fived. Wade glared at them, but he was afraid he couldn't keep denying that Roxy had him twisted tighter than a lug nut, and that he worried if he loosened up even a little bit, the wheels might fly off and leave him wrecked. "She's fresh from a divorce. I don't want to be a rebound romance."

"Ohh, that sounds serious," Nick said, greeting his pals, his cheeks bright from the cold weather, his dark eyes full of smiles. Impending fatherhood had given him a constant look of contentment.

Wait until the baby is keeping him up all night, Wade thought.

Nick draped his coat over an empty chair across from the booth, then shoved in next to Wade. "What are we talking about?"

"Wade and Roxy," Ian said, biting into a beef tart. "Damn. This is delish. I'm tasting onion and peppers and something else..."

"Secret ingredient. I'd have to kill you if I told you what it is," Quint said, reaching for his third tart.

Nick grinned at Wade. "Last man standing, huh?"

"Gonna be the biggest fall of all." Quint's eyes glistened with glee.

Wade said, "Fuck you, McCoy."

Quint laughed, then grew serious, leaning across the table, his eyes piercingly blue. "You might have set a Guinness record for 'man going without pussy' the longest. I get that you've been waiting for the right woman. It seems like you've found her. It's time, my friend, to climb back on that bucking horse."

"Don't book the church just yet." Wade shook his head, squirming, scrubbing his jaw with his fingers. He needed another shave. "We haven't even been on a proper date."

"Nothing wrong with an improper date," Ian and Quint said in unison, guffawing at their own humor.

"But you're going to ask her on one, right?" Nick said, helping himself to a tart. He seemed to be the only one of Wade's three friends who understood that he couldn't just take Roxy to a motel. First, she was currently living with her mother; second, he couldn't have sex-dates at the house he shared with his daughter; and third, he didn't want to treat Roxy like she was just a fling.

"Ask her on a date? Hell, he hasn't even had the balls to talk to her since..." Quint didn't have to finish. The guys burst out laughing.

"No shit?" Ian said.

"Damn," Nick said.

Wade took the teasing as good-naturedly as it was meant, but his pals didn't realize that his dating skills weren't just rusty; they'd never been oiled. He changed the subject, got Nick talking about Jane and the coming baby.

"They're both doing well. Jane's going a little stir crazy having to spend all that time in bed, but if I'm working, her mom or grandma are there. She is really missing work. God, but that woman loves baking pies. I'm going to take her home some pie tonight for a treat. She's avoiding sugar, but a little will lift her spirits."

"Andrea has a pie waiting for me at home," Ian said, a strange, awestruck smile playing around his mouth. He told them about Lucas calling him "Daddy" for the first time, and all the guys congratulated him.

At that moment, Wade envied his buddies. They were all past the dating stage in their relationships. Just the thought of a date made his gut ache and his palms sweat. Sarah had always arranged their evenings out—where they went, what they discussed, when it was over. He couldn't ask Roxy out and then ask her to plan the whole evening. This was on him. He had to step up and figure it out. Quint was right. She deserved more than he'd been giving her.

That thought stirred X-rated visions of what he'd like to give her, and blood pooled in his groin. A silent groan filled his throat. He had it bad all right. Really bad.

Chapter Eleven

⌒

"Where is Emily?" Roxy asked, gaping at the child Zoe had transformed into a teenage beauty.

Emily's new, shorter cut included bangs that brushed the top of her eyebrows and framed her pretty eyes, making them pop. Her hair was thicker than it had looked and was still long enough to put into a ponytail, but short enough to be stylish, touching her shoulders and showing off her graceful neck. The style was simple enough for a thirteen-year-old to deal with and keep fresh.

Roxy watched Emily seeing it for the first time, but what touched her heart wasn't so much the amazed look on the teenager's face, but the awe in her voice. "Is that really me?"

"Who else would it be?" Zoe laughed.

But Roxy didn't laugh. She was swept up in the wonder of watching the lanky, awkward little girl she'd brought into this shop an hour earlier start to appreciate and accept the change. On most days, a new hairdo was simply that. Today, however, this cut and style was life altering. Roxy could see that in the sparkle of Emily's eyes, and sharing this moment with Wade's daughter filled Roxy with unexpected reverence.

She was sorry Wade wasn't here to see Emily now, to experience this special moment, too.

A sudden cloud crashed across Emily's face. "What if I can't fix it this way tomorrow? Or ever?"

Zoe patted her on the shoulder, easing her back into the chair. "Are you kidding? I wish I had your hair. It's thick and full of body. This style was made for it."

"But I wanted some product."

"Well, duh. We women always need product," Zoe said, producing a mousse that she'd used on Emily's hair and then showing her a few tricks to do with the dryer and a brush.

Emily didn't take her eyes off Zoe, absorbing every word like a sponge. They left Trendy Tresses with the mousse, a hair dryer, and a brush exactly like those Zoe had used. Emily couldn't quit talking, her breath huffing out in little clouds into the chill afternoon. Roxy adored the sound of her happy chatter, even though it made her dream of that time when she too had been enthralled with the world of possibilities ahead of her, and without the knowledge of romantic heartache.

"Dad is going to be so surprised," Emily gushed, unable to stop glancing at herself in the reflection of the shop windows as they picked their way over the icy pavement to the Escalade. "What do you think he'll say?"

"I'm sure he'll think we've kidnapped his daughter and offer a ransom for her immediate return."

"No way. I'm never going back." Emily laughed, but she stopped in her tracks when they reached the Cadillac. "Is this yours? Are you rich?"

"No and no. It belongs to someone else. I'm just keeping it until he can take it off my hands."

Emily lifted a curious eyebrow at the explanation, but surprisingly didn't push. The new leather scent welcomed them as they climbed in, and Emily checked out all the gadgets in the dashboard as she put on her seatbelt. "It's sick."

Roxy's phone announced a text as she was buckling up. She started the engine to activate the heater and chase off the cold, then hit the seat warmers to give Emily another treat. "Huh. The text is from my mom. It's her Bunco night. She left early and forgot to feed Tallulah. So I have to swing by the house and take care of that, if that's okay with you."

"Who's Tallulah?"

Roxy was surprised Wade hadn't told her, considering the hat and the scratches he'd gotten from her pet. "My cat."

"You have a cat? Ooh, I love cats. I want a cat, but Dad isn't sold on that right now."

No surprise there. Guilt crept through Roxy. She and Tallulah might have sealed Emily's chances of ever owning a cat.

As though he knew she was thinking of him, her phone rang. At the sound of his voice in her ear, Roxy's heart did a jumping jack or two. "Hi, I was going to bring Emily straight home, but I have to stop by my house first." She explained the situation, and that his daughter was excited to meet Tallulah, cringing inside at his expected reaction.

He made a sound that might be a snort of derision, but then he said, "I'm picking up a pizza from Moose's. I'll bring it by. Don't say no."

Rather than having her join them at his house, he was bringing pizza to her mother's and risking the wrath of the Ragdoll? Who was this man of steel? This take-charge guy? "Okay, I won't."

"Beer or wine?"

The question surprised her, pleasantly. "Beer."

Another soft, unidentifiable sound from him. "A woman after my heart."

She was smiling when she hung up, and the smile lasted until she pulled into her mother's driveway, then Emily asked, "Do you like my dad?"

"Sure. He's a nice man."

"That's not what I mean. Do you *like* him, you know, like a boyfriend?"

Roxy wasn't sure how to answer. Was this about the rumors? Or something else? Better not give a specific answer without more of a clue as to exactly what Emily wanted to know. "Why do you ask?"

"I think he likes you ... like a girlfriend."

A part of Roxy swooned at this possibility, while another part freaked, wanting to run for the hills. The more she got to know Wade, the more she realized his affections were not to be toyed with or taken lightly. How had this gotten so complicated? She'd come back to Montana looking for rebound romances, not for some sweet, serious guy to fall for her, not for his daughter to also get attached to her. What was she going to do?

Hell, she knew what she had to do. After some of the conversations she'd been having today with her conscience, she needed to stop giving in to her attraction to Wade and find someone less complicated. A deep disappointment settled in her stomach. Wow, she was losing potential flings right and left. First Rafe, now Wade.

At this rate, she'd still be celibate when spring arrived.

* * *

Quint's words kept playing through Wade's mind as he drove toward Roxy's mom's house. The cab of the pickup smelled of the Beef Lover's Special, and the pepperoni and green pepper that both Emily and Roxy preferred. The paper sack holding the beer and soda pop rustled as he turned a corner. His palms were damp on the steering wheel, and his stomach felt full of butterflies. *Damn, I'm nervous as a teenager on a first date.*

The irony was that he hadn't dated in his teens. He'd wanted to, but he'd been too shy to ask anyone out. He'd only been with Sarah that once. They'd gone separately to the senior class hayride and when it broke up, somehow, they'd ended up alone together. A month before graduation. He hadn't even dated her after that infamous night. He'd been a bit astounded where a few kisses had led and overwhelmed with sexual desire afterward as though he'd just discovered a new game, one that was more fun than any present he'd ever gotten for a birthday.

He'd wanted to play the game with just about any girl who got too close for comfort. He didn't, though. The urges were too strong, and it was all he could do to control his reactions to girls once that floodgate had been shoved wide open. Only the thought of making a fool of himself kept him in check. He'd taken a lot of cold showers back then. Remembering how lame he'd been brought a grin now.

He'd been a kid, raw and inexperienced. Although he was now a full-grown man. More in control of himself. A wayward image of Roxy's creamy, exposed breasts filled his mind, making him instantly hard, eliciting emotions he struggled to rein in, and reminding him of how flustered he'd been when they were caught half-naked. He shook his head. *Yeah, right, Reynolds. You're a regular Don Juan these days.*

He parked behind the Escalade and stared at the ranch-style rambler, chickening out. But Quint's words started up again, and Wade knew he had to go after what he wanted or he'd regret it forever. Not that anything would happen tonight in Roxy's mother's house with Emily chaperoning.

He gathered his nerve, the pizzas, and the paper bag and walked to the door. He knocked and heard noise inside, then the door opened. Roxy stood there, looking so gorgeous his breath hitched. The light behind her bounced off her red hair, giving it the appearance that diamonds were nestled within its layers. "Your hair looks great."

"Trula's a find." She angled into him, and his pulse reacted as if she'd caught hold of his jacket and tugged him close, her orange scent invading his senses, turning the bones in his legs to sawdust.

"I should warn you," she whispered, hooking her hand around his wrist and pulling him inside, "you should brace for a shock, Dad. Your little girl looks very...different."

As he stepped into the foyer, he was struck by two things, the low ceilings and Emily being nowhere in sight. The floor plan was a familiar one: a typical ranch layout, small foyer with coat closet, a long living room with a fireplace on the end wall, and an open dining room completing the L shape. The kitchen would be behind the main wall. He lifted a brow at the ultra feminine décor—white carpet, red sofa, ruffled, flowery pillows. "Did you grow up here?"

Roxy smirked, shaking her head. "Mom bought this house after my dad passed away. She says the house that my brother, sister, and I were raised in was his style, his taste. This is hers."

"I see." Even the Christmas tree was white with red balls, the gifts all wrapped in white with red bows.

"Reminds me a bit of a little girl's bedroom, but she loves it."

"Where's Emily?"

"They're in the other room," Roxy said, relieving him of the pizza boxes and paper bag. "Put your coat in the closet."

He did as told, wondering who *they* were. Had Roxy picked up one of Emily's friends or was her mother home early? He absently dumped his hat on a club chair near the kitchen door as he passed, finger combing his hair, anxious to see his daughter and her new hairdo.

He had to duck to clear the kitchen door frame, only to find that the ceiling seemed even lower in this room than in the living room. It was like he'd stepped into a box, and the lid was slowly closing. He didn't usually get claustrophobic, but if he spent much time here that might change. He started to wish he'd asked Roxy to meet him at his house.

Even worse was being nearly blinded by the unrelieved white-on-white cabinets and countertops and floor. As his vision adjusted to the whiteout effect, he realized there were touches of red in the room, a heart-shaped cookie jar and miniature glass hearts in varying sizes occupied the windowsill over the sink.

But no Emily. He and Roxy were alone. *Ask her out now. Get it over with.* But as his gaze snagged on the slight sway of her hips in stretchy pants that enhanced her firm, inviting ass, his brain scrambled.

Roxy had set the boxes on the counter and was lifting lids. "My mother likes white."

For a second, he didn't catch the connection, his mind otherwise engaged with memories and fantasies about

Roxy, stirring a lust that strained his control. It hit him that she was talking about the décor.

"The only thing I know about your mother—" before coming into her house—"is that she writes an advice column of some sort, and that her name is Valentina." Which might explain her fondness for valentine hearts.

Roxy pulled paper plates and napkins from a cupboard and silverware from a drawer, then placed it all on the table. She walked to the door leading into the living room and called down the hall, "Emily, your dad's here."

A second later, Emily appeared in the doorway, but Wade didn't see her hair. His eyes caught on the giant furball she held in her arms. Monster cat. The Ragdoll spied Wade and growled. He took an impulsive step back, certain the she-devil would leap at him again. Instead, she struggled from Emily's grip and fled into the living room.

"Ah, Dad, you scared Tallulah."

He heaved a sigh of relief. "We have that effect on each other."

And then Emily moved toward him, and he got his first good glimpse of her. Whatever else he'd been about to say about the cat died on his tongue. No amount of preparation could keep the shock at bay. This girl sounded like his daughter, even had her eyes and mouth, but somehow, this was not the child he'd dropped off at the beauty salon. When had she gone from ten to...to this? How had he not noticed? How could a simple haircut turn a girl from a kid into a teenager? "It's incredible, Em. You look so...different, so...much like your mom."

The compliment spilled from Wade, surprising him even more, but Emily latched onto it with a widening smile, sounding breathless. "Really? Do you mean it?"

He did, and the acknowledgment brought a rush of emotion, not all of it good.

Chuckling, Roxy moved between them again. She dug into the paper bag, withdrawing the drinks. She twisted the top off a cold beer and handed the long-stemmed bottle to him. "You look like you could use this."

His neck grew hot, the temperature gauge a telling mark of how uncomfortable he was at this moment. "I could." But not because of the cat, or even because Roxy had his blood sizzling, but because he realized his daughter was growing up faster than he was prepared to face.

"Come on, you two," Roxy herded them to the table. "The pizza is getting cold."

Wade pulled out a chair and sat, feeling like a giant at the small table, his long legs not fitting under it. "Nothing wrong with cold pizza."

Both females chimed, "Eww."

Roxy sat across from him while Emily took the seat with the window to her back. Each one claimed a slice of their preferred pizza.

"How come you didn't tell me that you'd met Tallulah, Dad?" Emily asked as she plucked green pepper bits from between gooey cheese and pepperoni and plopped them into her mouth.

Wade let Roxy explain, happy that she gave an edited version of the night he'd met her and her devil cat. Emily was giggling by the end of it. But Wade kept staring at her, his daddy-brain still struggling to assimilate the change in his precious little girl, his emotions unsettled. Roxy exchanged smiles with him as Emily chattered about her first beauty salon experience, and then described the products she'd bought.

He couldn't recall having as nice an evening in a long time. Even though he'd had a few of Rafe's meat pasties at Big Sky Pie, he put a huge dent in the Beef Lover's pizza. He sent Emily to get her coat on and gather the supplies she'd bought for her hair, and he helped Roxy clear the table and pack up the leftovers she insisted he take home.

He said, "Oh, by the way, Molly wants me to look at the building next to the pie shop as soon as possible, and she thought you should be there with me to go over what you'll need for the remodel. Does tomorrow work for you?"

"Sure. I'll text you when I'm off work."

"Sounds like a plan." *Ask her for the date. Do it now*. Instead, what came out of his mouth surprised him. "This has been great, but you have to get up early and Emily has homework."

Roxy sighed, the sound a sensual humming. She gazed at his mouth with longing in her eyes, and damn near undid his control. "Yeah, you're right. Three a.m. comes early."

Coward. Mentally damning his lack of nerve, he

strode into the living room ahead of her. Where was his hat? But as the thought crossed his mind, his gaze landed on the Stetson. Upside down in the club chair. Tallulah was balancing on its brim, her bottom positioned over its bowl. Wade lunged for the cat, shouting, "No!"

Chapter Twelve

Tallulah let out a wail and leaped at Wade. Her bared claws caught him in the chest like the barbs of a Taser, her weight dragging her body lower, the talons cutting into his flesh as she slipped lower and lower. She dropped to the floor and then tore off into the hallway, nearly tripping Emily.

"Dad! Did you have to scare Tallulah again?" Emily scolded.

Roxy stood in the kitchen doorway, her hand to her mouth. "Oh my God, not again."

Wade gaped at the Stetson, afraid to check it. Roxy stood where she was, her eyes wide and full of dismay.

Emily glanced from one to the other and then at the Stetson. She started giggling. "Oh my God, did Tallulah pee in your hat again?"

"We don't know," Roxy said, making no move to find out.

But Emily marched to the chair, grabbed the hat, and peered inside, then sniffed it for good measure. "Nope. Bone dry."

Roxy exhaled loudly. "Oh, thank God. We caught her in time."

Emily carried the hat to her father. Wade accepted it reluctantly, picking a long cat hair off the brim, eyeing it suspiciously, not sure that Emily wasn't tricking him.

"It's okay, Dad, honest." She was still giggling. And now Roxy seemed to be smirking behind her hand.

Wade didn't find it one bit funny. His chest stung like hell where that monster fuzzball had clawed him, but he'd be damned if he'd let them know. He put on the hat, grappling with his dignity and silently cursing that hateful feline. He got his coat and quickly buttoned it. "That cat doesn't like me."

Emily hugged Roxy, thanking her again for sharing the beauty salon experience and for having them for dinner. She went outside carrying the leftovers, giving Wade a minute alone with Roxy to say his own good night.

But she beat him to it. "It was a lovely evening. Thank you."

His chest seemed too small for his heart all of a sudden. He didn't want the night to end, even knowing that it had to. He said, "Let's do it again. Soon. Just the two of us."

Her chin came up, and a smile played at the corners of her sexy mouth. "Are you asking me out on a date, Wade Reynolds?"

"Yeah, I am." Before he could chicken out, he bent and lightly kissed her mouth, then tipped his hat and walked out into the wintery night, feeling warm from head to toe, the stinging scrapes on his chest forgotten.

* * *

A date? At first Roxy had been charmed by the idea, but an hour later, soaking in a tub of orange-blossom bubble bath, she recalled every detail of that moment, right down to the sisterly kiss. At the time, she'd thought it sweet that he hadn't lingered for something deeper with his daughter so near. But something had niggled in the back of her mind. A warning. A signal she should have seen but had missed. What was it? She reviewed the clues. The chaste kiss, Wade's old-fashioned manners, his asking for a date. Horror washed through her as she realized what was going on. Oh, no. He meant to court her.

She scrambled out of the tub, not bothering to rinse off the bubbles, just grabbing the towel and frantically drying. She had to put a stop to this, right now. If they were going to act on their attraction, it was not going to be a courtship that led to a serious or permanent relationship. He had to understand that and agree. Or else. She didn't even glance at the clock or at her waiting bed as she tossed on clean panties, leggings, an oversized sweater, and Uggs.

"Don't look at me like that. You know I have to do this," she told Tallulah.

The cat, curled on the bed, had lifted her head just enough to see what the disturbance was all about, but apparently after deciding it was nothing to do with her, laid her head back onto her paws and shut her eyes again.

Minutes later, Roxy was sitting in the Escalade, letting the motor warm up, seat warmer on high, as she texted Wade. *We need to talk. Now.*

He responded: *Do you want to come here? Emily is asleep.*

She replied: *On my way.*

The front of the house was dark except for the porch light when she arrived. She hurried to the stoop and lifted her hand to knock, but he opened the door before her knuckles connected with it. He was barefoot, in a tight t-shirt over loose jeans, his jaw in need of a shave, his hair rumpled. He had no clue how sexy that unpretentious, easy look of his was. Didn't even realize how every cell in her body responded to his clean scent, his shy smile, his gentle touches.

"Come on in." He pointed to the ceiling, keeping his voice low. "Emily's room is at the front of the house. Mine is at the back."

As he hung her coat on the rack by the door, she kicked off her boots, noticing the pine scent that filled the air. He'd put up a Christmas tree since she'd been here last. It stood in the corner of the living room, the lights off, but the aroma as rich as a forest grove. She followed him into the kitchen. A half-finished beer and an open paperback lay on the table next to his cell phone. She was struck again by how inviting this room was, but her attention landed on Wade, a much more inviting sight. She ran her tongue across her lips, staring at his mouth. "Do you find me attractive?"

His eyebrows twitched, but his body stilled. "You know I do."

She inhaled, catching that clean soapy scent mixed with a hint of his spicy aftershave, and her mouth watered, her nostrils flared. Oh God, she wanted him so bad. "I feel the same way about you, but we are not going to have a romance."

"We're not?"

"No." She stroked a fingertip down the front of his solid chest, feeling his heart beating. Her pulse picked up. "I'm not looking for a husband."

He stared at her like a man mesmerized. "You're not?"

"No. And you're not looking for a wife."

His breathing increased as her finger went lower to his belly. "I'm not?"

"Are you?" She stopped the movement, meeting his gaze.

"I, er, I—"

"That would be a 'no' then. I don't want to date."

He swallowed, his Adam's apple bobbing. "You don't?"

"No. You don't need to spend money on me."

His gaze locked on her mouth. "I don't?"

"No."

"What do I want?" His voice came out like a raspy whisper.

"The same thing I want." So there would be no question about what she meant, she peeled off her sweater, exposing her bare breasts, her nipples swollen, sensitive, aching for his touch, just as she ached for the same. Slipping her fingers into his dense hair, she showed him that chaste kisses were not her thing. He didn't resist, not even when she pinned him against the kitchen wall, rattling the clock.

The kiss started an explosion inside her, little bursts of need and pleasure going off like miniature sparkles in the dark valley of her sexual deprivation. He tasted of beer and mint, and the odd combination sent her pulse into overdrive. He caught her to him, his hands groping her back, cupping her bottom, and leaving no doubt as to exactly how much he wanted her.

She brushed a hand across his fly. "I want this," she said, then pulled her mouth from his, realizing belatedly that she was topless in his kitchen, in the house he shared with his daughter. They needed to move this to a place where no one could walk in on them. "Where's your bedroom?"

"Up the back stairs."

They held hands, scurrying up the staircase, driven by the need coursing through their bodies. He guided her down a short hall and through a tall doorway. Roxy was surprised at how high the ceilings were on the second floor, at how large his bedroom was, and at how much space the extra-long mattress took up. The bed was neatly made, but the color scheme was a blur. The click of the door lock brought her gaze back to the only sight worth seeing in this room. The man in front of her.

In the soft light, he seemed dazed, staring at her breasts as though he couldn't believe they were real. She moved within touching distance and murmured, "They're all mine, but tonight I'll share."

Still he made none of the expected moves. Her confidence stumbled. Did he want this or not? The bulge in his pants said yes, but his inaction said something else. What, she wasn't sure. "Have you changed your mind? Is it still too soon for you?"

"Oh. God. No." But when he still didn't move toward her, she stepped back.

"What's the matter?"

"I'm... I haven't... done this in so long, I'm afraid I'll, you know, be too quick or too slow or too rough or—"

Relief flooded through her, and she closed the gap between them. "Then why don't you let me get things started? And if anything's too fast or slow or rough, I'll let you know." What she didn't say was that she shared his fear. At least the too-fast one. It had been so long and she was so ready that it wouldn't take much to pull her trigger. Perhaps this first time needed to be fast and furious. She stripped off his t-shirt, his jeans, and his boxers, then shimmied out of her leggings and panties. She stepped back to admire the gift she was about to receive.

Her heart nearly burst in her chest. He was the most gorgeous man she'd ever laid eyes on. His strong, muscled body came from physical labor, but it was more than that. He had the perfect amount of hair on his chest, on his arms, on his stomach. And he was so well proportioned; his male assets were just the right size, big, without being too big. She pushed him onto the bed, then took his hand and placed it between her legs so he could see she was ready for him. Then she dipped her mouth to his sex and stroked her tongue over rigid flesh, slowly until she reached the tip, tasting salt and eliciting a moan from him.

"Oh, man, Roxy, I can't wait…" He pulled her to her feet, pushing on a condom, then rolled her onto the bed beneath him and shoved inside her.

Lord, he was bigger than she'd thought, but her body opened to accommodate every inch, and her hips lifted to meet each thrust. She'd been dreaming of a long, glorious ride to climax heaven, but hers came quick and jarring, rocking her with decadent shudders that left her legs weak and her mind scrambled.

Wade cried out her name a moment later, and she felt another tremor, an aftershock that hit harder than the first. Instead of coming off the cloud together, though, he rolled to his side, his eyes closed, and lay there panting like a triathlon racer crossing the finish line. She was equally breathless, her body languid, like after a deep massage.

He went into the bathroom as she rolled over, realizing that she wasn't ready to call it a night. Hoping he felt the same, she struck a seductive pose. He looked surprised to see her still on the bed, still naked, crooking her finger at him. "How about another round, cowboy?"

His eyebrows twitched as if *seconds* weren't the usual in his wheelhouse, but the frown melted into a grin, and little Wade stood at attention. He joined her on the bed, pulled her into his arms and captured her mouth, his kisses deep and smoldering. Desire spread through her. This time he gave her breasts the attention she longed for, sucking and nipping and shooting desire to her every nerve ending. His fingers dipped between her legs, stroking, until she was on fire.

She didn't know where he found another condom, but he had it in place before she could return the favor. She wanted to climb on top of him this time, to watch his eyes as she rode him into oblivion, but he seemed a little taken aback by her actions and, as soon as she'd lowered herself onto him, as soon as she began to move, he reared up and turned them until she was under him.

Not to be foiled, she wrapped her legs around his body, meeting every thrust with one of her own, trying to slow him down, but her movements only seemed to incite his urgency. The friction was glorious. She climaxed twice before him, but even then, his release came too quick again. And the moment he was done, he pulled out of her.

Disappointment invaded her joy. Why? Wasn't this what she wanted? A sex buddy, someone who got her off without forming any bothersome attachments? Yes. Then why did she feel a little...cheated?

Wade obviously felt different, gazing starry-eyed at her. "Wow. That was, that was..." Words seemed to desert him. "Incredible."

Roxy snuggled against his side, sated, yet not. She still wanted more. Much more. She wanted prolonged foreplay, wanted to touch and taste and enjoy every part of him. She wanted him to do the same to her. She started tracing his flat nipple with her fingertip until it grew hard and he sucked in a breath. She traced kisses down his neck to his chest, noticing for the first time some small scratches within the sparse hair that looked like…cat scratches? Naw. Probably something that occurred at his work. She kept nibbling kisses lower, and lower, until she realized he was hard and arching his back at her every stroke. He groaned as though the pure torture was driving him mad. Since that was her aim, Roxy smiled.

He brushed at her hair, an earnest expression in those sea-green eyes. "I'm not real…experienced…I guess you could say. I was too shy to date in school. Sarah was my first. My only."

His only love? His only sex partner? Both, Roxy realized, bracing for a speech about his lost love. Though why she would brace was not something she wanted to examine at the moment.

Wade sighed and raked his hand through his hair. "Sarah didn't much care for sex. Especially spontaneous sex. She liked everything orderly. Planned."

"Even intimacy?" Roxy couldn't even imagine such a thing.

"Yeah, once a week on Tuesday nights. She didn't like to participate."

Pity welled in Roxy's throat. For Sarah for being unable to enjoy the pleasures her body could give, but more so for Wade, a healthy male in his twenties whose hormones had to be raging. She was amazed he hadn't sought out other women. "I'm sorry. I've heard that some women no longer enjoy sex after childbirth. There's a medical cause for it."

His neck reddened, and that shy smile pulled at his mouth. "I only told you in case you find my prowess lacking."

"The only thing lacking is I can't seem to get enough of you," Roxy said, her tongue gliding around his swollen member. The thought of teaching Wade the many wondrous ways that lovers pleasure each other filled her with desire. The first lesson he needed to learn was control. Otherwise foreplay would always be over before it began, but showing was better than telling.

She revved him up, then stopped when he seemed about to lose it. She smiled sweetly, "Hold onto your spurs, cowboy. You're about to ride out of your comfort zone."

Chapter Thirteen

❦

Three days to Christmas and Big Sky Pie was busier than usual, the kitchen bustling, pies going out the front door as fast as they could bake them. Roxy loved the feeling of accomplishment, getting the orders filled, producing a product that the customers were gleeful about taking home, thinking about families sharing the shop's scrumptious pies with friends and relatives. And just the joy of creating new recipes. Even after her long workday, she bubbled with pent-up energy.

It was Wade's fault. He was giving her more than lusty dreams. She woke up in a good mood that spilled onto others as the pie baking got underway. She couldn't help but think about Wade when she was stirring the rich cocoa mix for the chocolate cream pies, the color so like his hair, and that would lead to other thoughts of him, like the expression on his face when he'd seen Emily's new look for the first time, or the private smile when he'd begun gaining control of his libido. He was getting very good at that, even seemed a little more confident.

A small voice inside her head worried that she was letting him into her heart too much, but she shoved the voice away. She'd been miserable for so long. What was wrong with a little sunshine in her life? Nothing. Especially at this time of year.

"Well, now, don't that beat all," Molly said, pulling Roxy out of her musing in time to see her boss stuff her phone into her apron pocket. Molly's bright blue eyes lifted to the top cupboard in the Big Sky Pie kitchen as if it were a TV turned to late-breaking news. She blinked a couple of times, made a couple of strange faces, seeming to need a second to orient herself to where she was, then she caught everyone staring at her and her cheeks glowed pink. She spun toward the wall ovens, making a show of checking the timers on the baking pies.

Roxy exchanged a glance with Andrea that asked, "What was that about?"

Even Rafe had stopped slicing butter and was staring at their boss.

Andrea stepped toward the work island. "You can't say something like that, Molly, without explaining."

"That's right," Roxy said, carrying the pan of chocolate filling to the empty pie shells. "Inquiring minds and all that."

Molly's cheeks grew even pinker. She made a soft grumbling noise as if whatever "beat all" still had her head spinning. "That fool man."

Andrea said, "What man?"

"Charlie Mercer, of course."

"Of course." Andrea's eyes narrowed. "What'd he do?"

"He asked me out."

Andrea tucked her hair behind one ear, frowning. "But you've been out lots of times the past couple of months, right?"

Molly shrugged. "Going to a wedding reception and inviting him over to dinner or meeting him at Denny's isn't a date."

What did Molly consider a real date? Roxy wondered. "Where did he ask you out to, exactly?"

Molly's hands landed on her hips, and her eyes were wide with exasperation. "He wants to take me out New Year's Eve. Dancing at the Elks Lodge. Said I'd need a fancy party dress."

"Dancing?" Andrea's voice squeaked with worry. "Are you sure you're well enough for dancing?"

"It's not like I'll be doing any boot scootin', whatever that is, but a waltz or two probably qualifies as exercise." She went still for a moment and seemed to be glancing backward across the years. "My Jimmy never cared for dancing, but I always loved to dance." She came back to the present, her mouth pursing. "Then again, Jimmy never approved of Charlie, either. I wonder why. I haven't noticed any of the things Jimmy used to complain about. And now he's asked me to a dance. Do you suppose it's too soon? Would Jimmy be upset?"

She sounded like a cross between a giddy teenager who'd just been asked by the most popular boy in school to wear his ring, and the widow who was to wear black and mourn the rest of her life. Roxy's heart went out to her.

"It's not like you're going to marry the man," Andrea answered. "It's just dinner and a dance on New Year's Eve. Jimmy would want you to be happy."

Roxy agreed. She hadn't really known Quint's dad, but Callee always spoke so lovingly of him. She figured he wouldn't want his wife to be lonely.

"A real date," Molly said again. Then she glanced at her three employees and moaned. "I don't know how to date. I haven't been on a date since I was in high school. What am I going to do? How am I going to act?"

Rafe just shook his head, shrugging. Roxy wasn't sure how much of the conversation he actually understood since, whenever the female employees started talking about men, he either hummed to himself or made himself scarce. Like now. He stopped what he was doing and started for the hallway to the cold room. "I get more maize."

"Just be the same Molly you always are with Charlie and you'll be good," Roxy said, glad that she had decided not to formally date Wade. "You already know each other, so there won't be any of that awkwardness of dating someone you just met."

"You don't suppose he'll expect sex, do you?" Molly's expression was a mix of hopeful and appalled, and Andrea and Roxy stifled shocked grins.

Andrea said, "Are you expecting the evening to end with sex?"

Molly opened her mouth to speak, then clamped it shut. Her cheeks were pink again. "I haven't been with anyone but Jimmy, and I'm not that old you know, and I do still think, sometimes, that I might, er, you know, but so far Charlie's been a perfect gentleman. Hasn't even tried to kiss me. Oh my. Maybe he can't anymore."

Andrea made a little choking sound.

"Maybe he's just respecting Jimmy's memory," Roxy said, not wanting to know anything more about what Charlie Mercer could or couldn't do in the bedroom.

Molly thought about that, then smiled. "Yeah, maybe so. He wouldn't have asked me out if he didn't like me."

"That's true," Andrea agreed.

Rafe returned with a pound of butter just in time to hear Molly say, "But what am I going to wear? I don't have a dress suitable for dancing. Or for New Year's Eve."

"*Señora* Molly, no *preocupar*, no worry," Rafe said, pointing toward the café. "There mall *por ahi*, over there."

Molly burst out laughing, and her three employees joined in.

"What are you doing New Year's Eve?" Andrea asked Roxy a few minutes later, while Rafe and Molly whipped up a batch of meringue.

"Well, my mother is in Vegas with her bowling team, spending Christmas with my sister, who lives there. Wade invited Molly, Callee, Quint, and me to spend Christmas Eve with him and Emily, but my New Year's Eve is wide open at the moment."

"Wade, hmm? So things are heating up between you two?" Andrea looked a little too eager and curious for Roxy's liking.

"Nothing like that. We're just having *fun*."

"I'm glad to hear it. You both deserve some *fun*. Maybe you can even get him to take you dancing, but I don't recommend the VFW. The crowd is likely mostly seniors."

"Do you think Wade can dance?" He was so shy, didn't date in high school, hadn't gone to a prom. Maybe he'd never learned.

"He's actually a good dancer," Andrea said. "Nothing fancy, but he's graceful and doesn't step on your feet. Trust me, that happens more than you want to know."

Roxy grinned. She supposed there were a lot of things Andrea could tell her about Wade, but the subject was making her uncomfortable. Especially since most of what she kept learning just made her like him all the more. She changed the subject. "What are your holiday plans?"

Andrea rolled her eyes, wrung her hands, and grimaced. "Ian's parents are coming for Christmas, and frankly, I'm terrified that they're going to hate me and talk Ian into taking back his engagement ring."

"That's not going to happen," Roxy assured her. She set the filled pie shells into the Sub-Zero, then went to the sink to wash her hands. "Ian is crazy about you and those boys."

"He is. I know he is. But I'm having 'meet the celebrity in-laws' cold feet."

"I met a lot of celebrities in Seattle during my time at the bistro, and I found the bigger the stars they were, the more down to earth they were. It will probably be a treat for them to get away from the limelight and paparazzi. Eat some home cooking. And it looks like it's going to be a white Christmas, too."

"As long as they don't expect me to do the cooking…"

Roxy dried her hands and patted Andrea's arm. "You'll do great."

Andrea disappeared into the café, then returned with a mug and came up to Roxy. "Wade is in the end booth. He wants to speak to you if you can take a break."

"That man has good timing. I could do with a cup of coffee and to get off my feet for a few minutes." Roxy disappeared into the bathroom. She did a quick check of her hair and makeup and then headed into the café.

There were fewer patrons than earlier in the day. The after-school waitress was clearing off tables and setting up for the next round of weary, last-minute Christmas shoppers.

Roxy's heart did a happy dance when Wade came into view, his new Stetson on the seat beside him, his hair neatly combed, his jaw freshly shaved, with a hint of aftershave teasing her senses. A steaming mug sat in front of him, but there was a slice of pie in front of his companion. Emily. Roxy's smile grew larger as she met the teenager's gaze, noting that her hair looked almost as good as when she'd had it cut and styled. She was learning.

"This is a nice surprise," she said. "Let me get some coffee and I'll join you."

Wade gave her the full-on burn of those aqua-green eyes, the intensity warming her in places she didn't want heating up. Not here. Not with his daughter present. Wondering what he wanted to speak to her about that might include his daughter, Roxy got a cup of coffee, and Emily scooted in to make room for her on the bench seat. "What brings you two here, besides the awesome pics?"

"It's sort of about the pies," Emily said, digging into the slice of pumpkin piled high with whipping cream.

"Oh? I guess you're hoping I'll bring some pie for Christmas Eve?"

Wade chuckled. "Sure. My favorite is anything chocolate."

"Dad, that's not why we're here." Emily gave him an exasperated head-tilt, and he winked at Roxy.

"I better let her explain," he said, lifting his cup and smiling over the rim.

Emily laid her fork aside, wiped her mouth with her napkin, then inhaled as though whatever she wanted to say required a lot of oxygen. Her cheeks went as pink as Jane's sometimes did, and Roxy realized she'd inherited some of her father's shyness. "New Year's Eve is my thirteenth birthday, and I want to hire the pie shop to make my birthday pie. But Dad's paying for it."

Roxy made a face, not wanting to disappoint Emily, but afraid she had no choice. "The pie shop is going to be closed from New Year's Eve until January second, and we've taken all the orders we can fill until then."

Emily looked stricken. "But I was counting on having some of your pies for my celebration."

"I'm sorry," Roxy said.

Father and daughter released twin sighs of disappointment.

"Looks like you're going to have to settle for cake, sweetheart," Wade said, gripping her hand. "I warned you that we'd put this off too long."

Emily nodded, determined to be grown-up about her disappointment. "I know it was a lot to ask, especially since you're fixing our dinner for Christmas and all. But I had to ask anyway. I like pie better than cake, but—"

"You know," Roxy said, dragging out the two words. "A girl's thirteenth birthday is a pretty big deal, and I just had a thought."

Wade and Emily gave her their full attention.

Roxy spoke to the girl. "I don't think Molly would mind if I came in and made a couple of pies while everyone is gone."

"Oh, would you ask, please?" Emily clapped her hands together as she pled her case.

"On one condition."

"Anything," Emily said.

"You let me give you a lesson on making pies. So that you can serve a pie you've made yourself to your party guests."

"You'd teach me to make a pie?" Emily's hand went to her chest, her eyes filled with tears that she fought to keep from shedding, evidence of how much this child missed having a mother at home. Emily's mouth rounded, though, as she had another thought. "What if I ruin the pie?"

"You won't. I'll be right beside you all the way."

"Wow, this is going to be the best birthday ever. Thank you, Roxy."

The joy emanating from Emily filled Roxy's heart with gladness. Random acts of kindness paid both the giver as well as the receiver. "What kind of pies do you want for your birthday?"

"What are my choices?"

"Any pie we have the ingredients for. I'll bring a sample tray to Christmas Eve dinner, and you can taste and choose."

"Really. That would be sick." Emily rolled her head and smiled happily. "Oh, I almost forgot. I want you to come to the party, too. And you don't have to cook, 'cause we're having pizza."

"Emily, I told you Roxy might already have plans for New Year's Eve." Wade lifted his chin, his gaze questioning her. "Do you?"

Roxy arched an eyebrow at him. How could he even ask that? He knew he was monopolizing most of her spare time. But she supposed he didn't believe that Emily knew that. Maybe she should tell him she did have plans, that guys were lining up outside the pie shop by the dozens, and that she couldn't decide whether to accept the invitation from the bank president or the royal prince. "As a matter of fact . . ." she said, just to see Wade wince, "no. I don't have any plans. Not yet."

"It's a date then," Wade said, staring at his coffee, the corners of his mouth lifting up.

Roxy kicked him under the table, made him look at her, and mouthed, "No dating."

He grinned and got up to pay the bill. Roxy watched him walk away, fascinated by the way his jeans fit his fine butt. Damn, that man heated her blood.

Emily's hand landed on her arm. "Roxy, before we go, could I ask you a big favor?"

She glanced at the hand and then into the girl's earnest gaze. "Sure."

"Could you take me to the mall before my birthday and help me shop for a couple of outfits to go with my new hair?"

The question seemed to come out of nowhere, but did it really? This girl needed an older woman in her life to help her with things like how to make a pie and to give her shopping advice. She just hadn't pictured herself as that woman. And she wasn't sure it was healthy to let Emily come to depend on her so much. She waffled. "Well, I—"

Emily lowered her voice, speaking so fast Roxy had a hard time keeping up. "Dad means well, but he doesn't understand some stuff. I need a couple of sweaters and some new jeans and he thinks everything I like is too revealing. He doesn't get it. Plus I need a, a bra. I can't ask my dad to shop with me for a bra. I'd die."

Oh man. This was so not something a girl wanted to do with her dad. Roxy would have gone without a bra rather than shop for one with her father. Sometimes women just needed to stick together, no matter the age difference. No matter the risks or emotional consequences. But she could feel herself being sucked in, starting to care too much for Wade and his daughter. She had to step away before it was too late, before they all ended up heartbroken by her resolution to stay single. Right after the holidays. Let them have that. *Let me have that.* "I agree, but you have to help me pick out a couple of pairs of great jeans. I don't own a pair, and jeans really seems like *the pants* for most social occasions in Kalispell. Plus I wouldn't mind getting some great cowgirl boots."

"You should ask Andrea and Callee about the boots. They have some really sick ones."

Roxy made a mental note to do just that.

* * *

Roxy let herself in the back door of the place that Molly wanted to use for the Big Sky Pie spin-off shop. The detached building sat on the lot in such a way that it was perfect for adding a drive-through window, and the interior, while not large, would accommodate a nice-sized food prep space. The plan was to have an indoor order counter with a couple of picnic tables outside. The meat pasties were a carry-out item. This meant the shop didn't need to provide a public restroom or a café area.

The moment Roxy closed the door, she knew that she was not alone. The heat and electricity had been turned on, and the warm air chased off the chill she felt after walking over from the pie shop. She was moving through a compact storage/office area, the main room at the other end. A light beckoned ahead. A male voice humming a Garth Brooks oldie, about friends in low places, had her smiling. She stopped as the man moved into view, his back turned toward her as he studied a window frame.

The surrounding space seemed to fade away, until all she could see was Wade, his upper torso naked, sweat glistening on the muscles of his strong, magnificent back. In the light, he was every woman's fantasy, a man engrossed in his work, unaware of how desirable he was wielding a hammer to pull a nail from the old pane.

A pulse tattooed in Roxy's ears, music of some ancient tribe, the drumbeat taking her back to the beginning of time, to the creation of woman for man. The rhythm thrummed through her veins, sang to the sensitive nerve endings at the very core of her sex. She'd never wanted a man more than she did Wade at this moment.

He jerked, stopped, spun around, and caught her staring. He spoke her name.

The deep timbre of his voice chased off her fantasy, but had her heart climbing into her throat as he strode toward her.

"Hey, there you are."

His voice cut through her daydream. The room came back into focus, and she frowned. Not only was Wade not half-undressed, he was wearing a flannel shirt and a heavy work vest. She was losing it. Fantasizing with him right in front of her. She swallowed hard, grappling for composure. "Hi. I didn't want to disturb you while you were doing whatever it is you were doing."

"Checking for dry rot." He smirked. "Glad to report, however, that this building is in surprisingly great shape for its age. Hell, I should hold up this well."

Her gaze did a slow crawl from his boots to his face, finding not one flaw, and several points of interest. She couldn't breathe when he looked at her with that need in his eyes. "You're holding up fine as far as I can tell, but maybe I should give you an inspection, just to be sure. Wouldn't want to have to red flag you."

She advanced on him, dropping her coat to the floor, catching hold of his vest and pulling it off. A couple of weeks ago, he might have been taken aback at her being this bold about wanting him, but he seemed to be having no problem with it now. Soon, she suspected, he'd be initiating impromptu sex. He wasn't quite that bold yet, but she was unlacing him one lace at a time. Her chef pants fell to the floor, along with his jeans. She told him, "No waiting, no patience required today, cowboy, and no missionary style."

She wrapped her arms around his neck and then he caught on and lifted her legs until she locked them around his hips, and sensuously, she lowered herself onto him, moaning his name as he began to fill her, the ancient drumbeats starting anew.

He raised and lowered her, thrust after thrust, the sensations coursing through her body and enchanting her brain. She began to spiral out of control, crying his name in decadent release after release, the sound wanton and blissful, and he kept on, her words about no need for patience lost on him as he seemed to be enjoying his power to control and prolong his own release. Until he couldn't. And then he was crying her name, as loud as she'd cried his, not caring if the world heard.

Afterward, he clung to her, still inside her, kissing her neck. "Jesus, Red, you're driving me insane."

She smiled, feeling sated and a little decadent. "Good, because I don't want to be in this nuthouse alone."

Chapter Fourteen

Snow began to fall in the afternoon on Christmas Eve, covering the ground with a soft blanket of white and floating past the windows in Wade's kitchen. Roxy's holiday spirits were high. She had a glass of eggnog within reach as she plied her culinary skills on his five-burner gas range, the aromatic scents of shrimp scampi, baked salmon, and garlic mashed potatoes recalling her Seattle bistro on its best day.

Callee and Quint had brought Caesar salad and wine. Molly brought mincemeat and chocolate-crème de menthe meringue pies. Roxy half-expected her to also bring Charlie Mercer, but she said he was spending the evening with his daughters, and they would see him at mass later on. Many toasts were made to the reason for the season as well as cheers for the scrumptious meal. Roxy couldn't recall having a holiday this special in several years. Nothing beat getting together with her best friends. The laughter bounced off the dining room walls, with Quint and Wade telling fishing stories that had them all in stitches at the antics men played on their buddies.

The hours passed too quickly. The evening and the celebration had come and gone; the McCoys had departed for midnight mass. Only the snow stayed, inches deep, muting the world as if to make it sit up and take notice of this holiest of days. Roxy basked in the comfort and peace that enfolded her. She took another swipe across the stove, cleaning every butter and olive oil spatter, each parsley and onion bit, intent on leaving the range as spotless as she'd found it. How she envied Wade this incredible appliance, so like the one she'd cooked on in Seattle. When she finally decided on a place of her own, she wanted a stove like this one.

"I can't remember ever having had such an incredible meal," Wade said, as he and Emily washed the delicate china they'd used for this special occasion. "These dishes were a wedding gift, but your mom never used them. She was always afraid of breaking them."

"What good are fancy plates if you can't eat off of them?" Emily asked.

"No good at all," her dad said, accepting another one to dry. He set the plate into the cupboard then groaned. "I ate too much."

"If Roxy cooked for us all the time, Dad, you'd get fat."

"Oh, yeah? Well, so would you."

Emily squealed as Wade pretended to snap his towel at her. Emily returned the favor, wiping her soapy hands on his shirtfront, giggling, and asked, "Roxy, do you think Callee really thought my centerpiece was pretty?"

Emily had wanted to be in charge of the table. She'd set it with the good china and then arranged fir boughs, pinecones, and candles with a gold ribbon wound through it. The result was as good as any Roxy had seen some grown-ups attempt. Including herself. "No question, and coming from Callee that's a huge compliment."

"I know. She's a decorator." Emily's grin morphed into a yawn. "Oh, I'm sorry."

"It's late, babe," her dad said. "You should probably head to bed. We have to be at Grandma and Grandpa Jacobs's first thing in the morning."

Although Roxy knew that it was their tradition to go to Sarah's parents' on Christmas Day, she didn't relish spending the day alone. With her mother out of town, the rambler could feel empty, even with Tallulah as company.

"I know I have to be up early. Wait until Gram sees my hair." Emily tilted her head to the side, a wheedling glint in her eyes. "But you said I could open one present tonight..."

Roxy turned away, smirking. She and her siblings had pulled this same ploy with their dad when they were kids. Sometimes it worked, mostly it didn't.

Wade chuckled. "You've already opened one. Now get to bed so Roxy and I can finish cleaning up in here."

"Ah, okay." She gave him a kiss on the cheek, then came over and hugged Roxy, the gesture so unexpected that Roxy stood there like a tree, arms at her sides. She resisted the urge to sweep this darling girl into an embrace. She didn't want Emily getting too attached to her, and vice versa. She knew she was starting to care too much for this girl. And for her father. She might need to break off whatever she had going on with Wade sooner than she'd hoped. Emily squeezed her gently. "Merry Christmas and thank you for the amaze-ball dinner."

"You're welcome."

With that, Emily headed out through the dining room. Wade went with her to double-check that the lights were turned off on the tree and that the front door was locked. Roxy was still at the stove when he returned.

She said over her shoulder, "I didn't realize how much I miss cooking the dishes I used to in my bistro. Don't get me wrong, I love baking pies, but I miss doing it all."

"Oh, yeah?" Wade answered, his arm snaking around her waist from behind. He kissed her neck, pulling her back from the stove, her bottom bumping against the fly of his jeans.

Ah, this was what she'd been waiting all night for, she realized, as her body relaxed against his. She smiled, rocking back into him. "Is that a candy cane in your pants, Santa, or are you just happy to see me?"

"What do you think?" he murmured, nipping at her ear, eliciting tingles in every part of her.

"Dad!?" Emily called from the top of the stairs, and they sprang apart like thieves caught pawing their booty. They'd agreed not to show any intimate affection in front of Emily, or Quint and Callee, or Molly. They weren't dating. They weren't "a couple." Friends with benefits didn't flaunt their sexual romp as if it were a romance.

This is definitely not a romance. I am not falling in love ever again.

"What?" He walked over and glanced up the stairwell.

"Don't forget to set your alarm."

Wade glanced at Roxy, shaking his head and rolling his eyes. "Don't worry, I won't."

Once Emily had departed for her own room at the front of the house, Roxy asked, "Is she very close to Sarah's parents?"

"Reverend and Mrs. Jacobs?" The use of their formal names made it sound as if he didn't care much for them. "They're okay. They're good about watching her if I have a late night and on weekends sometimes. She's all they have left of their daughter. So, yeah, they're good to her."

Roxy sensed some undercurrent between Wade and his in-laws, but obviously he wasn't going to explain. She didn't really need to know. None of her business. Even if it did make her wonder. She carried the dishcloth to the sink and rinsed it out.

Wade flipped off the light in the kitchen, the only illumination coming from the outside light reflecting off the snow. He plucked the dish towel from her half-dried hands and pulled her into his arms. "I have a little something for you."

"It feels more like a big something…"

His chuckle was husky and sent sweet shivers over her skin. "No, this is something else."

She pulled back, her eyes adjusted to the dimness, and gazed up at him. "We agreed. No gifts."

She didn't want to have to explain to her mother or Callee or anyone some gift that Wade might have selected for her. Or to try and deal with a gift from Wade once she and he had moved on to other lovers. No thank you. She didn't want a gift.

"It's not in a package."

"It's you," she guessed, the best gift she could think of.

"Nope."

"Well, I didn't get you anything and now I'm feeling bad."

He smiled and kissed her. "Does that make it all better?"

"It might." She traced a fingertip around his inviting, soft lips, her pulse starting to thrum. "Maybe a couple more of those will do the trick."

He kissed her again, and once again, and her breath quickened. "Ooh, I like this present."

"It's not the present I have for you."

"It's not?"

"Nope." He was guiding her up the stairs as he spoke, stopping to kiss her every few steps.

"Okay, I give up." She inhaled his spicy clean scent, her need growing with each passing second. "What did you get me?"

"I didn't get you anything."

She grazed her knuckles down his flat stomach. "Are you being obtuse on purpose?"

"I am." He brought her to the landing, kissed her all the way to his room, then opened the door and held back as she went in first.

Roxy froze in wonderment. Rose petals covered the bed and the wooden floor, and softly glowing vanilla candles scented the air. Her hands went to her throat. "I didn't take you for the romantic type, cowboy. You constantly surprise me."

"Is that a good thing?"

"It is. And this, this is the best gift ever." Ty had never done anything like this. She hadn't thought she'd like it as much as she did.

"Yeah, this is okay, but it's not all."

"It's not?" She couldn't even imagine how he could top this. Well, that wasn't true. He had moves that could definitely put a cherry on this dessert.

"I was hoping you'd notice all night, but you didn't."

Notice? She turned to look at him as he stripped out of his western shirt and let it drop to the floor, then began undoing his jeans. The Levi's fell to his feet, and he kicked them off and peeled down his boxers. She still had no clue what he wanted her to notice, but now all she could do was stare at his arousal and smile. "That's a mighty impressive present."

"The gift that keeps on giving," he teased, closing the gap between them, catching the first button on her blouse and flicking it open. "But that's not it."

He kissed her again, his fingers moving into her hair,

her body melting against him. Then he began undoing the front of her blouse, his touch making her squirm, his actions as deft as his lovemaking was becoming. She shoved her fingers into his hair. "You got a haircut today?"

"Nope. Last week." Her blouse slithered down her arms and off her hands. He fondled her nipples through her lacy scrap of a red bra, and then his gaze moved to her waistband. "You look good in jeans. It was all I could do to keep my hands off your cheeks while you were cooking."

She knew he wasn't talking about her face, and she squirmed with anticipation as he lowered her zipper and tugged the new denim down her legs, dragging her panties with it. She stepped free of the garments and undid the hooks on her bra.

His eyes darkened with passion as the bit of red lace fell away, and he touched her budded nipples tentatively, a moan escaping his throat. He swept her up, carried her to the bed, stirring up the rose petals and filling the air with a rosy vanilla fragrance that she supposed would always remind her of Wade and this moment. His kiss drove her wild, made her want to do things to him to give him the same insane pleasure, but he held her hands above her head, pinning her in place, and his mouth moved from hers to her neck, then into the sensitive area beneath her throat, and finally to her breasts.

He inflicted such pleasure she cried out his name, arching into him, throwing her head back, aching for him to be inside her, but he wasn't in any hurry. Not yet.

Wade moved lower, nipping lightly over her tummy, trailing kisses, and setting tiny fires wherever he touched. He settled between her legs, finding the source of her need with his seeking tongue, his finger dipping inside to tease her more. She felt it coming, felt her control slipping, the pressure building and building until she was panting with the need for release, and when she thought she would scream with the urgency, the wave washed over and through her.

She opened her eyes to find Wade staring down at her, a smoldering grin in his sexy eyes. She reached her hand into his hair, pulling him to her for a kiss, felt him giving into it, and then she rolled him under her, and she pinned his hands over his head. His lusty chuckle warmed her from head to toe. She drew a fingernail through the spattering of soft brown hair on his chest, tracking kisses across his nipples, and over his ripped stomach, while her hand caressed his most sensitive male anatomy.

With her fingers on the inside pulse of his hard-on, she gently stroked, taking the tip into her mouth, licking, nipping, sucking. Although his control improved each time they had sex, he said her name now in such a way that she knew his restraint was reaching its limit. He handed her a condom, and their eyes stayed locked as she fit it to him, as she straddled him, as he filled her, as the rhythmic dance began.

Music played through her mind, as her hips rose and fell to meet his upward thrusts, the torturous joy expanding and expanding. It was naughty, it was nice, it was as incredible as finding every gift in Santa's sleigh under your tree. Need wound through her tighter and tighter, until she felt as if she might die from the sheer bliss of it, but the next second, she was spinning loose and free into the wild from the most glorious climax. Wade jerked, calling her name, and she felt him whipping through the freefall with her.

In the aftermath, she snuggled next to him. "That was the perfect ending to a perfect day."

"No complaints here." He stroked her hair. "I never knew it could be like this."

She propped up on her elbow, smiling at him. "You mean sex?"

'Cause you ain't seen nothing yet, cowboy. I've got plenty more I want to teach you.

"Yeah. Sure. Sex."

He didn't look like that was what he was talking about, though. She frowned, a disturbing thought flickering through her mind. Surely he hadn't been about to say the "L" word? No. That was absurd.

"You still haven't noticed, have you?" he said.

He was back to talking about her present. "Nope. Not a clue. I give up. What is it?"

He held up his left hand. It took her a second to realize the wedding ring was gone. "It was time that I stop letting the past hold me back. In order to commit to the future, though, I need to get rid of the things still binding me to it. Like that gold band. I'm going furniture shopping first of the year, too. All that stuff in the living room isn't me. I kept it for Emily, but it doesn't suit the house. I can't sit in one of the chairs without feeling like a linebacker in a doll house."

"I feel the same at my mother's house. That tiny sofa. The low ceilings." Roxy shuddered. She really did need to get her own place, get her furniture out of storage. In fact, her furniture would look great in this house, but she didn't mention that. She was still having trouble figuring out why Wade thought taking off his wedding ring was a gift to her. She'd heard some guys mistook sex for love—especially if they were inexperienced.

She had to make him understand that whatever he was feeling about her would go away when they were no longer sex buddies, but he'd begun stroking her between her legs again and her mind dove on board for the ride.

Chapter Fifteen

Christmas morning, alone in her mother's house, Roxy replayed all that Wade had said, discussing it with Tallulah. The cat seemed to think she was right. "He's falling in love with me. I know he is. I don't want that. I don't want to hurt him. Or hurt Emily either. I need to break this off." But memories of the night before, of the way he'd touched her, the abandon she'd shown, flushed through her. Wade made her feel as if she could conquer the world. And the problem was that was what she'd always wanted to do—not actually conquer the world, but cook the most exotic dishes for the world's most important people. She'd lost sight of that dream during her divorce, while deciding to return to Kalispell to start the next phase of her life. But the dream, she realized now, hadn't died.

She strode to the kitchen, poured another cup of coffee, and stared out the window over the sink, the backyard a pristine layer of snow like a blank piece of paper she could write her destiny on. If she could, what would it say? *Following her lifelong dream, lonely career woman spends life cooking for others but never finds the right recipe for a true and lasting relationship.*

The cat sideswiped her calves, and Roxy sank down to pet her. "Tallulah, when it comes to advice, you're absolutely worthless. Where's my mom when I really need her? *Dear Valentina, how do you break off with a guy who hasn't done anything but bring you happiness? Signed, confused in Kalispell.*

The cat meowed.

Roxy figured Tallulah was hungry, not trying to answer her question, and the moment the food hit her dish, she proved it.

Mom would probably answer, *"Dear Confused in Kalispell, just break it off. The longer you stall, the more it will hurt everyone involved."*

Yeah, that's what I thought. Roxy paced into the living room and stared at the tree with its red lights, red bulbs, and red-ribboned packages. No fun opening gifts alone. But she didn't begrudge her mother having fun with her gal pals or spending Christmas with her other daughter, especially since the trip had been planned for a year. She could have gone too. She'd chosen instead to stay and help out at the pie shop. She reached for her coffee, but realized she'd left it on the kitchen counter.

Back in the kitchen, she considered making some breakfast, but after using Wade's gas range, the thought of cooking on her mother's old electric stove killed her appetite. She put a piece of bread in the toaster, trying to figure out the right words to break it off with Wade. His handsome face filled her vision as if he were standing right there telling her, "I didn't know it could be like this…"

Her cell rang, interrupting the stress session. She grabbed the phone, surprised at how disappointed she was that the caller wasn't Wade, but equally as glad that it was her mother. "You think she knew I needed to talk to her, Tallulah?"

"Meow."

"Merry Christmas, darling," her mother said.

Roxy smiled. "It's great to hear your voice, Mom. I miss you."

There was a moment of silence before Valentina said, "You sound like you could use some advice."

"Yes, please." Damn. Even long distance, her mother could read her like an open book. She sank onto the sofa and curled her legs beneath her. "You know how indecisive I've been?"

"Yes."

"I can't seem to make up my mind about anything, and I don't know why. It's so unlike me."

"Roxanne, my darling daughter, don't you realize yet that you didn't come back to Kalispell intending to stay?"

"I didn't?"

"No. It was only a move diagonally to regroup and consider your next step forward. You've needed some time with the ones who love you most so that you could listen to your head and your heart. So you could figure out what you want and need. Since you were in your teens, you've chased your passion. You got a taste of fame, and you liked it. But you also discovered that a passion like yours can consume you, and that it comes at a cost."

She nodded as if her mother could see her through the phone. It was as if Mom's words had cleared away a dense fog, and she could see the truth of it. She had let her passion for cooking consume her, thinking of work to the exclusion of everything else, including her husband. "Hmm."

"You also discovered the big lie. Most women can't do it all. If you want to take your career to the next level, you need to live in New York or London or Los Angeles, or even here, in Sin City."

What her mother was saying made so much sense. She couldn't be the restaurateur that she'd always imagined herself in a town the size of Kalispell. It was why she'd moved to Seattle in the first place. She'd thought she might scale down, pursue her passion in a smaller venue, but her heart apparently had never gone along with that idea. "You're right."

"Mother is always right, darling. Once you know what will make you happy, you'll start making decisions again without any doubts or regrets."

"I love you, Mom. Thank you."

She hung up, feeling as if she'd been given a priceless present. The gift of understanding herself and her motivations. If her mother really was right, and Roxy knew she was, then she would soon be leaving for another mega city to reestablish herself as a major player in the culinary world.

But you can't leave before Emily's birthday. You promised to teach her how to bake pies.

Roxy hugged herself. That didn't mean she couldn't make all the other necessary arrangements in the meantime. She might have to visit all of the major cities. Yeah, that's what she'd do. Starting with Vegas, since she could stay at her sister's while she scoped out the place and hunted for the right gig.

* * *

Roxy pulled into the back parking lot of Big Sky Pie. Callee had some plans drawn up that she wanted to show to her and Wade. Wade wasn't here yet. Regret slipped through her. She'd spent the last couple of days with Wade and Callee at Big Sky Pie Too, going over ideas for the design and sleeping with Wade at night. Every day, she meant to tell him about her plans to leave town, but she kept getting caught up in her own desires. He'd look at her a certain way, and she was a goner. She knew they weren't fooling Callee. Or Quint. Probably not fooling anyone.

And in its own way, that also made it more difficult to break it off with Wade—especially since he seemed so much more animated than he'd been when she first met him. Emily did, too, actually.

The sun was brilliant in the sky, but the day was

frosty, the snow crunching under her new cowgirl boots. Although the pie shop was closed today, when she stepped inside the aroma of fresh coffee greeted her. Callee looked up gleeful, doing a little happy dance. "Oh, I'm so glad you got here first. Ian and Andrea are getting married. On New Year's Day. Here in the shop. Small. Private. Secret. Two Hollywood celebrities in attendance. Andrea is a wreck."

"Oh my god, I bet she is." Roxy laughed as she shrugged off her outerwear. "Apparently she met the approval of her prospective in-laws. I assume they're the reason for the rush and the hush-hush."

"Absolutely. But it's more like she found a way to forgive them. Ian might have made peace with them, but I'm not sure Andrea ever will one hundred percent." Callee filled her in on Ian's sad childhood, and as Roxy listened to the story, her heart when out to Ian, and she finally understood why Andrea had been so nervous about meeting his parents. Knowing Andrea, it was more about how she'd react to them than being starstruck as Roxy had assumed.

Wade grinned when Callee told him the news a few minutes later. "Ian is a great guy, and Andrea deserves a great guy. I'm glad for those little boys, too."

He looked extra yummy this morning, in faded jeans, an aqua shirt that brought out the blue in his sea-green eyes. But all this talk of weddings and love had Roxy itching to change the subject. She pointed to the papers spread on the work island. "Hey, are those the plans?"

"Come see if this meets with your approval, Roxy, and

then Wade, you can see if I'm staying within the budget," Callee said as they gathered on either side of her.

A few adjustments were agreed on, and Callee had to run, leaving Wade and Roxy alone. He grinned at her, crooked his finger. "Come here, sexy lady."

Damn, when he looked at her like this she melted, putty in his hands. She closed the distance between them, slipping into his arms as if doing so were the most natural thing on Earth, as if this was where she belonged. Forever. But even as he began kissing her, as she returned those kisses with the passion she couldn't contain, she knew she didn't belong with Wade. Not forever. Maybe not even for now.

He pulled back, gazing into her eyes, his expression so adoring, so adorable, that her heart swelled to bursting. "I think I'm falling for you, Roxy. I want to tell everyone about us. No more sneaking around at night. No more pretending in public. I want to hold your hand when we're with our friends. It's killing me. But I know you're not ready for that."

Roxy's heart lurched. How did she tell him that she would never be ready? That she was leaving? Her head began to throb. She couldn't put this off any longer. He tried pulling her back, but she raised her arms, warning him off. "I think we need to get something straight between us right now. Before we—"

A knock sounded on the back door. They both jumped, looking at the door as though they could see through the blinds covering the windows. Wade asked, "Who the hell has such bad timing?"

He strode to the door and, without even looking outside, yanked it open before Roxy could caution him. She supposed he didn't expect much of anything to intimidate him given his size. The man on the other side of the door, however, was equally as impressively built and a lot more bulked up. But while Wade's muscle came from the labor of doing his job, the other man's came from hours in the gym.

Wade said, "The pie shop's closed until the second."

"Is Roxanne Nash here?" The bruiser had a messy bunch of blond hair that came to his shoulders, a baseball cap with the Seahawks logo, and a leather jacket that creaked when he moved. He sidestepped past Wade and into the shop. He spied her and flashed his killer grin. "Roxy."

Roxy's stomach hit the floor. "Ty, what are you doing in Kalispell?"

"Didn't you get my text, babe?"

"No." How could she have? She'd blocked his phone number from her phone.

"I'd like to talk to you…alone, if you wouldn't mind."

But Wade showed no sign of leaving. He walked up to Ty and said, "Aren't you going to introduce us, Roxy?"

Ty didn't wait for her. He stuck his hand out. "I'm her husband, Ty Buckholtz."

"Ex-husband," she said, her temper stirring.

Ty ignored that, still squaring off with Wade like a football opponent he was about to tackle. "And you are?"

Roxy held her breath. She could see Wade wanted to tell him "her lover," but he was too much of a gentleman to say something that might hurt Roxy. She hoped. "Wade Reynolds, Roxy's contractor."

"Oh?" Ty glanced at Roxy, his gaze crawling over her with the same anticipation a carnivore has eyeing a steak. "You building a house or something, babe?"

"Something," she said elusively. He'd torn apart her life. She still hadn't put it back together, wasn't sure when or if she'd manage to land on her feet again. But she'd be damned if she'd let him know that. "You didn't say why you're in town."

"But I did say I'd prefer to speak to you alone."

Roxy wasn't afraid of Ty. He might be a rat as a husband and a fierce baller on the field, but he was never a violent man. "Sure. Wade and I were just wrapping up."

Wade was scowling at Ty. "Aren't you supposed to be in a playoff game somewhere?"

Ty looked bemused. "Yeah, but we have a bye this week."

Roxy didn't like where this was heading. "Wade, I'll talk to you later, okay?"

"Sure." He didn't seem to like it, but he gathered the plans Callee had drawn up and left.

Ty stepped between Roxy and her view of the door. He wanted her attention on him. That killer smile reappeared, and his gaze devoured her. There was a time she would have fallen for that, but no longer. He said, "God, babe, you look incredible."

She shook her head, her mouth curved in a half-smile.

"I'm sure you didn't fly from Seattle to tell me that, and equally as sure that your fiancée wouldn't appreciate knowing that you're hitting on your ex." He flinched. "What do you want, Ty?"

He started toward her, reaching for her, but she backed him down with a look. He shrugged and retreated. "Suspension's been lifted. My bank account unfrozen. I came for my Escalade and—"

She interrupted him. "Did you bring my check?"

"Sure did. I have it right here." He held it up. "Along with the papers from my attorney to release the title back into my name."

Their respective attorneys could have, should have, handled this, but Ty was always impulsive. He had to have what he wanted when he wanted it. And he wanted his Escalade now. "Then let's go directly to the bank, and as soon as that check is verified and the money actually in my account, I'll give you the keys, sign all your papers, and you can head on home."

He burst out laughing. "God, I've missed you, Roxy."

Like hell. But she couldn't help wondering why he kept coming on to her. "Why didn't Ms. SeaGal come with you?"

His shoulders slumped, his whole demeanor deflating as if she'd punched the air from him. He seemed unable to look at her. "We split up."

So you thought you'd pick up with me like nothing ever happened? Asscap. Roxy stifled the urge to throw something at him. "What happened? She catch you cheating?"

He had the audacity to look wounded. "*She* was the cheater."

Roxy considered asking him how he liked the feeling, except that two and two weren't adding up to four. "Wait. I thought she was having your baby?"

"It was a lie. She claimed she had a miscarriage but I found out she'd been using birth control all along." He lifted the ball cap, smoothed his hair back, and met her gaze. "I guess it's what I deserve, considering."

Despite everything, Roxy actually felt a little sorry for him. "So, she was after the fame? The money?"

"Yeah, once my salary was frozen, she started showing her true self. She made a mess of running the bistro, too."

"No." Roxy's heart froze. It was what she'd expected would happen, but to hear that it actually had caught her off guard. "Did you have to shut it down?"

"No, I hired someone to run it who knows what they're doing. But it would all be better if you'd come back, Roxy. Come back. Come back to the bistro. Come back to me. I promise I won't ever stray again."

Seriously? The chance to take over her bistro again, to shop at Pike Place Market again, to regain her dream life, only a better version this time? She closed her eyes, hugging herself, imagining it. But when she did, Ty wasn't anywhere in the picture. A couple of months ago she would probably have packed her bags in a heartbeat, but she realized now that if she did go back, it would only be for the job. And oddly enough, even that didn't entice her. She'd changed. She might not know what she wanted yet, but she finally knew what she didn't want. She mentally scratched Seattle off the list of big-city choices.

"Ty, answer me this, and be honest. I'll know if you lie. Don't tell me what I want to hear. Tell me what you really feel."

A leery look entered his hazel eyes, as though this was a trick question, like "does this dress make me look fat?" that all men dreaded answering. "Okay."

"Why did you cheat on me?"

He tilted his head back, as if the answer were written on the ceiling, his tongue playing the inside of his cheek, his breathing loud. Finally, his eyes met hers. He shrugged. "To be honest, I guess I was flattered by the attention. Hell, you never had time for me."

"Let's be really honest, Ty. The truth is, our schedules clashed. You weren't around when I needed you either."

He sighed. "Yeah, I guess that's fair."

"So why would I want to take you back, knowing I'd be getting right back into the same routine that sent you into another woman's arms?" As she studied Ty now, she wondered if she'd ever been in love with him. Or had it just been a combination of lust and excitement about the bistro?

He huffed. "Well, I, er, I don't know, babe."

She had to face it and so did he. "Ty, our marriage was ill-fated from the beginning. We were young and most likely in love with the idea of being in love, but we're older, wiser, and we both still have ambitions taking us in opposite directions. One thing I've learned since our divorce is that you can't build a relationship on a lie. I think you've learned the same lesson. I would suggest you think long and hard about what and who you really want and need in your life, then be honest about it. With them and with yourself."

She took the check from his hand. "Now, let's go to the bank."

An hour later, the money was in her account, all ready to be spent any way she wanted, and the Escalade was all Ty's. He was driving her back to the pie shop when he said, "I'm starving. Is there a place in this town a man can get some grub?"

Roxy named a couple of places, then she had a thought. "You know, everyone goes to Moose's Saloon to watch the Seahawks. They serve the best pizza in town, but they have more than pizza on the menu, if you'd rather have a sandwich. And how cool would it be for the management to have an actual Seahawk player walk in and maybe sign a couple of posters, chat with some of your fans?"

She knew his ego was up for something like this.

The smile in his eyes confirmed it. "Are you coming with me?"

She considered. It was well past noon, and she hadn't eaten either. Why not? "Yeah, let's do it. A final farewell meal."

The second they walked in the door, Ty turned on the Buckholtz charm. Roxy had been right. The manager was so excited that Ty had dropped in, she sent over free pizza and a pitcher of beer. The noon crowd was more rowdy than during a big game. Music blared, and pool balls clinked amid raucous laughter. But no one bothered them once they started eating.

After gulping down two glasses of beer and five slices of pizza, Ty leaned back from the table like a man who'd had his fill, but she knew he was only about halfway done. He required more carbs than the average person. Tons more. He took a sip of his beer and wiped his mouth with his forearm. "So, you gonna open another restaurant with that money?"

As friendly as they were being with each other, she didn't consider Ty a friend, and she wasn't keen to divulge anything about possible plans with him. Why should she? But she had to say something. "First, I guess I'll have to get a car."

"I'm sorry, babe." He put his hand over hers. "What're you thinking about buying?"

"Not your concern." She shook her head and smirked. She was about to pull free of his grasp when she felt someone staring at her. She glanced up, around the room. Wade stood at the end of the bar, holding a couple of pizza boxes, his gaze glued to her booth, to her hand locked in Ty's. Before she could shake her head, the waitress blocked her sightline to give Wade change. She pulled free of Ty and said, "I'll be right back."

But when she started out of the booth, she realized Wade was gone.

Damn. She waved the waitress over and ordered another pitcher of beer. No more car. Probably no more lover. Talk about the best of times, the worst of times. No sooner had the thought crossed her mind than an

even worse time appeared on the horizon. Tippy...
Tappy...or whoever she was. As usual, the blonde wore
too much makeup and a knowing look. Her balloon-
sized boobs looked ready to pop out of her skintight,
V-necked sweater.

Holding a glass of white wine, she'd sidled up to the
booth near where Ty sat, her gaze on Roxy. "Well now,
it seems you've traded up, Red."

Ty's eyebrows lifted questioningly, but before Roxy
could think how to explain that suggestive remark, he
seemed to get his first good look at the blonde and
her overblown assets. From the smile in his eyes, Roxy
guessed he liked what he saw. The Buckholtz charm
made another dazzling appearance. "Just who might you
be, pretty lady?"

"I'm Tabby."

"Oh, yeah? Like a cat?"

"Meow..." Tabby said, Roxy no longer on her radar.

Ty laughed and made a purring sound. Roxy's mouth
dropped open, disgust souring her stomach. She shoved
her pizza aside and gulped some beer, thanking her
lucky stars that she had escaped their marriage when
she did. She contemplated ways to escape this awkward
meal.

"Say, you wanna dance?" Tabby asked Ty as a
country-western fan favorite issued from the speaker
system. Ty usually liked hip-hop.

"I think they're playing our song." He winked at
Roxy and started to scoot out of the booth.

She caught his wrist. "What are you doing?"

He shrugged. "What you said I should do. I'm figuring out what I really want."

Fair enough. Roxy released him. "I hear she can cook, too."

Roxy left them to it. She went outside. The sun shone on the snowy patches, melting them just enough to make the sidewalk slick. *What now? Call a cab? Call a friend? Call Wade?* She noticed he hadn't texted or phoned her, and she wasn't sure how she felt about that. *I guess I do need to figure out what kind of car or SUV or pickup I want. STAT.* Otherwise she'd be borrowing her mother's ancient, baby-pink Mercedes. She shuddered at the thought.

She texted Callee, asking for a ride home. Callee texted back that she was at the pie shop. Roxy said she'd be right there. Roxy glanced across Front Street, over the top of slow-moving afternoon traffic, and saw there were a couple of vehicles parked at the pie shop.

Wondering what was going on, she arrived a couple minutes later, and the female laughter coming from within made her more curious. Callee, Molly, and Andrea were sitting in the back booth, eating pie and drinking wine from coffee mugs. Champagne, to be precise. Her hands landed on her hips. "What's going on?"

"We're celebrating Andrea calling off her wedding," Molly said, raising her mug and taking a sip.

"What? You're not going to marry Ian?" Roxy couldn't believe it. Okay, so she was against marriage, but even she knew if any couple belonged together it was Ian and Andrea.

"Oh, we're still getting married," Andrea said, her words slightly slurred. "Just not this week. That was his father's idea, and then his mother sided with his father. But just because they're richer than sin...or richer than Molly's chocolate meringue pie...doesn't mean they get to pick my wedding date because it's convenient for them."

Callee grimaced. "Told you she hadn't quite forgiven them for the way they treated Ian as a kid."

"I'm working on that, I swear I am, but it's not easy. I might never get past it, even though Ian says he has." Andrea tucked her hair behind one ear. "Besides, Big Sky Pie is closed for vacation, a much needed one at that. I don't want Molly and you having to come in and bake on your time off. That's just inconsiderate."

Molly said, "Sit down, Roxy dear. I'm getting a crick in my neck staring up at you. Right here beside me. You look like you could use a little wine and some pie, of course."

Callee served her a slice of the pie, handed over a fork and napkin, and poured her some champagne. Roxy took a bite and, although she'd been making this pie for weeks now, she'd hardly had time to actually enjoy some of it. The crust flaked apart in her mouth, tasting freshly baked; the filling was pure decadence. *What is that extra ingredient? Brandy?* She sighed just enjoying it. "Where did you get this pie?"

"Well, you don't expect me to sit around home and not bake pies, do you?" Molly glanced at each one of them, defying them to tell her otherwise.

"Yes, we do," Callee said. "It's your day off."

Roxy almost choked on her pie, laughing along with the others.

"What's so funny?" Molly wanted to know. And they all laughed harder.

"I wouldn't have minded having the wedding this week," Andrea said, "if I'd known about it at least early enough to plan for some things, like a dress and flowers. Plus, my mom didn't get to attend my first wedding or help with the preparations since we eloped and she was fighting cancer. This is a chance to rectify that."

"Do you have a date yet?" Roxy asked.

"It will be close to the first day of spring. Everyone keep that time period open. And remember, it will still need to be secret, private, and small for Ian's parents to attend. I'll let you know as soon as I can."

"Well, if we can help with anything..." Callee said, downing more bubbly.

"Thank you. Mom has enlisted Rebel, Jane's mother, to help me find a dress on the down-low. She's going to order the flowers we choose under a false name."

Given how nervous Andrea had been before meeting her celebrity in-laws, Roxy was impressed with how she'd stood up to them and taken charge of something so important to her. "How's Ian handling the tension between his parents and his bride-to-be?"

"He's on my side." A secret smile lifted the corner of her mouth as though it had just hit her how special this was. "And really, I think they respect me for not letting them run all over me."

Callee grinned and lifted her mug. "Then you have indeed found the right man for you."

"Here, here," Molly said, and mugs clinked all around.

Callee said, "To love and marriage."

Roxy forced a smile and downed more champagne. She'd had her eyes opened today and realized she knew less than nothing about love and marriage, except that she intended to avoid them both and concentrate on getting back her career. She would have to tell Molly at some point that she wouldn't be sticking around to run Big Sky Pie Too. But it could wait for another couple of days.

More pie and champagne were consumed, and it quickly became apparent that none of the ladies of the pie shop were fit to drive themselves home. Callee texted an SOS to Quint. He arrived with Ian and Wade.

At the end of the shuffle, somehow, Roxy found herself alone with Wade in his pickup. Did everyone know they were sleeping together? Yeah, probably.

Wade glanced across the bench seat. "Quint tells me you need a new vehicle."

"True. The luxury loaner is back in its rightful custody, either heading to Seattle or to Tabby's house."

"What?" Wade almost put them both through the windshield when his foot jerked on the brake. Roxy giggled and told him about Ty and the blonde meeting in Moose's. Wade snorted. "Damn, I'm sorry I missed that."

"Trust me, you're not." She couldn't stop staring at

him, wondering why he had to be the cutest thing she'd ever seen. His tender eyes, his mind-halting grin, the deep vibration of his voice. It would be easy to fall in love with a guy like Wade. *With Wade.* But she already knew that her passion for her career would trump any love match that might come her way. All she could do was enjoy the ride while it lasted and hope to leave as few broken hearts along the path as possible. For now and until it ended, the only thing happening between Wade and her was great sex. Not love. Nothing long-term.

As if to prove that, they went to his house, where she got a lot drunker... on lust. Afterward, she curled in his arms, more certain of that than ever. She adored Wade. As a friend. As a lover. But she most certainly was not "in love" with him. And he should be grateful for that.

Chapter Sixteen

⁓

Roxy had all the pie ingredients ready to go when she heard tires crunch on the gravel behind Big Sky Pie. She opened the door in anticipation, but had to check her surprise when Emily and Misty, Tabby's daughter, spilled out of the gray Subaru along with a short woman whose hair was the same shade as her car. Sarah's mother? Her features were delicate, her skin pale, her eyes intense.

That gaze on Roxy felt like a laser beam about to carve her open.

All three came into the kitchen. Emily caught Misty's hand and began showing her around, impressing her friend with her knowledge.

Greta Jacobs introduced herself and asked if she could have a private word with Roxy. Roxy had cocoa for Emily ready to go, and fortunately, she'd made enough for two. She sent the girls into the café to drink it.

From the worrisome expression on her grandmother's face, Roxy's first thought was that something had happened involving Emily. "Is Emily okay?"

Greta was about six inches shorter than Roxy. She rubbed her neck and pointed to the stools at the work island. "Could we sit over here?"

"Of course." They settled side by side.

"I just wanted to meet you," Greta said, studying Roxy like a teacher checking test papers for errors. "Emily talks highly of you, you see. Truthfully, I've been worrying about her for a while now, facing all the changes that a girl goes through at this age. She needs the steady influence of a devout woman in her life, someone who will raise her the way God had in mind, someone like her mother was."

From what little she'd learned about Wade's deceased wife, Roxy considered herself the polar opposite of Sarah, and she worried a little that this woman's beliefs would stifle Emily. That would be a shame. But it wasn't her job to rock this boat. "I agree."

"Oh, I'm so very glad to hear that," Greta said, placing her hand on Roxy's. The hand was cold and clammy. Roxy tried not to recoil or yank it free as Greta continued, "I feel deeply that Wade has grieved long enough. Sarah couldn't expect more. Nor does He."

Roxy nodded, trying to ease her hand from beneath Greta's.

Greta leaned in closer. "You seem to make them both happy."

As the direction of this conversation became more clear, Roxy squirmed. "Well, I..."

"I guess I sound like a protective father asking a suitor what his intentions are toward his daughter, and I hope you'll forgive me, but I would like to know exactly that. What are your intentions toward my daughter's family, Ms. Nash? Are you prepared to take on a teenager? Are you planning on having children with Wade? Are you willing to give yourself over to the Lord's work?"

Roxy's jaw threatened to hit the island counter, but her temper flared through the roof. "Excuse me? I don't know what you're implying, but you're completely off base. Wade and I aren't even dating. We're just... friends. I'm helping Emily as a favor to her father, my *friend*. That's all." *Liar.* "And how I practice my religion is none of your business."

Greta's face went as red as the Jeep Roxy was considering buying. She huffed, obviously offended. "Don't you break their hearts, Ms. Nash. I'm warning you. You'll answer to me. And to Him." With that, she stormed out, head high, shoulders back, strutting like she'd done the Lord's work by putting the Devil's temptress in her place.

Reeling in her anger, Roxy swallowed a slew of nasty names she'd like to call this self-proclaimed saint. This was supposed to be a fun day for the two young girls in the café, and she wasn't going to let Wade's mother-in-law ruin it. She called the girls into the kitchen.

The pie baking was a huge success. Emily and Misty paid close attention, and between the three of them, they made four pies. The finished product might not be as eye-appealing as the usual pie shop desserts, but they would taste just as delicious as any she or Molly made. All in all, a perfect way to spend the afternoon. Could she handle a teenager? *Greta Jacobs, I can handle more than one at a time.* Of course, as the conversation replayed in her mind, she rethought her response, wishing she hadn't taken umbrage at the questions. She couldn't really blame the woman for watching out for her granddaughter's well being, even if her methods were flat-out rude.

But as the day wore on, Roxy realized Greta had a point; not telling Wade she was leaving Kalispell for good was selfish. She hadn't broken the news to Callee either. Or to Molly. She'd been telling herself that she didn't want to ruin their holiday, but the truth was she felt bad about misleading them into thinking she would put down roots here. Even though she'd thought that was her intention. She knew Molly and Callee would understand, but she had to tell Wade first; he couldn't hear this from anyone else.

And yet, as she lay in Wade's arms that night, snuggling in his bed after a passionate bout of lovemaking, the words seemed to stick in her throat. He lifted his hand to her cheek, brushing her hair aside, studying her as if he knew something was weighing on her mind.

"What's wrong?" he asked. "You seem like you're hundreds of miles away."

She blanched at how close that was to the truth. She caught his left hand, stared at his long graceful fingers, and the words she couldn't find began tumbling out of her. "Do you remember on Christmas Eve when you told me you'd given me a gift by removing your wedding ring?"

"Yeah," he said, memory and uncertainty dancing in his aqua-green eyes.

"It was a milestone, a significant act, but that wasn't your gift to me. That was my gift to you."

He frowned, clearly not understanding. "How so?"

She traced her fingers down his strong jaw, memorizing the feel of it. "Removing that ring symbolized that you were ready to step out of the past, to return to the present, and to move forward toward your future. I will always treasure whatever part I played in helping you find that renewed sense of self."

He lay back on the pillow, his handsome face contemplative, but his gaze remained on her. She could see he was absorbing what she'd told him, examining it like he might a piece of lumber he was about to transform into a support beam, realizing that she'd shored up the sagging foundation of his life.

He finally smiled and pulled her to his chest, his voice a husky whisper, full of sensuous need. "It seems I still owe you a present, lady..."

She kissed him, desire teasing through her, but she couldn't give in to it. Not yet. "You have given me a gift. Something more precious than you can ever understand." Her fingers tangled in the fine hair on his chest.

"Ty's betrayal stripped away everything I'd believed in, including me. I was left feeling not only unloved, but unlovable. I no longer trusted men. Or myself. Or my decisions. Losing my business was the final blow, robbing me of my career and my direction."

"Ah, Roxy..." He kissed her, hugged her. "Nothing should ever make you feel any of that."

She snuggled against him, letting his body reassure her, warm her, and then she rose just enough to meet his gaze, wanting him to know how much his gift meant. "You gave me back my confidence, my balance, my drive."

He sat up, propped on his elbow, frowning as if sensing what was coming. "Why do I feel that I'm not going to like where this is heading?"

She swallowed over the lump in her throat, tears welling in her eyes. "I'm the luckiest woman alive to have had these past six weeks with you, Wade, but it seems like Kalispell was just a stopover on my way to the next phase of my life."

He started to protest, but she touched a finger to his lips. "No, don't. We both knew going in that this was sex and nothing more. No promises, no permanency. Neither of us was looking for love. Just some much needed fun."

"Yes, but—" He broke off, wiping at the tears streaming from her eyes, looking as though his heart were breaking.

She felt a twin fissure slicing through her own heart. "You've given me the courage and the emotional tools to take that next huge step. I won't ever forget you, but we both need to move on."

He didn't look convinced.

"You know I'm right." She threw her arms around his neck, stemming her tears, and whispering in his ear as she climbed into his lap. "Make love to me, cowboy. Make me forget that this is good-bye."

* * *

"If the ladies can drink wine here, then we can drink beer," Quint told Wade. They were in the pie shop, after hours, the night before New Year's Eve.

"Thanks for meeting me here," Wade said, pulling up to the work island. Sweet aromas teased his nose, mouthwatering scents that made his stomach growl, but tonight he needed something stronger than pie to assuage what ailed him. "Roxy's leaving tomorrow for a potential job opportunity in one of the high-end steak houses in Vegas. It won't be the same as owning her own bistro, but it's a means to an end."

"Yeah, Callee told me." Quint accepted the beer Wade offered him, shoving his overlong hair out of his eyes. "Are you okay with it?"

"Not really, but I knew at the onset that she wasn't looking for love. Hell, neither was I. And when she kept waffling about where to live and what business she wanted to open, and even what kind of vehicle she wanted to buy, I knew she wasn't going to stay. I think I knew it before she did."

"I'm sorry. I thought the two of you could have a good time and then move on. Otherwise I would never have suggested that you hook up."

"Hah. You had nothing to do with it."

"Well, I did make sure you guys were alone a few times together."

"Yeah, but you weren't in charge of the chemistry we have. The first night I met her, when her cat pissed in my hat, I felt it then. Never met anyone like her. Didn't think she was my type, but considering my lack of experience with women, I never did know what my type was."

Quint straddled the bar stool opposite Wade like it was a saddle. "I always knew you were shy, but I figured you were getting some in high school, captain of the basketball team and all."

"Much as I hate to admit it, Sarah seduced me. Until Roxy, she was the only woman I—" He broke off.

Quint took a tug on his beer, empathy in the set of his mouth when he set it down. "I know how rough it is losing someone you love."

He was speaking of his dad, and almost losing his mom, but Wade grimaced, then confessed, "I didn't love her."

"What?"

"Sarah." Wade sighed. There. He'd said it. Out loud. Finally. Guilt bubbled up inside him. "I've never told anyone that."

"But...why the hell did you marry her?"

"I told you I never dated much in high school, but the truth is, I didn't date at all."

"Never?" Quint reared back, his expression incredulous. "Never?"

"Nope. Remember that senior class hayride, a month before graduation?"

Quint nodded. "Yeah, yeah, I do. Great night. Warm. Loud music. Dave brought a flask of Jack Daniels."

"Well, I came alone, but somehow, at the end of the night, Sarah and I ended up together. Alone, by the bleachers. She started kissing me and, and you can guess what happened. We only did it that once, but she ended up pregnant. I had to marry her. She was having my baby."

Quint's bright blue eyes filled with sympathy. "Shit. I never even guessed."

"Oh, you guessed something was off. You didn't think much of Sarah."

"Well, I . . ." Quint looked ready to spew out a mouthful of denial, but Wade knew he was too good a friend to lie. "I didn't always like the way she treated you."

Wade ran his finger around the rim of the glass beer bottle. "I thought maybe someday I'd learn to love Sarah, but she wasn't affectionate; she didn't like me touching her much. I figured I was too rough or something. Still, she was Emily's mother, so I stuck it out. And then one day, Emily fell and cut open her arm when she was around four years old. She lost a lot of blood and needed a transfusion."

"Yeah, I remember that," Quint said. "I came to the hospital to donate blood for her, but Sarah told me they wouldn't use it. She only wanted family to donate the blood."

Wade shook his head as he reached for a second beer. "That's when I found out Sarah's big lie."

Quint spit beer across the counter. "What?"

"Emily's blood type showed she couldn't be mine. I decided not to speak to Sarah about it until I had a definitive answer. Without telling anyone, I ordered a DNA test. The results determined that I'm not Emily's natural father. I stewed about it for weeks, until it was eating me up. Finally, I confronted Sarah, showed her the proof. She laughed. She admitted that she was pregnant the night she'd seduced me on the hayride. Emily's father was some drifter who'd worked at her father's church. He hadn't given them his real name."

"Holy shit." Quint didn't call Sarah any names, but it was obvious that he wanted to. "Talk about a knife in the balls."

"Yeah, I was devastated. Furious as hell. I would have left Sarah then and there, except she'd just been diagnosed with cancer."

"Even then, no one would have blamed you."

"I would have blamed me. And once I'd calmed down, I realized it didn't matter what a piece of paper said, or what a DNA test proved. Emily was my daughter from the moment they placed her in my arms."

Quint nodded. "I hope I'm as good a dad as you someday."

"You're gonna be great."

"So, if you weren't in love with Sarah, why wouldn't you date any of the women I kept trying to hook you up with?"

"Guilt. Believe it or not, I felt guilty that I didn't love Sarah, as if she'd gotten sick and died because I didn't love her. Then along came Roxy, who made me look at my life honestly. Her divorce was painful too, but she'd come to terms with it. I've accepted that my marriage sucked, but I have Emily, and she was and is worth it all."

"So Roxy unlocked the chains that bound you," Quint said on a laugh. "Look out, Kalispell. There's a randy new cowboy in town."

"I think I'm in love with her, Quint," Wade said.

Quint sobered. "Naw. More like you're fuck-struck."

"What?"

"Guys who've been sexually deprived can often find themselves falling for the first seriously good lover they have. Most often the cure is another woman, or two."

"I don't want another woman."

"You won't know that for sure until you try."

* * *

The look of approval in Wade's smoldering gaze stole her breath. One last secret date and then good-bye. "Damn, I'm going to miss you, woman."

"You'd better," she joked, although she hoped she'd given him the courage to start dating. She wanted him to find someone he deserved. Someone who wanted to live in Kalispell and build a life with him. Someone who loved him as much as she did. Even more.

He pulled her into his arms and began kissing her, but

moments later, he leaned back, his hands loose around her waist. "Do you know what you want?"

"I want you to carry me upstairs, to take off my clothes, to kiss all of my sensitive places until I can't stand the sheer pleasure of it, until you can't stand not being inside me. I want you to set fire to my body as never before. I want you to make love to me like there's no tomorrow."

Because for us, there isn't.

* * *

A couple of days later, Wade met the guys for coffee and pie in the new offices of Adz R Taz, Nick Taziano's advertising firm. Wade had left it a clean, empty space that Nick had brought to life with his intriguing photographs that begged you to look. Deep, wide seats anchored a round table that invited a customer to sit and browse through notebooks to see the many ways Nick could put a business on the map.

The floor-to-ceiling windows overlooked ample parking space for the other businesses on this street, as well as the planters that held winter foliage, but would be planted with flowers when spring came. The room smelled like new paint and leather with an overlay of freshly brewed coffee. Wade headed straight for a mug.

"You look like hell, Reynolds," Ian said, but the softly spoken acknowledgment held a large dose of sympathy.

His friends seemed to share his pain. "Feel like someone stomped on me."

"That's tough, man." Quint clamped his shoulder.

Nick set out paper plates as Quint lifted the dessert from the Big Sky Pie box.

"Roxy was the best thing to happen to me in a long time. It was like I'd been in prison, then she showed up with the key." Although his heart was broken, he was in a better place than he'd been before Roxy came into his life and turned it on end.

"Well, it's a new year and a new pie." Quint cut into the two-crust goodness revealing a rich red center, sending a fragrance into the air like warm shortcake covered in strawberries. "Strawberry cream."

Silence and moans of pleasure escaped as the men dug into the newest addition to Molly McCoy's menu. Then Nick asked, "So, what went wrong with you and Roxy? I thought you two were going to end up together."

Wade set his fork down. "Bad timing. It was too soon for her, and it had been too long for me. She was looking for an affair, not to fall in love. She needs time."

"Do you think she'll come back?"

He didn't know for sure. He hoped, prayed she would. "Maybe, when she's ready."

The guys nodded as though that could definitely happen, but a niggling doubt stirred in Wade. *What if she never comes back?* The question haunted him the rest of the day, and as he climbed into his bed that night, inhaling the orange-y scent that lingered on the pillows, his heart squeezing, he told himself he'd wait for her. For as long as it took.

What if she never comes back? Then he'd be putting

himself into another cage, like the one he'd just escaped, and this time, he might never get out.

There was only one thing he could do. What Quint had told him to do. What Roxy had told him to do. Move on. Find someone else.

Chapter Seventeen

Two months later

Roxy strode through the casino, barely registering the boisterous voices rising from around the gaming tables or the *clink-whirr-whistle-pop* from the slot machines. Her chef uniform drew gazes as she passed. It had been a long, satisfying night of preparing her favorite dishes in the fabulous kitchen of this resort's five-star restaurant. She was living her dream, producing plates that looked like artwork and food that tasted like nirvana. The clientele ranged from world-famous celebrities to little-known millionaires to everyday common folk on a luxury vacation.

Unfortunately, this gig wasn't permanent. Five weeks into a six-week contract, she needed to regroup and figure out her next move. She strode down a long marble hallway past the spa area and the pro shop to the private bar tucked into this secluded part of the resort. This Las Vegas property was owned by a billionaire businessman with hotels, casinos, and golf courses all over the country. Probably the world.

More than anything, she wanted to be part of this organization. If not here, then at another of his high-end resorts. One of her kitchen staff had told her to fill out an application and take it to the bartender who worked in the bar near the pro shop in the basement level. She settled at the bar two seats down from a man in his mid-fifties, dressed like a typical tourist—cargo shorts, golf shirt, and sandals. She ordered a beer from a bartender in his mid-thirties with stylish black hair and warm blue eyes.

As she waited for her drink, she pulled the job application from her purse along with a pen and jotted down her name. Roxy stared at the page, not seeing it, wondering instead what Wade would say about this place, about the elaborate accoutrements, and she imagined his handsome face lighting up as he told her about the thingamabobs that beefed up the whatsit to support the marble floor.

A bittersweet smile tugged at her mouth, but a nagging ache in her heart kept it from becoming a real grin. God, she missed that man. The only time the heart pangs subsided was when she was at work. But the moment she walked out of the kitchen, a deep loneliness embraced her. Why did she have to have either a man or a career? "Why couldn't there be some way to balance both?"

"A problem in the kitchen?" the tourist asked.

Roxy didn't realize she'd spoken out loud. She

glanced up at the man. His bushy brows were knit, and he gestured to her uniform.

"No. I'm just...no."

"Don't mean to be nosy, but I see you're filling out a job application, so I can only deduce you aren't happy working here."

She laughed with irony. "Just the opposite is true. But I've been standing in for the head chef in Le Château. He'll be back next week, and I'll be out of a job. I hear that the owner of this resort, Nathan Bardos, has restaurants all over, and I want to run one of the kitchens in one of those restaurants."

"Ambitious."

She gave him a wry grin. "I've been accused of worse."

He laughed. The bartender, who'd been listening to their exchange, kept a bland expression as he delivered her beer and asked the tourist if he wanted another scotch. The tourist said his wife was waiting for him, placed a twenty on the bar, and nodded good-bye to Roxy.

She took a long swallow of beer, the cool liquid clearing her head. She bent over the application, trying not to think about Wade, not to worry about ending up in Europe somewhere and likely never ever seeing him again.

The bartender came over to her. "I hear Mr. Bardos ate at Le Château last night and had the shrimp scampi."

"Really?" Her palms dampened. "Did you hear whether or not he liked it?"

The bartender wore a vest over a white shirt and bow

tie with black pants. His face was rugged, but clean shaven, his smile quick. "I think he liked it. A lot."

"I hope you're right. I created that recipe when I owned a waterfront bistro in Seattle."

"You owned your own restaurant, and now you're working part-time for someone else's?"

Roxy sighed. "Married the wrong guy, had to start over. Life happens, as they say."

"Tell me about it." He gave the pristine bar top a swipe with a damp cloth.

She stopped writing and caught his eye. "Someone told me that if I wanted this job application to reach the higher-ups that I should bring it to you. Is that true or just a rumor?"

"It's true."

Relief flooded through her. She decided not to ask why he had better connections than human resources. Maybe he was related to Mr. Bardos. As long as her application went where she intended, she didn't care if a carrier pigeon took it. Incredible salary and great benefits with none of the pressures of owning her own restaurant. Dream job. She signed the application, clipped a résumé to it, and handed the papers to the bartender. "My name is Roxanne Nash, by the way."

He pointed to his name tag. "John Smith." He scanned the application, apparently making sure she hadn't missed filling in any of the important boxes. He said, "This says you're from Montana, not Seattle."

"I grew up in Kalispell, a town very near Glacier Park in northwestern Montana."

"Is that anywhere near Tall Mountain and White-fish?"

"Very near. Why?"

"Just something I heard someone say today." He shrugged. "Don't worry; I'll see that this gets into the right hands."

"Thank you." She finished her beer and headed to the parking garage. Her cell phone rang as she got off the elevator. Mom. She ignored the call, not wanting to drive and talk, but once she reached her sister's, changed into her sleepwear, and curled up on the bed next to Tallulah, Roxy returned the call to her mother.

Her mother picked up on the first ring. "How is the job going, sweetheart?"

Roxy caught a fretful note in her mother's voice, and—for likely the first time—appreciated how lucky she was to have a mother who fussed over her, who cared about her well-being, even if she sometimes gave her grief.

"One more week, Mom," Roxy said. "And then I'm out of work again."

"Oh dear."

"Don't worry. I have other irons in the fire."

"Then you're happy about the move to Vegas?"

"I am." She was. Most of the time. Except when the loneliness that had crept through her heart like an insidious weed came on full force. Although when things got crazy in the Le Château kitchen, she couldn't deny that she missed the relative calm of Big Sky Pie. And she missed her mother and Callee something awful. Missed

Molly and Andrea and the girlfriends' wine chats. She missed Emily. But most of all, she missed Wade.

"You don't sound convincing," Valentina said.

Roxy changed the subject. "So, how's your bowling team doing?" As her mother indulged her, rattling on about the games won and lost, Roxy's mind wandered back to Wade. Although Emily texted her almost daily, he had neither texted nor phoned. Okay, in his defense, she'd told him a clean break was best. But still. According to Callee, she and Quint had set him up on a couple of blind dates, and he had been doing some dating on his own.

She kept remembering their last night together; Wade had been so gentle one minute, so rough the next, making her feel more alive than she'd ever felt. She couldn't get past that night, but he had moved on. She should be happy for him. So why was she crying herself to sleep every night?

"Do you plan on staying in Vegas, sweetheart?" her mother asked.

"I doubt it. If I can land another job with Nathan Bardos's company, it could be anywhere, maybe even in Europe."

"Europe. Oh, dear. That's so far away."

"I have to go where the job is."

"Of course you do."

Why then did she feel such a deep sadness about her decision to go wherever the job took her? Tears welled and a fissure spread through her heart, the pain radiating through her. She curled into a ball on the bed. Her only comfort was the warm cat pressing against her back. She was too ambitious, and that had cost her a man who made her smile, who made her feel loved—a man, she realized with a jolt, that she had fallen in love with.

Her cell phone rang. She didn't recognize the number. She answered cautiously. "Hello?"

"Hey, it's John Smith...though most people call me Nathan Bardos."

* * *

"You've done an excellent job on this, Wade," Molly said, admiring the finished interior of the building next door to the pie shop. "You and your crew working on this like speed demons, finishing ahead of schedule, with this as the result. I'm so pleased. Big Sky Pie Too is just as I'd imagined."

Wade said, "It will definitely be ready to launch next month."

"Music to my ears," Molly said. "I'll leave you to it. I've got pies baking."

She turned to leave and stopped in her tracks. "Roxy. Hello. Tell me you've come back to run this new shop for me."

"I've come back to run this new shop for you."

"Stop teasing and give me a hug. It's so great to see you. We've all missed you."

As Molly hugged her, Roxy looked over her shoulder at the man standing rigid behind Molly. Her heart kicked into high gear at the sight of him. "Hi."

"Hi," he answered, a tentative smile hovering on his lips. God, he was possibly more handsome than in her dreams.

"You're—you look—it's great to run into you," she stammered.

Molly released her and excused herself, doing a lousy job of hiding a smile.

When they were alone, Wade asked, "How's the new job?" His voice sounded thick with emotion.

"It's everything I dreamed it would be and more. So much more."

He nodded, his face shadowed by the tan Stetson. "I'm happy for you, Roxy."

"I was hoping you would be."

"I didn't know you were coming to town."

"Everything happened so fast, I didn't have time to tell anyone, not even Mom. My boss flew me here in his private jet." She ached to close the distance between them. Hated that they were acting like polite strangers when she yearned for him to open his arms and welcome her home as she'd hoped he would. "Molly's right, Wade. You've turned this old building into something both modern and rustic. It's perfect for the meat tarts and pies."

"Thanks." His crisp answers tightened the knot in her stomach. Was he glad to see her or not?

"Since you're finishing up here," she said, "does that mean you're free to consider doing a really big job?"

He frowned as if she'd been speaking Greek. "What big job?"

Roxy stepped closer to him, desire racing in her veins. "My boss, Nathan Bardos, is building a Pro-Am golf course, hotel, and spa resort in Whitefish. It will include his signature restaurant, Le Château, which he wants a local chef to run for him."

"You?"

"Yep. Apparently, he likes to hire locals for the construction work whenever possible, and I suggested you."

"A clubhouse, a hotel, spa, and restaurant. That's a year or two's worth of work for me and my crew. When can I meet him?"

"Now. He's in Big Sky Pie enjoying the special of the month."

Wade grinned, then frowned. "The restaurant won't be open for over a year, either. So, where will you be until then?"

"I'll be overseeing the building of the restaurant. And I'll also be running Big Sky Pie Too, as long as Molly still wants me."

"Oh, she wants you."

Is she the only one who wants me? She twisted her hands together, and blurted, "Are you dating anyone?"

He lifted his Stetson, his expression cautious. "Uh, yeah...about that...no, I'm not."

"You're not? But..."

"I hate to admit this." His neck reddened. "I swear I tried dating a few women since you left. Nothing came of it."

"I'm sorry to hear that."

"Really?"

"Yes." She took a step toward him.

"Then why are you smiling?"

"I'm not smiling."

"Yeah, you kind of are."

"I guess I was hoping that maybe you still wanted me."

"Are you ever going to pack up and run off again?"

"Not unless you come with me."

Wade eliminated the gap between them in three strides. His slow, sexy smile spread across his face, lighting his aqua-green eyes and melting the frost from her ravaged heart. How could she be so blessed to have both the career she craved and a man who would always support her passion for cooking, yet be there waiting for her with open arms? She was having her pie and eating it too.

He cupped her cheek in his palm, kissed her softly, then fiercely, pulling her against him, whispering over and over, "I love you, Roxy."

The sweetest words she'd ever heard or ever said. "I love you, too, cowboy."

"We're going to city hall in the morning," he said, separating his mouth from hers long enough to catch his breath. "I'm not spending another night without you in my bed as my wife. No more sneaking around. No more not-dating."

"No more hesitation. No more indecisiveness. We'll throw a reception in a few months." A thought gave her pause. "Do you think Emily will be okay having me as her stepmother?"

"Are you kidding? She's as crazy about you as I am."

Roxy thought her heart might burst from joy. "Uh, there is one thing you'll have to agree to before we can be married."

"Anything."

"Tallulah."

Wade burst out laughing and held her even tighter. "Damn, woman, I'd really have to love you a hell of a lot to agree to that." And he did.

Decadent Chocolate Meringue Pie

ALL-BUTTER BASIC CRUST INGREDIENTS

- 2 1/2 cups all-purpose flour, plus extra for rolling
- 1 cup (2 sticks or 8 ounces) unsalted butter, very cold, cut into ½-inch cubes
- 1 tsp salt
- 1 tsp sugar
- 6 to 8 tbsp of ice water
- 2 eggs, lightly beaten

DIRECTIONS

To make the crust, combine flour, salt, and sugar in a food processor. Pulse until mixed. Add cubed butter. Pulse 6 or 8 times until the butter is pea-sized and the mixture looks like coarse meal. Next add ice water 1 tbsp at a time. Pulse until the mixture just begins to clump. If you pinch some of the crumbly dough and it holds together, it's ready. If the dough doesn't hold together, add a little more water and pulse again. Caution: too much water will make the crust tough.

Place the dough in a mound on a clean surface. Shape the dough mixture into two disks, one for the bottom crust, one for the top. Work the dough gently to form the disks. Don't over-knead. You should be able to see flecks of butter in the dough. They will result in a flakier crust. Sprinkle a little flour around the disks. Wrap each disk in plastic wrap and refrigerate from 1 hour to 2 days.

Remove a crust disk from the refrigerator. Let it sit at room temperature for 5-10 minutes. This will soften it enough for easier rolling. On a lightly floured surface, roll out the dough to a 12-inch circle and about 1/8 of an inch thick. If the dough begins to stick to the surface below, sprinkle some flour underneath. Carefully place the bottom crust into a 9-inch pie plate, pressing the dough gently into the bottom and sides of the pie pan. Trim the edges to about ½ inch over the edge all around the pan and place in the refrigerator to chill for about 30 minutes.

PIE FILLING INGREDIENTS

- ¾ cup sugar
- 5 tbsp of baking cocoa
- 3 tbsp cornstarch
- ¼ tsp of salt
- 2 cups of milk
- 3 egg yolks, beaten
- 1 tsp of vanilla

DIRECTIONS

In a saucepan, mix sugar, cocoa, cornstarch, and salt; gradually add milk. Cook and stir over medium-high heat until thickened and bubbly. Reduce heat, then cook and stir for 2 more minutes.

Remove from heat. Stir about 1 cup of the hot filling into the egg yolks. Return the mixture to the saucepan and bring to a gentle boil. Cook and stir 2 minutes. Remove from the heat and stir in vanilla. Pour the hot filling into the pie crust.

Preheat the oven to 350° F

MERINGUE

- 3 egg whites
- ¼ tsp cream of tartar
- 6 tbsp sugar

Beat egg whites with the cream of tartar until soft peaks form. Gradually add the sugar and continue to beat until stiff and glossy. Spread evenly over the hot filling, sealing the meringue to the pie crust. Bake for 12-15 minutes or until golden.

See how the Big Sky Pie
series first set up shop!

When Quint McCoy returns from a long trip,
he discovers his office has been turned into
Big Sky Pie—with his soon-to-be ex, Callee,
working at the shop. They soon realize that
some couples are so good together that one
delectable taste is not enough...

Please see the next page

for an excerpt from

Delectable

Chapter One

I am one sorry son of a bitch, Quint McCoy thought. *A complete, total fuckup.* He didn't have a clue how to rectify the wrong he'd done. It had taken thirty days fishing in the wilds of Alaska, starting in Ketchikan, then deeper inland to the Unuk River, to bring him to his senses. To make him realize he couldn't run from the pain of losing his dad, or from the grief, or the guilt. He couldn't shove it all away. Or cut it out. It would always be inside him, wherever he was—as much a part of him as his black hair and his blue eyes.

Now that he was back in Montana, in the empty house he'd shared with Callee for two short years, he faced another raw truth. He'd bulldozed his life. Leveled every good thing about it. Nothing left for him but to move on and recoup. Somehow.

He grazed the electric razor over the last of the

month-old beard, leaving his preferred rough skiff of whiskers on his chin, and slapped on cologne. After four weeks in a small cabin with three other guys, he appreciated the scent of a civilized male. He took note of new lines carved at his mouth and the corners of his eyes, lines that bespoke his misery. *Losing your dad, and then your wife, will do that to you.*

He wasn't proud of the man in the mirror. He didn't know if he ever would be again. He'd trashed his marriage to the only woman he'd ever loved, or probably ever would love. Treated her like the enemy. And worse. Her mother died when she was seven, leaving her to be raised by a taciturn grandmother. She'd grown up feeling unwanted and unloved. He'd made her feel that way all over again. He hated himself for that. If Callee never spoke to him again, he wouldn't blame her.

But then, he wasn't likely to have a chance to speak to her. She'd left his sorry ass, let their lawyers hash out the equitable property settlement, and moved to Seattle right after he told her to divorce him. It took twenty-one days for the paperwork to go through the legal system. By now, he was a free man. And he didn't like it one damned bit.

Quint glanced at the mirror once more, expecting to see *Dumb Shit* stamped on his forehead, but only noticed that he needed a haircut. He pulled on dark-wash jeans, a crisp blue dress shirt and tie, and his favorite Dan Post boots. His dirty clothes went into the duffle on the floor. A scan of the bathroom showed nothing was left behind. He swiped his towel over the sink and counter and stuffed it on top of his laundry, then a second quick perusal, and a nod of satisfaction. Nothing forgotten.

He plunked the tan Stetson onto his still-damp hair and grabbed the duffle. His boot heels thudded on the hardwood floors, echoing through the empty split-level as he strode the hallway, and then down the stairs to the front door.

As he reached the door, his cell phone rang. He snapped it up and looked at the readout. A fellow real estate agent, Dave Vernon. "Hey, Dave."

"Quint. Well, hang me for a hog. 'Bout time you answered your phone. You still in the land of igloos and Eskimos?"

"I wasn't that far north, Dave. But, no, I'm in town."

"Well, now, that is good news. Glad to hear it. How was the fishing?"

"Okay." If the trip had been about the fish, then the fishing was actually great, but it hadn't been about salmon twice as long as his arm. It had been about his inability to deal with the loss of his dad. His inability to stop setting fire to every aspect of his life.

"You still want me to sell your house?"

"That I do."

"Well, as you know, I had it sold...until you decided to skip town. The buyers got tired of waiting for you to return and bought something else."

"I'm sorry, Dave." Although Dave didn't convey it, Quint imagined he was pissed. Quint had cost him a sale. He'd been as irresponsible as a drunken teenager—

without the excuse of adolescence. "I'm leaving the house now."

"All the furniture was moved out while you were gone."

"Yeah, I found the note about the storage unit and the key on the kitchen counter." He'd had to crash on the floor in his sleeping bag. "I just picked up the last of my personal items."

"Well, okay, that's good, actually." Relief ran through Dave's words. "I can put this back into the system immediately if you'll swing by and renew the listing agreement."

"Sure. I have to stop at the office first." Quint stepped outside into the overcast day. The end-of-May gloom suited his mood. "Give me an hour or so, and I'll head your way."

"I'm counting on it."

"See you around eleven." Quint stuffed the duffle into the back of his Cadillac SUV and gave the house one last glance before climbing behind the wheel and backing out of the driveway. The development was small, full of similar homes stuffed between Siberian larch and Scotch pine, the kind of place where newlyweds started their futures. *Started their families*. Like he and Callee had hoped to do when they'd moved here.

A heaviness as dense as the cloud cover settled on his heart. He kept his eyes on the road ahead and didn't look back. He didn't need to see the regrets in his rearview mirror; they were etched in his brain. As he drove north toward town on I-93, the vista vast in all directions, he wondered how it could all look so familiar, so un-changed, when he felt so altered.

But something about the crisp Montana air and the wide-open spaces gave him heart. In contrast, the wilds of Alaska—with giant trees pressing toward the river's edge and just a patch of sky overhead—had made him look inward, at acceptance. Here, he could look out-ward, at possibilities.

Like what, if anything, he might do to salvage his business, McCoy Realty. He knew he'd be lucky if he ever got another listing in this town, but by God, he meant to try. It had taken him three years to build his reputation and clientele list into one of the best in Flat-head County, and three months to destroy it. He'd gone from Realtor of the Year two years running to a pariah. The only reason the office was still open was because he owned the building.

And his office manager, Andrea Lovette, hadn't given up on him. Although he'd given her enough reason. Was she at the office yet this morning? He dialed the number, but the female voice that came on the line was elec-tronic. *"I'm sorry, the number you are trying to reach is no longer in service."*

Huh? Had he misdialed? Or had the phones been dis-connected? He sighed. One step at a time. Instead of hitting redial, he pulled to the side of the road beneath a billboard and punched in the office number again. Slower this time. The response was the same. He dis-connected. One more grizzly to kill.

He tried Andrea's cell phone. The call went straight

to voice mail. As he waited to leave a message, his gaze roamed to the billboard. A gigantic image of his own face smiled down at him. An image taken a month before his dad died. Happy times, he'd thought then, not realizing he was already on the track to losing it all. Overworking, ignoring his wife, his mama. His dad. He shook his head. At least this was proof his business on Center Street still existed, sorry as it was. Right across from the Kalispell Center Mall. *Location, location, location*. If nothing else, he had *that* in spades. He supposed it was one positive to hang on to today.

He pulled back into traffic. He needed to confer with Andrea and figure out what steps to take to get the business back on its feet. Starting with getting the phone service reconnected. He called her cell phone again and left another message. Nothing would be easy. He didn't deserve easy.

"Quint, my boy, there isn't a problem so big a man can't solve it with a piece of your mama's sweet cherry pie in one hand and a fishing rod in the other."

Fishing wouldn't solve what ailed him, but a piece of his mama's sweet cherry pie might take the edge off this morning. The thought made his mouth water, but pie for breakfast? Aw, hell, why not? His spirits could use a lift.

His phone rang. He didn't recognize the number. Business as usual for a Realtor. "Quint McCoy."

"Quint," his mother said, warming his heart and his mood. She'd had that effect on him for as far back as he could remember.

"Mama, I was just thinking about you." He'd missed

hearing her voice. "How's my best girl? I'm hoping she'll take pity on her poor, homeless son. Maybe do my laundry? I just left the house for the last time, and I'm feeling lower than a rattler's belly. I have some business that can't wait, but—"

"Uh, that's why I'm calling."

"How about I pick you up for lunch and you can tell me how the pie shop is coming?" She was remodeling the half of his building that he wasn't using into a take-out pie shop. It was set to open later that month. The plans he'd seen before leaving for Alaska included a kitchen in back and a display case and counter in front. Small and compact—like his mama. He smiled. "Yeah, that's what I'll do. I'll see you around one, then after lunch, you can give me a tour of your little shop—"

Call-waiting beeped. "Quint, will...please...I—"

He glanced at the phone's screen. A client. *Thank God for small blessings.* "Mama, I have to run. Say, you haven't seen Andrea, have you? She's not answering her cell phone, and I'm hoping to get together with her today. See what we can do to salvage my realty business."

"Well...as—" Call-waiting beeped.

"Look, I gotta take this call, Mama."

"Quint, about Andr—" Call-waiting cut off his mother's words again.

"See you at one," he said, and switched to the incoming call, realizing as he did that some small part of him kept wishing every incoming call would be one from Callee.

* * *

Callee McCoy pulled the small U-Haul truck into the parking spot at the Kalispell Center Mall, cut the engine, and listened to the motor tick-tick as it cooled. One more thing to do. Her hands gripped the steering wheel as though the vehicle careened downhill at uncontrollable speed and an ensuing crash could only be prevented if she hung on tight enough. But the crash had already occurred, rendering her marriage a pile of bent metal and smoking ash, rendering her shell-shocked at the velocity with which the devastation struck.

She felt as someone might who'd been hit by lightning twice—surprised, certain she was immune to any second such occurrence, given the first had been so devastating. Callee thought nothing could ever hurt as much as when her mother died. She'd been wrong. Losing Jimmy McCoy, the only real father she'd ever known, had knocked the pins out from under her again. This time, however, everything should have been different. After all, she had Quint.

A bitter laugh spilled from her, and she gave herself a mental shake. It was all water under the bridge. She was moving on, sadder, but wiser, the Kalispell to-do list almost complete. After landing at Glacier Park International yesterday and renting this U-haul truck, she'd visited the storage unit she'd leased before leaving for Seattle and retrieved the belongings she'd negotiated in the equitable settlement part of the divorce. This morning, she'd met with her attorney, finally given him the go-ahead to file for the final decree, and signed the required paperwork. One loose thread left to tie, and then she was out of here. Montana would be a distant memory that she could look back on whenever she felt maudlin or needed a reminder of how good her new life was.

Live and learn, her mother used to say. Of course, she always said this after bundling Callee out into the night to somewhere her latest disaster of a romance couldn't find them. According to her grandmother, her mother was a tramp. She'd pounded this into Callee's head from the day she came to live with her, hoping, Callee supposed, to make sure that Callee didn't turn out the same. But the mother Callee remembered was a free spirit, always laughing and hugging and promising adventures.

When she was old enough to understand such things, she realized her mother had been acting out, rebelling against a too-strict upbringing by running wild, by living fast and hard as though she knew somehow it would all end too soon. Callee was the end product of both upbringings, as emotionally unequipped for a long-term relationship as a mother who had no idea who'd fathered Callee, and a bitter, taciturn grandmother. As proof, the first punch life threw landed squarely on Callee's chin and knocked her clean out of the ring.

The ring. She glanced at the third finger of her left hand, at the diamond and emerald ring that had belonged to Quint's grandmother. The family heirloom had a fragile, antique beauty, the platinum band filigreed. As much as she adored it, she couldn't keep it. She tugged it off, surprised at the sudden sense of disconnection it brought—as though she'd pulled something of herself loose. Silly. She should have removed it the moment Quint walked out on her.

But she hadn't had the courage to let him go then. Not then. Had she the courage now? Or was shaking Quint McCoy loose from her heart going to be as painful as shaking Montana from her red Dingo boots?

Callee tucked the ring into her coin purse next to a business card, trying to ignore the naked-finger sensation, but knowing it was responsible for her thoughts rolling back to the first time she met Quint. She was in Seattle, about to start cooking school, when she'd received a call that her grandmother had had a severe stroke. Callee flew back to Kalispell immediately, and it soon became apparent that she'd have to sell the house to cover the cost of a nursing home.

Quint represented the buyers. He'd come to present the offer, and one exchanged glance tilted Callee's world. Some might call it love at first sight.

A dinner date led to a kiss; a kiss led to an endless night of lovemaking. She lost her head, her heart, and everything she'd ever meant to be in that conflagration of sensuality. They were like a Johnny Cash/June Carter song—hotter than a pepper sprout, hotter than the flame on Cherries Jubilee, the sizzle and burn an irresistible blue blaze.

Just the memory of those erotic months could melt steel, but then the fire of excitement and sexual discovery calmed to a slow burn. She still craved Quint physically, sexually, but he was so intent on building his real estate business that he no longer had time for her. Somehow, she never got around to telling him that the classes she was about to start just before they met were at a cooking school. Callee feared he might laugh, given she could do little more in a kitchen than boil water. She'd never worked up the nerve to share her secret desire to become a chef or the secret fear that she was incapable of learning to cook.

But the adventurous part of her, which she'd inherited from her mother, was making her try. She'd re-enrolled in that same Seattle culinary college, and her first classes started next week. *Here's hoping the second time is the charm.*

She reached for the truck's door handle and hesitated. She had come to say the toughest good-bye of all...to Molly McCoy. Quint's mother had treated her like the daughter she'd never had and been the closest thing to a real mother since Callie lost her own. Staving off tears, Callee jumped down from the cab into the gloomy day and felt a sudden shiver, like a portent of something dreadful. Probably just her mood. She zipped her jacket and locked the U-Haul.

Her phone vibrated in her pocket, a text from her best friend, Roxanne Nash. Roxy owned a Seattle waterfront bistro, and she'd opened her heart and her home when Callee arrived on her doorstep after leaving Quint. Roxy was always egging Callee on, making her try new things and face her phobia of learning how to cook.

Roxy wanted to know if everything was okay, if Callee was okay, and if she'd started the eleven-hour drive back to western Washington yet. She answered the text, then stepped to the curb at Center Street, her gaze skipping across the road to be caught by a new sign: Big Sky Pie. She knew Molly was renovating the largest part of Quint's office building into a pie shop, but her brows rose at exactly how much of a renovation had occurred.

She smiled, thinking of the treat that awaited Flathead County residents. No one made pies better than Molly McCoy. But it was the example Quint's mother was setting that filled Callee with pride and happiness. Molly had grieved the loss of Jimmy McCoy worse than anyone, yet she'd turned her sorrow into something positive and productive. Callee wanted that end result for herself.

She patted her purse to make sure the ring was still there and hastened across the street, admiring the exterior of the pie shop. Bay windows wore white awnings, and the exterior was painted a rich ruby red with white-and-tan trim and lettering, reminiscent of Molly's specialty, sweet cherry pie made with fresh Bing cherries from the orchards around Flathead Lake. The color scheme was one Callee had suggested when Molly first mentioned she might open a pie shop one day. Callee felt honored that her mother-in-law had remembered and taken the suggestion to heart.

She pasted a smile on her face and tapped on the door, prepared to give Molly an "I love what you've done with the place" greeting. But she startled and then grinned at the woman in the doorway, Andrea Lovette, Quint's longtime office manager and Callee's friend.

Andrea lit up like a delighted child at the sight of a favorite toy. "Oh my God, Callee. I didn't know you were in town. Does Molly know?"

"Not yet, and I'm not staying." They exchanged a quick hug, and then Callee stepped back and looked at her friend. "I'd ask how you're doing, but you look fabulous."

"I look ragged. Two little boys will do that to you." Andrea laughed, her brown eyes sparkling as she shoved at her long, thick blond hair. She was taller than Callee, a fact made more pronounced by the skinny jeans and platform pumps she wore. "Since you're not staying, what brings you back to Kalispell?"

"Tying up some loose ends."

Andrea nodded, her lips pressed together. "Well, whatever the reason, I'm delighted to see you. And Molly will be, too. Besides, I hate being the only guinea pig."

Guinea pig? Callee found herself being pulled farther into the shop. "I don't know what you're talking about. Where's Molly?"

"In the kitchen with Rafe, her new assistant pastry chef. She's teaching him something, I think."

Muffled voices issued from the kitchen, one female speaking English and one male speaking Spanish. Callee smiled. "Do they even understand each other?"

"No clue, but Molly will be out in a minute. I'm sitting over there." Andrea pointed to a booth. "Go ahead. Sit. I'll bring you some coffee."

"Okay, but I can't stay long." Only long enough to give Molly the ring and a hug good-bye. Callee settled into the booth and began to take in the décor. The interior reflected the colors used outside, but in reverse. The walls were tan, the crown molding and trim white, and the tablecloths and napkins a ripe red. This was all café, display cases, cash register, and an espresso/coffee and tea counter. Seating consisted of a row of four high-backed booths on one wall and round tables scattered throughout the space.

"Isn't it great?" Andrea handed her a cup of steaming coffee. "The kitchen consumes the largest portion of this building, an L-shaped chunk that isn't visible from this room."

"It's wonderful. Right down to the framed, poster-sized photos of juicy pies with sugar-coated crusts."

"Mouthwatering, huh?" Andrea took a sip of coffee.

"That's the idea, right?" Callee couldn't get over the size of the room. "I didn't know she was going to do a café. Last I heard, the pie shop would be take-out only."

"Yeah, well, the café was kind of last-minute," Andrea said, quickly downing more coffee. "Molly told me the design was yours."

Callee shook her head. "Nope. Only the colors."

"All the same, I think you missed your calling, lady."

Callee smiled. "I missed a lot of things."

"So, how are you doing?" Andrea touched her hand.

The gesture made Callee feel less alone. Andrea had once been where she was now, figuring out how to be single again. The difference was that Andrea had had the burden of two little boys relying on her to get it right. Callee had only herself. *Thank God.* "I'm looking forward, not backward."

"I'm glad. I've been worried about you." Andrea offered a commiserating smile.

"I promise, I'll be okay, eventually." She smiled weakly.

"This whole thing is such a tragedy." Andrea shook her head, but never one to hold back how she was feeling, she added, "When Quint comes to his senses, he's going to be real damned sorry. I wish you'd stick around, Callee. I know he said and did some awful things, but that man loves you. Even if he can't see past his grief right now."

"If that's what he thinks love is, I want no part of it." It didn't matter if he did love her, or even if she still harbored tender feelings for him. He was, after all, her first true love, but she had never been a priority with him, and watching the love his parents had shared, she realized she deserved better than what Quint was giving. One day, maybe she'd find her Mr. Right. But Quint McCoy was not that man. "My U-Haul is parked right across the street. As soon as I have a minute with Molly, I'm on my way to Seattle. I've enrolled in college," she said, keeping the type of college to herself. If she ended up with her degree then she would share details with trusted friends, but for now, it was her secret. "Classes start next week."

"That's awesome. I'm so excited for you." Andrea's smile flashed, then quickly faded. "Uh, by the way, Molly just spoke to Quint. He's on his way here."

"What? I thought he was still in Alaska." The news tweaked Callee's nerves, and she gulped down a swallow of coffee, the hot liquid burning its way to her stomach.

Andrea was studying her. "He got back last night."

Callee set her mug aside, snatched hold of her purse, and scooted toward the end of the banquette. "It's been wonderful visiting with you, but right now, I need to see Molly and get out of here."

"Okay, Andrea, I hope you're hungry," Molly called, emerging from the kitchen. Quint's mother, a bubbly, middle-aged redhead with short spiky hair, was followed by a tall, handsome Latino in his early twenties, who carried a serving tray with fragrant goodies on dessert plates.

"Callee!" Molly squealed, foiling Callee's attempted escape. Molly wiped her hands on an apron spotted with flour, chocolate, and fruit juice and hugged Callee. "Oh my God, you're like a gift from Heaven."

Callee returned the hug, wishing she never had to let go, but she did, and since the memory of this moment would have to last her a long time, she held on a beat or two longer than she might have. Even though Molly would always welcome Callee into her home and her heart, Callee understood their relationship would never be the same once she left here today. Tears stung her eyes.

Molly stepped back, and Callee did a quick assessment. There was a smidge of flour in her choppy red hair and on her pert nose. The bedroom eyes she'd passed on to her son seemed weary, and the wide smile that lit up any room she entered seemed less brilliant. She was like a clock someone forgot to wind; not quite up to speed. Still missing her husband, Callee figured, still worrying about her son. At least the shop would joyfully fill a lot of lonely hours.

Callee glanced at the wall clock, wondering how soon before Quint arrived. She had to leave. Now. But Molly urged her back into the booth.

"I know why you're here."

How could she know that? Callee lowered her voice. "In that case, could I see you in private—?"

"You're going to stay and come work for me." Molly cut her off, hope erasing the worry lines near her mouth.

"What?" Callee's eyebrows rose. "Work for you doing what?"

"A pie shop can always use more than one pastry chef." She handed Andrea and Callee forks and napkins.

"A pastry chef?" Callee blushed, recalling the time Molly tried to teach her to bake a pie. Callee kept hearing her grandmother's voice, taunting, telling her that she was only fit for washing dishes and taking out garbage. Not for cooking or baking anything. The end result had been a crust that resembled lumpy clay, and although

Molly had been kind, Callee couldn't stop cringing at the memory.

Callee gave Molly an indulgent smile. "You know perfectly well that my kitchen skills are limited to coffee and scrambled eggs. Period. Not pies."

"Oh, all right." Molly sighed. "But since you don't have anything against *eating* pies, you can help us figure out which of these three items belongs on the menu."

"I really need to go."

"I'm opening next week, and I need to tick this off my to-do list."

"I can't st—"

"Nonsense. It'll only take a few minutes." Molly slipped into her side of the booth, blocking her in. As stuck as gum in cat fur, her grandmother was fond of saying. Resigned, Callee turned her attention to the tray, which held three colorful pie slices. Her mouth watered. Her early morning breakfast had consisted of a grande latte. Eating something now meant one less stop along the road later on.

Andrea said, "If presentation means anything... wow."

Molly beamed. She handed Andrea a small green tart. "It's key lime."

Molly gave Callee a slice of chocolate pie and gestured for Callee to try it. "This is tar heel pie."

Callee tried a bite. "I've never heard of it."

"It's chocolate chips, coconut, and pecans. A word of caution. It's very rich and should probably only be eaten in tiny increments."

"Ooh, I like this," Andrea said. "A definite ten."

"This is to die for," Callee exclaimed, her sweet meter tilting off the charts. She shoved the slice toward Andrea. "Try it."

Molly pointed to the next item. "This last one is Daiquiri pie. Cream cheese, condensed milk, concentrated lemonade, and my own twist, ninety-proof rum."

Andrea and Callee dug in while Molly watched, waiting for their verdicts.

But Callee and Andrea could only moan in pleasure.

Molly glanced at Rafe. "So much for narrowing the menu."

He muttered something in Spanish that sounded like "a bucket of Tequila" and headed back to the kitchen.

Outside, tires crunched on the gravel parking lot. Inside, forks stopped halfway to mouths. The three women exchanged knowing looks. Molly scooted out of the booth, then stood frozen beside the table. "Quick, Callee, go see if it's Quint."

"Me? Why me? I don't want to see Quint." She would just mail the ring to Molly. Feeling none too composed, Callee slipped from the booth. "Do you have a back door?"

"Please, Callee." Molly's face had gone a worrisome gray.

"What's going on?" Callee looked from Molly to Andrea.

Andrea winced. "A sort of intervention."

"Shock therapy," Molly said.

"What?" Callee had no clue what they were talking about, and she didn't want to know. She stole to the window and peered out through the blinds. The second she saw Quint, her heart began to thrum with a rhythm akin to a love song. He was sitting in his SUV, phone to ear. "It's him."

"It's for his own good," Molly muttered, as though to herself, as though her actions needed defending. "It's true what they say about tough love. It is harder on the giver than on the receiver. If I hadn't spoiled that boy to the edge of redemption..."

"What's he doing?" Andrea asked, still seated in the booth, sucking up Daiquiri pie like she was downing shots in a bar and ignoring her cell phone, which kept announcing a new voice mail.

Callee had a bad feeling. "He's putting his phone away."

"What's he doing now?" Molly asked, her face drained of color.

"Getting out of the car."

"Does he look angry?" Molly asked.

He looks heart-stopping delectable—like always. Damn. Callee hated that her pulse still skipped whenever she laid eyes on Quint, hated that every nerve in her body seemed to quiver as he shoved back the Stetson revealing his incredible face. God, how she adored that face. His smile, his touch, the things he did to her body, the responses he elicited...just recalling left her breathless. *No. Stop it. You're over. He never put you first. Never.* "He's glancing up and down the street as though he can't understand why he isn't seeing what he expects to see."

"Like he's wondering if he's on the right street?" Andrea said, sounding...anxious?

And then Callee realized. *Shock therapy.* "You didn't tell him you were turning his office into the café portion of your pie shop?"

Molly gulped. All the answer Callee needed. Before she could ask what the hell Molly was thinking, a fist hit the door. All three women jumped. But no one moved to let him in.

Fall in Love with Forever Romance

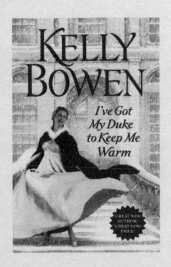

I'VE GOT MY DUKE TO KEEP ME WARM
by Kelly Bowen

Gisele Whitby has perfected the art of illusion—her survival, after all, has depended upon it. But now she needs help, and the only man for the job shows a remarkable talent for seeing the real Gisele...Fans of Sarah MacLean and Tessa Dare will love this historical debut!

HOPE RISING
by Stacy Henrie

From a great war springs a great love. Stacy Henrie's Of Love and War series transports readers to the front lines of World War I as army nurse Evelyn Gray and Corporal Joel Campbell struggle to hold on to hope and love amidst the destruction of war...

Fall in Love with Forever Romance

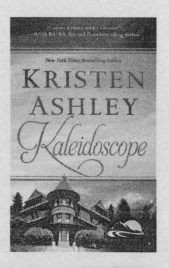

KALEIDOSCOPE
by Kristen Ashley

When old friends become new lovers, anything can happen. And now that Deck finally has a chance with Emme, he's not going to let her past get in the way of their future. Fans of Julie Ann Walker, Lauren Dane, and Julie James will love Kristen Ashley's *New York Times* bestselling Colorado Mountain series!

BOLD TRICKS
by Karina Halle

Ellie Watt has only one chance at saving the lives of her father and mother. But the only way to come out of this alive is to trust one of two very dangerous men who will stop at nothing to have her love in this riveting finale of Karina Halle's *USA Today* bestselling Artists Trilogy.

Fall in Love with Forever Romance

DECADENT
by Adrianne Lee

Fans of Robyn Carr and Sherryl Woods will enjoy the newest book set at Big Sky Pie! Fresh off a divorce, Roxy isn't looking for another relationship, but there's something about her buttoned-up contractor that she can't resist. What that man clearly needs is something decadent—
like her...

THE LAST COWBOY IN TEXAS
by Katie Lane

Country music princess Starlet Brubaker has a sweet tooth for moon pies and cowboys: both are yummy—and you can never have just one. Beckett Cates may not be her usual type, but he may be the one to put Starlet's boy-crazy days behind her...Fans of Linda Lael Miller and Diana Palmer will love it, darlin'!

Fall in Love with Forever Romance

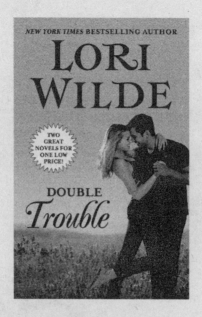

DOUBLE TROUBLE
by Lori Wilde

Get two books for the price of one in this special collection from *New York Times* bestselling author Lori Wilde, featuring twin sisters Maddie and Cassie Cooper from *Charmed and Dangerous* and *Mission: Irresistible*, and their adventures in finding their own happily ever afters.